I0573348

Funny Old People

Gene Murray

A Wings ePress, Inc.
General Fiction Novel

Wings ePress, Inc.

Edited by: Jeanne Smith
Copy Edited by: Christie Kraemer
Executive Editor: Jeanne Smith
Cover Artist: Trisha FitzGerald-Jung
Cover images: Woman by Mikhail Nilov from Pexels,
Cat by angeleses from Pixabay

All rights reserved

Wings ePress Books
www.wingsepress.com

Copyright © 2022 by: Gene Murray
ISBN-13: 978-1-61309-500-3
ISBN-10: 1-61309-500-7

Published In the United States Of America

Wings ePress Inc.
3000 N. Rock Road
Newton, KS 67114

Dedication

To the humorists from Mark Twain to James Thurber to
Douglas Adams.
It's not as easy as it looks.

* * *

One

"But he's not the boss anymore," he said, leaning on his polished, empty desk, growing irritated.

"But he ought to be," she said calmly.

"He had a coronary three weeks ago. You think he should come to work with one of those oxygen things stuck in his nose?"

"You know I don't mean that. But the fact that he isn't here doesn't mean you should be."

"You're just upset because I mentioned the 'R' word. It's not a swearword, Anna."

"The 'R' word? Sure it is. You want me to, you know, while I'm still in the prime of life? Nuts to that."

"Anna, you are seventy-four years old. In what retirement village is that considered the prime of life?"

"And there it is. You used the word again. 'Retirement.' I am not retiring and you can't convince me that I should. I have worked here for too long, and I know every crook and nanny of this operation."

He smiled. "You mean 'nook and cranny.'" He pointed to his head, "See, your mind is starting…"

"Right there is the problem, Sebastian. 'Crook and nanny' is a play on words. A joke. The thing we do here. You don't even get the jokes. How are you supposed to edit this magazine if you don't get the jokes?"

"I have people."

"No. Your uncle, if he's really your uncle, has people. And I'm one of the people."

"Not after you retire."

"And you already forgot what I just told you. I'm not going to retire." She pointed to her head. "See, your mind..."

He sat down heavily. "Anna. Anna. I know your eyes are beginning to fail, but can you focus for a moment? Look at this desk. This one right here in front of you." He tapped it a couple of times.

She sighed and looked over at the desk. "I certainly know that desk. I was the one who figured out how to get it through the door in 1992. You would have been on a changing table with your legs in the air at the time."

He tried to smile, but it turned into a sneer. "This is a very big desk," he continued flatly, "and its purpose is to make a clear statement. It's solid oak, with a Carpathian Elm veneer top. I know because I googled it. It has three storage drawers and two locking file drawers. As you can see, there is a graceful curve along the front and a cutout for the user, in this case me, to be close to his work. The size and the curve of the desk are designed to indicate the relative positions of those in front of the desk and those behind it."

"It's made of pine with veneer glued on," she said. "Your uncle, if he is your uncle, wanted a compressed-wood five-footer from Jersey City Premium Furniture. I talked him into this one."

Sebastian's face turned pink, but he continued. "You are in front of the desk. On the carpet, literally. I am behind the desk, which signals clearly that I am in charge here. I am commander of this base, admiral of this fleet, the buck where it all stops."

She pointed to her head again. "Not quite right, pal. The quote is, 'The buck stops here.'"

"Whatever."

She snorted. "With you running this magazine, the base will cave in, the fleet will sink, and the buck will probably be counterfeit."

He breathed deeply and leaned back in his chair. "Retirement, Anna, is the topic at the moment. It's the reason I called you in, remember? I...called *you*...in."

She paused to let herself calm down and pulled a chair close to the desk. "Sebastian, I am asking politely. You know retirement is not for me. I will shrivel. I will peel into shreds and blow away. I apologize for being snarky with you, but—"

"Don't misunderstand. You aren't being fired, Anna. And if you want to work somewhere else, I will give you a reference. But that word 'snarky' will be prominently mentioned as one of your prime personality traits."

"Sebastian—"

"I've already spoken to Human Resources about this, and we think two weeks will be sufficient for you to finish up any little projects you have and pass on whatever practical knowledge you have developed over a long and valued career. We'll have a little breakfast for you on the," he opened a drawer and pulled out a calendar, "on the eighteenth."

Anna sighed and stood to leave. She looked down at him and said, "The eighteenth is a Saturday. That's last month's calendar, Admiral." She walked out, leaving the office door wide open. She knew he hated that.

~ * ~

One step outside his office and she felt like she was on leave from a war zone, like stepping from the moon into a friend's house. She waited while the blood left her face, her shoulders lowered, and her pulse leveled off. Her 'friend's house' consisted of fourteen desks occupied by fourteen reasonably talented people who would much rather be somewhere else. Out on the floor, she recognized signs of the daily afternoon slump. Four of them were up and strolling with no apparent destination. A few had their arms high in the air, either stretching or signaling a field goal. Mike was sitting on the corner of Chloe's desk because no other woman in the office would let Mike sit near her. Chloe, that lucky copy editor, had allergies and often could not smell a thing. Mike, a puzzle for Anna, but sweet in a way, was not an enthusiast of rigorous personal hygiene. Even his friends occasionally referred to him as 'Pepe Le Pew,' and maneuvered to stay upwind.

Anna stood silently in front of Chloe's desk until Mike got the hint and went back to his own. Chloe smiled. "Why the long face, like the bartender said to the horse."

Anna said, "Oh, I love that joke. My grandpa used to tell that one before he shipped out in World War One."

"I'm gonna take a wild guess that your meeting didn't go well." At first Anna misunderstood 'meeting' for 'beating.'

"My beating?"

"Do," she said. "Dot beating, beating. With an 'mb.' Mmmmmeeeting." She wiped a little spit off her chin with a tissue.

Chloe had been with the magazine for about three years, and was everything an office manager hoped for. She was quiet, friendly, and efficient. She did her job and, when it was done, she said good night and went home. She didn't gossip, talk to herself or curse at her computer. She didn't make fun of Mike, and didn't steal office supplies. Naturally, everyone except Anna and Mike was suspicious of her.

"Oh, my meeting," Anna said. "It ran the usual gamut of conversations with Sebastian. He proceeded from feigned ignorance to genuine ignorance to condescension and then back to genuine ignorance."

"It's comforting to know there are still people in the world you can rely on," Chloe said.

"The upshot is, my sentence is scheduled to begin in two weeks."

"Your sentence? I don't...oh, the 'R' thing."

Anna pointed under her nose. "You got a little, you know, there."

Chloe wiped her nose quickly with a tissue. "Are we gonna do the usual breakfast farewell? A bibosa, mmmmimosa and a doaster?"

"So he said. He picked the eighteenth to do it."

Chloe looked at her calendar. "The eighteenth is a Saturday."

"I did mentioned that."

"Well, you'll change it."

Anna nodded and started to walk back to her desk, but stopped. "I don't think I will change it. I've planned every retirement party here for years, but I think I'll just be the belle of the ball for this one. I'll let someone else buy the toaster, send around a card, and mix the mimosas."

She turned back to her desk and noticed Sebastian had closed his door. There would be faint music soon, a string quartet probably, something soothing, something that would blend into the background while he was woolgathering.

Her desk was about twenty feet distant and angled away from Sebastian's enclosed office. She had chosen that spot years ago so the managing editor could not see her from behind his desk. He, or someday she, would have go to the corner of the office and peer out the window, or else open the door and look out. Privacy had rarely been an issue for the years Bernard had been managing editor, except when his latest wife visited the office, but it was a concern now that Sebastian had claimed squatter's rights.

Early in the life of *Propriety Magazine*, the late seventies, there had been departments for commentary, short stories, literary criticism, world news, and politics. The rapid increase in both weekly and monthly magazines with similar content obliged the owners to branch off, and *Aplomb* was launched as a younger and more hip choice for a sophisticated audience. Over the years, humor, both written and drawn, became their *métier*. Under the stewardship of Bernard Holloway, a minority investor in *Aplomb*, it found its niche, and blossomed. *Aplomb* published two issues per month and a special holiday issue in December.

Anna had been a copy editor when gentle wit and sophisticated humor were the primary product of *Aplomb*. She had interviewed to be in the typing pool, but when the managing editor at the time, Albert, learned that she had two years of college, he hired her as a copy editor. She bought a dictionary, a thesaurus, and a book of grammar, and ignored the stares and sniggers she drew as the only female member of her department.

Forty-one years later, those same three books were still on her desk. The building where she worked was new, the room was larger and busier, even her desk was different, but the books were the same.

A little after five o'clock, she waved goodbye to Chloe and watched her walk to the elevator with Mike tagging along like a puppy. Sebastian was long gone, as usual without even mumbling 'good night,' and the stalwarts left were clearing their desks and putting on coats. There was one more article Anna wanted to look at. She knew it was not a good fit for her magazine, but the title intrigued her.

She could see the janitor, Malcolm, at the far end of the office, with his push broom and the trash bags sticking out of his pocket. Malcolm pushed his wheeled trash barrel up close to her desk. "Your friend, the lady who works at the desk there, told me a joke. Wanna hear it?"

"Hello, Malcolm. Sure, always ready for a good joke."

"Okay then, how do you make a bandstand?"

"I don't know. How?"

"Easy, just take away their chairs."

"Oh god, Malcolm, that is the second corniest joke I have heard all day. And Chloe, that's the lady at that desk, told me the other one."

"Yeah, but you gotta love it," he said. "You know, in this world you got to laugh." He moved away and started emptying trash cans.

She took her time with the last article of the day, reading it carefully and pausing at points that seemed to fit her situation. The title of this article, *How to Start Your Own Magazine,* was not a humorous piece, and certainly not funny to her. She read it over twice, smiling and nodding, and left it in the middle of the desk to read again first thing in the morning.

~ * ~

The next two weeks, which she feared would be filled with regrets and teary nostalgia, were nothing of the kind. Sebastian drifted in around ten, a little early for him, and occasionally stopped by her desk. He said nothing, just smiled until she looked at him, and then went into his office and closed the door. Someone, probably Donna, had let it be known around the office she would be retiring. A few people wished her well, a few others knew this was not good news for her, and kept their distance.

But she wasn't upset or angry at Sebastian, or flooded with memories. She wasn't thinking of Albert, who had hired her, or Bernard who had trusted her; she was organizing her new magazine. The article she had read supplied the spark, and by mid-week after her conversation with Sebastian, her 'little engine that could' had built up a full head of steam.

Donna brought Sebastian his coffee, his second cup, and stopped at Anna's desk. "I hear congratulations are in order," she said.

"Oh, it's not true, Donna."

"It's not?"

"No. I'm not really pregnant. I just said that to trap Sebastian into marrying me. He saw right through my ruse, though. That man has a mind like a steel trap. Everything intelligent skirts around it."

Donna just stood open-mouthed and blinked for a moment. She did that a lot during conversations with Anna. "I meant your retirement," she said. "Seb told me this morning. You've certainly earned the rest."

"Oh, Sebastian told you. Well, yes, I am rrr... wait, just give me a moment. I am rrree, rrree..."

It occurred, dimly, to Donna that Anna may be ill, or worse, having a stroke, which didn't bother her much, except for all the fuss it would cause. "Anna, are you okay?" she said.

"Yes, I'm all right. I just have a problem with that word. Always have had. Rrrrreeeee. Nope. Can't get it out. Maybe after I, you know, stop working."

"That's kind of odd, isn't it? Being stuck on one word?"

"I think it may be some kind of reaction to a trauma. What they call 'post-traumatic stress.' Something that happened right here in this office when I was much younger." She thought she had her hooked, but wasn't sure.

Donna looked around slowly at the office and shook her head. "I see," she said. "Please don't worry too much about it. You can just say 'leaving work.' That says it all."

"Yes, yes. Thank you for the suggestion. I'll just say 'leaving work.' Everyone will understand."

"Of course they will. And by the way, Seb asked me to make the arrangements for a little retir— um, going away breakfast for you."

"Oh, how nice. That will be lovely," Anna said. Donna smiled her most gracious smile, and walked back to her desk. She sat and looked through some papers, but within a few minutes she was back.

"I don't mean to pry, or be in any way morbid, but what *did* happen? I mean the trauma thing here in this office."

"Do you really want to know? It happened years ago, but it still isn't easy to talk about."

"Well, maybe talking it out will help a little. Like therapy."

"Maybe, I guess. Okay, years ago we had a little get together for someone who was moving to Florida to, you know, stop working. And, well, it wasn't my fault. We didn't know, she never told us about her problem."

"What was her problem?"

Chloe had walked back to Anna's desk to see what was going on. She stopped and listened. "Oh, I don't think I ever heard about this."

"It was years ago, Chloe, before your time. Debra, I think her name was. She was the sweetest woman, too. Very personable. A hard worker. She used to sit at your desk, Donna, if I recall."

"So, what happened? What was her problem?" Donna asked.

Anna took a few moments to answer. "I made brownies for the party, with peanut butter, and she had a peanut allergy. I didn't know, really, I had no idea. I felt so bad when her face swelled up all red and she had trouble breathing. Her breath made this awful scraping noise, you know? I can still hear it sometimes. I thought she was in really big trouble. I even called nine-one-one. She was okay by the time the EMTs got here, but boy did she give me some hard looks."

"I can imagine," Chloe said. "Poor thing."

"The 'R' word has had special meaning for me ever since. She got over it, though, and I guess she forgave me. A few months later, I got a very charming email from her, and she even included a joke."

Donna frowned. "A joke, really? She sent you a joke?"

"Yeah. Something about a rock band named Peanut Brittle? They broke up."

Chloe giggled. Donna turned quickly and walked away, shaking her head.

"I guess you can get away with tweaking her now," Chloe said.

"I could always get away with tweaking her." Anna said, smiling.

Chloe asked how she was feeling. "You were a little bit down the other day after your meeting. Your mmmmeeting." She blew her nose in a balled-up tissue.

"I am actually good," Anna said. "Better than in a long time, I'm surprised to say. Since Sebaceous..."

"Sebaceous? Is that Sebastian?"

"Yeah. I finally came up with a good name for him. It just popped into my head this morning. Actually, a bunch of things popped into my head this morning."

"But Sebaceous? I was just getting used to 'Underperforming Unctuous.'"

Anna laughed. It was no longer a suitable-for-work, ladylike titter, but a full-throated guffaw. "I loved that one, especially the alliteration. But 'sebaceous' is easier to say. The sebaceous gland is a little thing that secretes oil into skin or hair. Sebastian is as oily as they come, so, he's officially Sebaceous."

Chloe laughed and blew her nose again.

"Anyway," Anna said, "I was feeling pretty crummy, I guess. I was feeling my age, since Sebaceous dropped that 'R' bomb on me. But I'm good now. It's like that saying 'when one door closes, another one will hit you in the ass'."

"On a different topic, have you heard anything about Mister Holloway's condition? I haven't had a chance to go see him, and he makes me a little nervous anyway."

"Yeah, well, I called him an ignorant jackass one time and I thought he would fire me. He laughed and said, 'How many educated jackasses do you know?' He didn't make me nervous after that."

"Do we know how he's doing?" Chloe asked. "Has anyone gone to see him? "

"I tried once, but he was still critical; only family permitted. I asked Sebaceous about him but he just said something typically unctuous like, 'Well, we'll have to wait and see.' I have a feeling he hasn't visited, either."

"Poor Mister Holloway," Chloe said. "He's not a bad guy. He doesn't deserve to be afflicted by this family."

"Paula is still doing Europe, I guess, although it's really strange to travel so soon after getting married. I think there's a whole backstory there."

"I've only seen her once or twice," Chloe said, "and she seems nice enough. I wonder if she even knows he's sick, poor guy. He deserves better."

"He had better once. His first wife was a lovely woman, and the nice ones always die young. I guess that says something about me."

"Yes, Anna, it says you beat yourself up too often. Anyway, I'd better get back. I'm working on that *Famous Couples* series. The piece on Hillary Clinton and her husband is not going to edit itself."

Anna made a face. "She had a husband? Who knew?"

She was never formally part of management, but grew into what she called a 'funnel' position at the magazine. Anything not assigned to someone else swirled down until it landed on her desk. Usually, at this time of morning, she would take a short break and stroll through her dominion, just to quietly remind everyone to stay on task. She had read somewhere this was called MBWA; Management By Walking Around, and it seemed to keep people focused. Bernard always liked the idea.

She stood and took a couple of steps but did a quick detour to the ladies' room. She had noticed Donna was strolling, looking casually over the shoulders of people at their desks, and not saying anything. With Donna it was more like DBWA; Distraction By Walking Around. She could see heads turning to keep an eye on her. But with only seven working days left, Anna was surprised to find she didn't really care. Her head was elsewhere.

In the empty ladies' room, she leaned on a sink and talked to herself in the mirror. The list in her head, growing by the hour, felt like it was spilling out of her ears. Plans and ideas and numbers were darting around, crashing into each other. She mumbled the list to the woman in the mirror: "Office space, office furniture, computers, salaries and benefits, printers and internet service, web design, payroll services, an attorney, a bookkeeper." She had, over the years as unrecognized office manager, successfully wrestled with all of those issues, but usually one at a time, and with someone else's money.

As she was splashing cold water on her face, Suzanne came in. "Oh, congratulations, Anna! I hear you're leaving us for a life of rest and relaxation," she beamed. Suzanne always beamed. She had a bright smile and spoke fluent cliché.

"Yes," Anna said, checking herself in the mirror. "I'm finishing up a few things and leaving at the end of next week."

"Oh, the golden years. Time for gardening projects and world cruises and finally having the time to read *War and Peace*."

"Oh, I've already seen that movie," Anna said. "Everything is cold and snowy. Henry Fonda marries Audrey Hepburn, and Napoleon has to retreat with his hand inside his jacket."

Suzanne grinned at her. "Movies are so educational, don't you think?" Suzanne was from the art department and a talented, if somewhat callow, illustrator.

The remainder of Anna's day and week shifted between automatic pilot on her current job and excited preparation for her next one. She ignored grins from Sebastian and sidelong glances from Donna, and amiably accepted warm wishes from everyone else in the office. From Chloe and Malcolm, her genuine friends in the office, she got her daily dose of bad jokes.

On Friday, she left work right at five o'clock and rode the subway to New York Presbyterian Hospital to see Bernard. She got in this time after being told his condition was 'stable' and she should only stay for fifteen minutes. Hospitals always made her eyebrows meet in the middle and her shoulders rise to her ears. One of her uncles had been an army surgeon, and she was enamored with doctors, especially the television variety. At one stage, she had considered becoming a nurse, maybe even a doctor, but one scary experience as a candy striper turned that dream inside out.

She passed the elevator and went up the staircase. *I haven't thought about that in years*, she thought. *Wonder where that SOB is now? I hope somewhere with a lot of mosquitoes.* She stopped at the first landing and thought about him. He was a doctor, or at least an adult with a white coat and a stethoscope around his neck; skinny, glasses, not especially good looking. They were riding the elevator together and he reached over to the panel and pressed 'Stop.' He smiled and put his hand on her shoulder. She smacked his hand, pushed him away and pressed all the number buttons on the elevator. "Little snot," he said.

The elevator stopped on the next floor and he got out without even looking back at her. She was sixteen and shaking.

It was years ago, she reminded herself. *Years and years ago.*

She found Bernard sitting up in bed, pale and haggard, but smiling, with a pulse monitor on his finger, a blood pressure cuff on his arm and sensors on his chest, all cabled to a monitor over his bed. A plastic tube ran down from an IV bag to his arm.

"No need to tell me how good I look, Anna. I know how I look."

She said, "You don't look great, Bernie, but you look okay."

"Thank you," he said in a low and raspy voice that surprised her. "And thank you for coming to see me. Being sick is bad, but boredom is like hell right after purgatory."

"They wouldn't let me see you before. Family only."

"Yeah," he said. "Family. Sherilyn has been here a few times. She never stays very long, and the nurses have asked her to leave." He had a slight, sly smile as he said this.

"Really? They asked your *wife* to leave? Why?"

"They told me it was because of the monitors. Whenever she was with me for more than a few minutes, all the monitors reacted. Electrocardiogram, blood pressure, pulse, all the dials shot right up, double quick, when she was around. One nurse even told me she thought Sherilyn could block the IV tube from across the room. I told her, 'You have no idea.'"

"Oh, Bernie, I'm sorry. Did they think it was some kind of biology thing? Like electro-biology or whatever the hell?"

"No, she was just too loud. *Is* too loud. Also, they think her perfume may contribute to the problem. The stuff she uses is called *Eau de Marais*, or *Eau de Marisal,* or something like that. It costs me seventy bucks for a chintzy little bottle and she goes through about one a month. Douses herself with it, maybe takes a swig or two, for all I know. I hate the smell of it. One of the nurses' aides here speaks French and she said *eau de marais*, roughly translated, is 'swamp water.' Don't those French people have a way with words? So, now they have brought in a team of specialists, instrumentalists they're called, to figure out if the problem is her perfume or the monitors. I have an opinion, but it doesn't much matter to me. I'm screwed either way."

Anna had to turn away and stifle a laugh. Then Bernie laughed, softly, and it was all okay. Laughter meant he wasn't just a sick man in a hospital bed anymore. He was Bernard, 'Bern,' 'the B,' her boss, her old friend. "Good to see you still have your sense of humor," she said.

"Yes, that I still got. And a wife, I'm pretty sure she's my wife, who runs barefoot through my money and picks fifty-dollar bills from between her toes. And I got a nephew, if he is my nephew."

"You're still not sure about those divorce papers, huh?"

"No. Which is my fault. In a fit of pique that lasted about two weeks, I shut Paula out. I just, ah, you've seen me get that way, and I shouldn't get worked up about it. You get it."

"Yeah, I guess I do."

"So, the inevitable question. How are things at the magazine?"

She made a face. "You know, Bern, I don't want to stay too long and I don't want to get into all that. They warned me not to tire you out."

"Anna, please. Tell me something I can think about. If I have to lie here counting these ceiling tiles one more night, I think I may scream. And think what that would do to the monitors."

Anna pulled a chair over. "That's what old friends are for, right?" she said. "To give you bad news right after a heart attack."

"I know it's bad over there. I know that. But news? Not so much. Sebastian, right? It's gotta be Sebastian. What's little Seabass done?"

"Seabass! Ha! I like that."

"Oily, scaly, not that bright," he said. She tried not to laugh, and snorted. He just smiled.

"What's he done?"

Anna sighed deeply and took a few moments to answer. "Well, Bern, bad news and good news. I am retiring, a casualty of his daily campaign of whining and carping."

"No," he said quickly. "Not carping, seabassing."

"Ha! I didn't see that one coming. But the good news is I found a way to be happy about it. Excited, actually."

It isn't easy to look surprised when you're pale and motionless in bed, when even subtle facial expression is a struggle, but Bernard managed. His eyebrows raised and his mouth opened. "I could never imagine you on a shuffleboard court. Unless someone invents full contact shuffleboard."

She laughed as if he were the old Bernie, but saw how pale he looked, and remembered where she was. "Okay, Bern. You have to stop making me laugh or they're gonna throw me out of here, too."

He took a raspy breath and groaned a little. "Maybe we *should* call it a day, Anna. But will you come back? Soon?"

"Tomorrow. Count on it."

"Smuggle in something to read," he muttered. "*The Times*." She looked back as the door was closing, and his eyes were almost closed.

His room was on the third floor. She walked down the hall, stood and stared for a full minute at the elevator door. A nurse came over and asked if there were something wrong.

Anna said without looking at her, "Just remembering a time I got lucky, years ago. Thirty seconds in an elevator and I was cured of the plague of hero worship forever." She took the stairs down.

Two

Next morning, she was up early and walked to Herman's Deli for her usual: coffee, a bagel with a schmear, and two newspapers.

Herman had a slight German accent, except when he was angry, when it became no longer slight. When something outraged him, a common occurrence, he veered into an outbreak of throaty, rapid German. The words were foreign, but the meaning was clear. He was gray haired, big boned, big bellied and had all the physical equipment needed to bellow.

He looked stern, generally, and presented himself as gruff and impatient, but his customers warmed to him quickly. Anna, like many, was initially intimidated by him, but kept coming back. He was part of the 'warp and weft' of Forest Hills. *That's my mom's phrase, 'warp and weft.' Thanks for everything, Mom.*

"Anna," Herman said. "Anna is here so I know it is Saturday. I have little need for a calendar as long as there is Anna."

She smiled at him. "What would you do on a Wednesday, Herman?"

He frowned. "Simple. I would wait until Saturday, and then I would know."

"Your logic is impeccable, Herman."

"A gift of my German heritage. Throw me a problem, I will catch it in the air and solve it with one hand."

"Well, tell me then, where are you keeping your *Daily News*? I got the *Newsday* I wanted, but I don't see the *News* on the rack."

He shook his head and walked to the rack. He lifted up several *New York Times* newspapers and pulled out a stack of the *Daily News* underneath. "Surrounded, Anna. *Ich bin von dummköpfen umgeben, Anna! Dummköpfen.* My nephew! Such a simple thing I asked. Put the newspapers there on the rack. Simple! *Einfach! Dummköpfen!*"

"A nephew? Please don't talk to me about nephews."

"You are plagued by a nephew too, Anna?"

"Yes. No, not my nephew. The nephew of my boss, who has now become my boss. He could not stack your newspapers without pictures and a tutor to explain it to him."

Another customer came into the deli and Herman slipped behind the counter. Anna breathed more easily. She paid the *Dummköpfen* nephew for her coffee, bagel, and newspapers, and brought them home.

She sat at a small table in her Forest Hills kitchen and pored over the real estate ads to find a home for her business. Money, of course, was a problem, but she was not afraid to take out a loan if she could get one. Her only collateral was her car, an eight-year-old Honda, her only income, social security and her pension from the magazine. A bank, though, could find a way to squeeze a monthly payment out of her. She looked slowly and carefully through anything with a label of 'commercial real estate,' but everything was too new, too large or else prohibitively expensive. What she had in mind, dimly, was a big room with a few desks, with space in the middle for a large table where she and her staff, *her staff* she thought, could hold conferences and make decisions. One of the phrases ricocheting around her head since last week was, 'what to leave in, and what to leave out.' Getting consensus, smoothing things over to get people to agree, was Bernard's skill, one she envied, and she was both anxious and daunted, realizing that role might soon be hers. "Maybe just some desks we can arrange into pods, or basic departments," she told her cat. "We'll stick signs on the walls, like Art Department, or News of the Day, or Profiles Without Courage. Yeah. Yeah. Departments. Infant, developing departments. Yeah. That'll work." She took a bite of her bagel and a sip of coffee.

"No. No, no," she told herself, louder. "Don't get smug about this, Anna. Actual departments seems a bit ambitious. You are going to start small, and will probably stay small, and that's okay. You aren't Henry Luce. You aren't Harold Ross. If the stars are in alignment and there's a soft breeze from the east, you may cobble together a small, intelligent, classy, humorous publication. You're going to have to work your foundation undergarments off to get it to fly, but it's better than shuffleboard."

Anna cleaned her glasses, took another bite of her bagel and went back to studying the newspaper, feeling a little concerned that suddenly she was talking to herself. The cat had left the room.

By late afternoon, she was back at Presbyterian Hospital climbing the stairs to the third floor. Bernard looked a little better, but just a little. He was sitting more upright than yesterday, too.

A nurse was checking his monitors and watching him take his medicine. She saw Anna and gave her a nervous little smile. "It's okay," Bernard said to the nurse. "That's not my wife."

"No, no. Not a wife. Just a friend. A co-worker," Anna said. She handed him the newspaper.

The nurse sniffed the air discreetly and smiled. She said, "Please, Mr. Holloway, stick with the crossword and the entertainment section. The stock market pages are not recommended for someone with your history." She smiled at Bernard, nodded at Anna and left.

"You came back," he said to Anna.

"Yes. I did. But a word to the wise. If your queen sails in here, and I might smell her before she gets through the door, I'm gone. I'll try to be polite enough to say hello and goodbye, but I'm not promising anything."

"Fair enough. Oh, look at this! A newspaper! Words! All right in a row, running down a page! Perhaps providing some information about the outside world! Thank you, Anna. You have brought joy to my toxic ticker."

"You're looking a little closer to human, Bern. You have color in your cheeks. It isn't a color often seen on this planet, but better than yesterday."

He folded the newspaper and tucked it under his pillow. "I'm not sharing this with anyone."

"That's why God made single rooms. For curmudgeons like you."

"He was really thoughtful that way."

"Yeah, I think She was." She laughed, he smiled. It was a real smile this time, wide and toothy.

"So, what did you not want to tell me yesterday? I can always tell when you have something you need to share. So, what? Give me some grist for my mill."

She sat on the side of the bed without any tubes or wires. "Okay, so Seabass wants me gone, which really had me walking in circles for a while. But things have turned around."

"They do that when you're walking in circles. So, come on. What is it? What's the good news?"

"I made up my mind not to retire. To hell with Seabass. To hell with full contact shuffleboard. I'm going into business. I'm gonna start a magazine."

He said nothing for a long minute, then the eyebrows moved slowly up. "You're...you're gonna do what?" he said slowly.

"Yep."

"Anna."

"Bernard." The looked at each other without speaking, Anna with sadness, and Bernie with surprise. Finally, Anna said, "Oh, not you. I knew someone was gonna throw stones at this, but not you. I didn't think it would be you."

Bernard shifted a little in his bed. "I think you misunderstand. I'm not throwing stones. I'm not throwing anything. I'm worried. And I'm a little jealous."

"Worried?"

"Yeah, worried. About *Aplomb,* for one thing. If you're not there to stamp out the fires Seabass starts, the magazine doesn't have six months. I've been there for thirty-four years; you know my story. I sunk every nickel I had into it and if it had failed, I would still be living under a bridge. I was a smart-ass twenty-something that got lucky and found a home. And it *was* a home for all that time. I'll hate to see it go."

Anna struggled for something to say. She had known him for all those years, and knew *Aplomb* was even more important to him than it was to her. Age carries the sad reality that the landmarks in your life have vanished: loved relatives, the house you grew up in, your best friend in fourth grade. Losing his job was the final rug being pulled out from under a man who was once young. The sincerest words of consolation are hollow and anemic, and she did not want to minimize their friendship by mouthing them.

"Okay, I get it Bern," she said after a while. "If I wasn't angry about being pushed out, I would be worried about the magazine, too. I think it's easier to be angry."

He thought for a moment. "Angry *is* better than sad. The hell with all that 'gently into that good night' crappola. My problem is, with this dickie ticker, I may not have much choice."

"Is that where the jealous part comes in? Do you resent me doing this?"

"No, not resent. It's more complicated than that. Partly, I'm worried about you. Launching a business, especially a magazine, is a lot of work, a lot of stress, a lot of headaches. And once it's launched, it's still a lot of work, stress, and headaches. I would hate to see you in here, prodded and beeping and hoping someone comes to visit."

"You're gonna be fine, Bern, and so am I. You know I'm a hardy specimen. Feed me coffee, and I can go all day."

"'Feed me coffee and I can go all day.' Wow, that sounds familiar. I said those exact words, *those exact words*, just before my lights went out and I was carried in here."

"I know the risks. But I've thought about it, and I'm not toddling off gently into any good nights, Bern. And I doubt you will be either. I'm betting by summer you'll be up and shufflin.' And I don't mean shuffle-boarding."

"Harumph."

"There it is. I've been waiting for you to 'harumph' me. I've really missed it."

"No, you haven't. You hate it when I 'harumph.'"

A voice outside the room said, firmly, "I know who you are, Mrs. Holloway, but you can only stay for fifteen minutes. Those are hospital rules, not mine."

Sherilyn Holloway swept into the room like Scarlett O'Hara in a hoop skirt gliding onto her veranda. Her perfume preceded her like a mist before a rainstorm. She looked at Bernard, and then more pointedly at Anna, and said, "Hello. I see you're here."

"Yes," Anna said, and appealed to the nurse still standing by the open door. "There is a rule that limits to one visitor at a time, right?"

The nurse nodded. "That's right. Cardiac wing. One visitor."

She pulled her jacket off the back of the chair and said goodbye to Bernard. She nodded at Sherilyn and said, "Have a nice visit. It's nice to see you again, Sherilyn." Sherilyn smiled and nodded. As the door was closing behind her, Anna heard Bernard sneeze.

~ * ~

The Sunday papers didn't advertise anything that looked useable for an office. Space in an industrial park was the cheapest per square foot, but the spaces offered were enormous, and usually not easily accessible. Office rental space was smaller, more convenient, and made a more pleasant environment, but was pricey and subject to the usual *sturm und drang* of New York real estate—corruption supported by rapacious greed and seasoned liberally with taxes and sudden, unexpected costs. Anna always felt the welcoming symbol of New York, the Statue of Liberty, should have been constructed with a wink and one palm up.

Her fallback plan was to move to a larger apartment, where one room could be dedicated to the magazine. That was probably illegal, contrary to copyright laws, zoning laws, municipal tax code, fire regulations, the Book of Revelations, and at least one article of the Constitution. But with a small staff willing to be flexible and discreet, maybe it was manageable. *Temporarily,* she thought. *Until we get some momentum, and a little working capital.* She decided to call a local real estate agent the next day, and maybe stop by after work. *After work,* she thought. *If the magazine ends up in my apartment, 'after work' will have a very different meaning.*

With a dish of ice cream and a handful of pretzels, she settled on the couch and started reading the rest of the paper. Paging through the Queens section of *Newsday,* she scanned a small article about a preschool that was transferring its students to another building. It was labeled as an 'auxiliary' preschool, named after a beloved secretary who had done the payroll for years in the previous millennium. The school was in a cottage, a mile away from the other school buildings. The article explained that registration of the under-six population had fallen off sharply, and there was now adequate room for all the kids in the regular building. The article was entitled, "The Little Red Schoolhouse Gets Left Back."

She finished the article, folded the paper, yawned, and went to bed. Up early as usual, she was almost out the door early, as usual. She hesitated with her hand on the doorknob and said to the cat, Mrs. Roosevelt, "I don't really care if I'm late. It's too late for Sebaceous to fire me." She poured another glass of juice and picked up the paper. Right where she had folded it was the article about The Little Red Schoolhouse, and this time she didn't scan it. She read it once, and then again, and then a third time with the care and focus of a copy editor. Those plans and ideas that were careening around in her head last week started up again, but this time with more focus.

Instead of a depressing interview with a real estate agent, she drove past the schoolhouse. It was in a wooded section of Forest Hills, appropriately, and was indeed, little and red. It was a cottage with a screened in front porch, a side entrance, a driveway leading to a garage, and even a small fenced-in back yard. It was too dark that evening to see anything inside, and too cold to get out of the car, but Anna felt she had a toehold on something. She looked up the phone number for the school district and for the public works department. *Maybe,* she thought. *Maybe.*

Most of last week, Sebastian, aka Sebaceous, aka Seabass, had given her a wide berth, with just an occasional smirk. This morning he turned off the music and called her in.

Anna stood in front of him. "Wow," she said. "That really is an impressive desk. Big. Polished. Curved in just such a way as to clearly indicate who is in charge."

Sebastian ignored the barb. "I talked to my aunt last night. She had me over for dessert."

Anna said nothing.

"You visited my Uncle Bernard on Sunday. Can I ask why?"

"I had finished running the Zamboni for the Rangers after the second period, so I had some time to kill. Why?"

"Running the what?"

"Zamboni."

He shook his head in frustration. "Stop it, Anna. Stop gaslighting me. There's no such thing as a Zamboni, and if there were, why would park rangers ask you to run it?

She laughed. "You amaze me, Seb."

"Don't call me Seb," he snapped. That surprised her. She was used to him accepting her gibes meekly.

"Okay then, Sebastian, but you still amaze me. I can't even kid around with you. A Zamboni is a real thing. It's a machine, like a big truck they drive around to smooth over the ice during a hockey game. It's a funny name, but it's a real thing. Google it. Learn something."

"Fine. A Zamboni is a real thing. But you didn't answer my question. Why did you visit my uncle on Sunday night?"

She looked at him with that subtle head tilt that said, 'are you kidding?'

"Seb, um, Sebastian, I'm going to sit down because this is looking like it may be a long discussion. I promise I'll sit directly in front of the desk to get the full effect."

"Heh, heh. Sarcasm just spills out of you, doesn't it?"

"I would like to show you the kind of respect you demand, Sebastian. But it's hard when you ask questions like 'why did you visit my critically ill uncle in the hospital, just because you have known and worked with him for over thirty years?'"

"Don't give me that. Aunt Sherilyn always thought there was something between you two. And now that he's about to cash in, you're looking to, you know, cash in."

She leaned back in her chair and stared at him. He just stared back.

"Cash in? *Cash in?* That's cold," she said. "Even for you."

"So, then why? Why were you there, and why did you make a bee line as soon as Aunt Sherilyn arrived?"

"Severe respiratory problems."

"Bernard has respiratory problems, too? In addition to the heart thing?"

"No, not Bernard. Me. When Sherilyn came in, I had trouble breathing."

"Oh, yeah. That."

"And, to answer your question, I was there for a couple of reasons. Because I like him. Because you don't visit. And because I wanted his advice."

"Advice about what?"

"About the 'R' word, what else? In three days, I no longer have a place to go, a schedule, a routine."

He made a face. "What's the big deal? Do what all the other creaky blue hairs do. Go to Florida. Take a cruise. Learn to knit. Complain about your arthritis. But leave my uncle Bernard alone."

She felt her anger rising. "If you don't want my sarcasm, you need to cut me a little slack. Take it down a little. Give a little, get a little."

"Bah! I'm the boss here, and you're a soon-to be-former-employee. I don't have to give you squat."

That was the final button he needed to push. "There is something important missing in you, Sebastian. I mean Seb," she said.

He yelled, "Don't call me Seb!" She smiled at him.

"You can't really believe, Seb, that I'm after his money, Seb. Even your aunt is smarter than that, Seb."

He glared at her, pointed to the door, stood and turned his stereo on. A Bach fugue stretched across the room, and the conversation was over. She left the door open.

~ * ~

It took Anna two days of calling from the privacy of the ladies' room before she got the supervisor of buildings and grounds for the Forest

Hills School District. He was very pleasant, in a vague and unhelpful way. He opined that, yes, the schoolhouse might be available for lease, and, yes, he was fairly sure it was structurally sound and habitable for both children and adults. But no, it was not he that was empowered to make arrangements for a lease. In all likelihood, it was either the office of the superintendent, or else the office of the attorney for the district. Or, perhaps the superintendent with the *consent* of the attorney. He was not sufficiently familiar with the legal transfer of district resources to say for sure. But yes, he would have his administrative assistant get the phone number for both offices if she would kindly hold on. Anna wanted to ask if she could get a tour through the building, but she was afraid that requesting the assistant to find two phone numbers was the limit of his administrative abilities.

~ * ~

Chloe came over with a cup of coffee for Anna, who needed it. "How you doing there, short timer?"

"I'm good, Chloe. I don't understand why I'm good, but I feel like I am. Every step, every turn, every idea runs me into a brick wall, and still somehow, I'm good."

"When you turn your head at a certain angle, I can see the bruises on your head. That one's really turning a lovely combination of black and blue."

Anna thought of Chloe as a younger version of herself: organized, focused and serious. She also had the same sense of humor, and both Sebaceous and Donna disliked her for it. That was another reason for Anna to trust her. Chloe, for her part, thought of Anna as family. Anna had been friends with Chloe's mother.

Anna sipped her coffee. "Would you come with me for a minute? I want to show you something."

"Oh, some of your bruises? Ew."

Anna laughed. "Come on, I promise not to gross you out."

Anna poked her head into the ladies' room, but Donna was in there talking with Suzanne. Donna was saying, "So, the husband says, I told her to get out of my fort." Suzanne hesitated, waiting for a little more, and then realized it was the punchline and laughed.

"Oh, yeah I get it. She says he's immature and he tells her to get out of his fort. That's funny."

Anna closed the door quickly and went around the corner to the entrance to the stairway. "You want to show me the stairway?" Chloe said. "I have something a lot like this at home. Just smaller."

"Breaking news, here, kiddo. I'm not retiring. I'm going to start my own magazine. That's why I've been kind of preoccupied lately."

Chloe was wide-eyed. "Your own magazine? Really? You can do that? I mean, you really think you can do that? That's, uh, wow."

"It won't be as big as *Aplomb*, or as classy. But it will be a smart, funny weekly. Or maybe bi-weekly. Monthly, maybe. I haven't worked out all the details."

Chloe was still wide-eyed, and now she added an open mouth. Anna gave her a nervous little smile and shrugged.

"Wow," Chloe said. "I may have mentioned that before, but it bears repeating. Wow. Your own magazine. Wow."

"Lots of details, Chloe. Lots of stuff to work out. I think that's why I'm feeling so good. I think it's like a lion or a cheetah or something that been just lazing around licking her paws. But all of a sudden there's a herd of unicorns or heffalumps or something, and she just springs into full predator mode. I feel like Elsa the lioness stalking a heffalump."

Chloe hugged her. Words were insufficient, tears not necessary. So, a hug. "I wish I could help."

"I think you just did. I needed to blurt it out to someone, and you were the one. That helped."

They heard Donna and Suzanne come out of the bathroom and giggle their way down the hall, and when the coast was clear, they went back to the office. Chloe sat at her desk and smiled broadly at Anna, who was still paying close attention to the ideas and plans and numbers that were bouncing around in her head.

Three

Friday arrived, Anna's final day, and the day of her 'Rrr' party. Years ago, in a quasi-poetic flurry, someone had come up with the theme 'mimosas and toasters,' and succeeding generations at *Aplomb*, probably for lack of creativity, continued the tradition. Donna made the mimosas, with minimal champagne as directed by Sebastian, and someone was dispatched to buy a cheap toaster and wrap it. Anna was subdued, a little bit nostalgic, but mostly preoccupied with those plans and ideas and numbers that had taken up residence in her mind. Like all people who are highly organized, she carried around a list of things that need to fall into place. She had the inventory on paper in her pocketbook, but it soon was memorized:

A place, (fingers crossed about the Little Red Schoolhouse), furniture (this one is easy, just expensive), technology (also easy, also expensive), people (people are easy, the right people much more difficult), a magazine layout (easiest of all, right in her wheelhouse). She went to sleep with this list, woke up with it, rode the subway with it, and ate her meals with it.

The party slipped into gear shortly after nine o'clock. There was, of course, a giant card with a picture of someone snoring in a hammock with the caption "You Earned It!!!" Anna suspected you could measure the sincerity of a greeting card by how many exclamation points are included. She was satisfied with three.

There was coffee and peanut-butter-free brownies, and as Anna looked around, only a few ghosts made an appearance:

Bernard, of course, walking around with his hands behind his back mumbling his favorite phrase, "You have no idea."

Beverly, Anna's predecessor as chief-cook-and-bottle-washer. She was a friend and mentor to Anna, essential to Bernard, and gone too soon.

Aloysius, whom Anna spotted near the fire exit, and ignored. He soon disappeared, and she breathed a deep sigh,

The Chorus, three smiling women with hands clasped in front as they had been coached. She could see them clearly, but could not hear them. That was a disappointment. She would have dearly loved to hear them again, just once.

After all the hugs and 'let's stay in touch' comments and the stony looks from Donna, Anna gathered her coat, her card and her toaster and stopped in to say goodbye to Sebastian. He had not made an appearance. Beethoven's *Für Elise* was playing, the only classical music Anna recognized, and Sebastian's desktop was, as usual, clear.

"Sebaceous," she said.

"Anna, how many of those mimosas have you had? You're slurring already."

"No, Sebastian, I'm not having trouble saying your name, because you are much more Sebaceous than you are Sebastian."

"I have no idea what you mean, but anyway, goodbye."

She reached in her jacket pocket. "I know it's backwards, but I have a going away gift for you."

"Oh, something explosive?"

"You misjudge me, Sebaceous. I'm old and cranky, but not violent." She handed him a small package, neatly wrapped with a bow on top. He was suspicious, but he opened it. It was a book of jokes.

"Something to help you develop a sense of humor," she said. "And I put a note in there with a website for some Zamboni jokes."

He shook his head slowly. "I had braces when I was a kid, Anna. I'm going to miss you even less."

She turned to the door as he said, "And stay away from my uncle Bernard."

"Oh, thank you, Sebaceous, for the golden opportunity for my final words to you to be 'hell, no.'" She walked out, and left the door open.

~ * ~

The 'mimosa and toaster' was over by ten-thirty. She stopped for a cup of tea, and was home by noon, nervous, because she had a two o'clock appointment with the Forest Hills School District Superintendent.

A dress, she wondered? *A pants suit would look more business-like. A briefcase, maybe? Earrings, those dangly ones? Heels?* She tried on three outfits, each with different shoes, and tried her hair two different ways. Nothing she did screamed 'successful business woman who just needs a break.'

"To hell with it," she said to her mirror. "I hate to sound like Sammy Davis Junior, but *I Gotta Be Me.*"

Just before two o'clock she was outside the office of Keith Dannell, the superintendent. A tall, rangy African-American man with bright eyes and a broad smile. He shook hands and pointed to a seat at a table in the corner of the office.

"It's an unusual request," he said. "That pre-school has been here as long as I have, and the need to rent it has never come up. An unprecedented situation," he said.

She had opted for the pants suit and comfortable shoes. "In the business world," she said, "unprecedented situations can often generate wonderful advantages." He nodded.

"Forgive me," she added. "That came off as a little pompous."

He smiled. "A little, but I do see what you mean. It could be one of those rare 'win-win' situations. But tell me more about what you plan to do with the cottage. You mentioned a magazine."

She relaxed a little. "I've worked for magazines, well, one magazine, most of my adult life, and I know how they work. But recent circumstances have forced me into retirement."

"Recent circumstances. Health?"

"No. Bureaucracy."

"Ah, that one. That's the big one."

She laughed. "It is. So, my plan is to develop a magazine of my own."

"Huh. A big job."

"I've done most of the jobs within a magazine, with the exception of management. I'm sorry if this comes off a pompous as well, but I am convinced I can handle it. I've arranged for the financial backing, and I have a plan for the format of the magazine. If I can get the right staff and a place to set it up, I know I can run it."

He leaned back and rubbed his head. "Who was that Greek guy looking for a fulcrum? I'm trying to remember."

She was confused for a minute, and then smiled. "Archimedes, the leverage guy. All he needed was a place to stand and he could move the world."

"Yeah, that's the guy. You're planning to move the world?"

"Maybe just nudge it a little."

Anna had noticed over the years that people did one of three things when they were thinking: some were nodders, following some private conversation with themselves. Others were tappers, either with a finger on the desk or with a pencil to serve as a drumstick. Others were gazers, looking around for a picture to stare at, or a window to stare out of. Keith Dannell was a tapper. He looked steadily at her, tapped a few times, and said, "You feel confident that our schoolhouse has everything you're looking for?"

"Yes. Mr. Clemente had one of his custodians walk through with me, and it fits all my needs. There's enough space, there's heat, air conditioning, electricity, plumbing, a kitchen, even wi-fi. I already have a business loan, I have a contact for office furniture and computers, and I have someone in mind to do building maintenance, unless the district wants me to contract with them."

"Unprecedented," he said softly. "Mr. Clemente was a little hesitant about this, but he's the nervous type. He wears both a belt and suspenders."

Anna laughed again and said, "I know the type."

He started tapping again. Anna said, "I have whittled down my 'to-do' list, at least for the start-up. Once I have a physical office space, I can start developing a staff and planning articles and drawings. I have in mind about six people to begin with, and I will admit to you I am very excited about this."

He smiled. "I envy you. The beginning of things, the start-up as you call it, is usually more fun than the middle and the end."

Apparently, he had made his decision. He took an envelope out of his desk. "I had our legal department draw up this contract. It's not too involved, and I'm sure you can imagine most of what's in it. Feel free to consult your attorney, but you may not need to. Surprisingly, it's mostly English." She nodded a few times, because she couldn't think of anything to say.

"I had them add one special item I hope you will agree to. Our high school has a literature club, and they have a contest at the end of every school year. There is a prize for fiction and a prize for non-fiction. It would be a real boost to the winners if, as part of the prize, we could promise publication in your magazine."

"Wow, that is just a great idea. Another 'win-win.'

"In the education business, we call it incentive."

"In the magazine business, we call it quality content."

~ * ~

Anna lived in one of the older, and smaller, apartment complexes in Queens: brick buildings, only two stories high, with eight apartments in each building. They were a throwback to the days of a smaller, less dominating cityscape. It was a group of seventeen buildings that, over decades, had become a mecca for senior citizens. Anna had lived there for twenty-three years with her mother, and was comfortable enough to stay after her mother passed away.

It was, in a very real sense, a community. There were stores nearby, there was a swimming pool, a pool table, a library of sorts, and a multitude of clubs. There were well-maintained gardens in the pathways between the buildings, and most residents knew each other. Anna was a regular in the Thursday evening bridge game, and was trying, so far without success, to establish a weekly poker game.

She hadn't mentioned yet to anyone that she was retired, and when she was recognized on the grounds, was reluctant to admit it. She did mention it to a couple she knew that had been friendly with her mother.

"Nothing to be ashamed of," Carla and Robert told her. "We're both retired and we love it. We don't fight any more than we used to, now that we're home together all day," Robert said.

"But then, we don't fight any less, either," Carla said. "It's just that we have fewer things to fight about, and our fights are a lot shorter. It's, you know, the same old stuff, so we've developed a kind of shorthand."

"Yeah, like a code, a secret language, just to save time and aggravation."

"Really?" Anna said. "A code? How would that work?"

Carla and Robert looked at each other. Carla started speaking and Robert interrupted. "Suppose," he said, "we're going out somewhere, to dinner, or maybe a friend's house, and Carla is running late. She's making herself even more beautiful, probably, which seems like it shouldn't take very long, being so naturally close to perfection."

"Or," Carla said with a chuckle, 'Robert is early, because it's easier for men to get dressed up. They don't fret much about accessories or shoes or make up. And if they had the same underwear on yesterday, who's to know?"

"So, if she was late," Robert continued, "I would say, 'Time and tide,' honey. And then Carla would say, "Speaking of Tide, it's your turn to do the wash. And that would shut me up, *post haste*; argument avoided, mostly because I hate doing the wash."

Carla said, "That worked for years, but gradually it morphed into...oh, is 'morphed' a word? Anyway, pretty soon all one of us had to say was 'it's your turn to do the wash,' and the argument would collapse like a punctured Thanksgiving parade balloon. Or another one. Sometimes he'll wear white socks with black shoes. I used to say, 'You look like Willy off the pickle boat' and the spat would begin. Now, I just call him 'Willy,' and he gets it. Argument avoided. Magic. Works every time."

Anna, slipping into editor-in-chief mode, saw the nucleus of an article for her magazine. Around the curve of the walkway, they waved and turned toward their apartment. Anna called after them. "Robert, what did you do for a living?"

"I wrote advertising copy for a supermarket chain for almost forty-two years. I was the best in the business. 'Where meat becomes dinner' was one of my gems. And the one that won an award, 'We're not trying to be fresh, but we strive to be fresh.'"

"Carla, what did you do?"

"I was a middle school English teacher, and I have the x-rays to prove it," she said. The ideas and plans and numbers that had bounced around in Anna's head a few weeks ago started bouncing again, but softer now, slower, and she thought, funnier.

"I hope to see you again soon," Anna called. She looked at them as they walked away, Robert wore white socks with his black sneakers, and they were holding hands.

She made a note in her little memo book, an accommodation to being in her seventies, 'Robert and Carla. The code.'

~ * ~

Herman's Deli was a few blocks down Gateway Boulevard, only a ten-minute walk, but today Anna turned right instead of left, walked a couple of blocks, just looking, and then turned around. She didn't think about it, she just did it because she was now, officially, a woman who made her own hours.

Herman was in the back, stocking cereal. "Oh, no," he said when he saw her. "I'm not ready for this yet."

"Herman, what is it? Are you okay?"

"I must be getting old, Anna. Senile. I would have sworn it was only Tuesday, and yet, here you are, so it must be Saturday."

She laughed. "No, Herman. It's Tuesday. Your calendar is still accurate, but you may need to adjust it a little bit. I am retired now, so I can get my coffee here other than Saturdays."

"Oh, that's good. I mean, not so good for you maybe, but good for me. I thought I was, um, what is that thing, non-compost-able?"

Anna thought for a moment, translating.

"*Non-compos mentis?*"

"Yes, that. Those foreign words always escape me. But yes, that's what I mean. Losing my mental agility." He was tearing the corners of the cardboard cartons and flattening them.

"You seem pretty sharp to me, Herman." She wondered how old he was but was too polite to ask. He was broad and steely grey, and his face was unlined; she thought he could be anywhere from fifty to seventy.

"But retirement for you, Anna? Well, I guess, congratulations and all the best to you."

"Thank you, Herman. It wasn't my idea, but I am figuring out a way to survive it."

"I am not a believer in retirement. It may be a Deutschland belief, but I think a man is meant to work, not to fish. Unless he is a fisherman, of course."

"I imagine there are a lot of Deutschland beliefs that are different from American ones."

He sat down on a crate with a small groan. "You are a woman who sees clearly through things, Anna. I came here when I was only seven, and a lot about the United States seemed odd to me. A lot still does, even after so many years."

"Really?" said Anna, thinking she had been lucky enough to stumble on a second article for her magazine. "Like what, for example?"

He crossed his legs and rubbed his chin. "Pets, for instance. We love our dogs and cats, but one time I laughed at a lady who had dressed her dog as a reindeer, and foolishly, I lost a customer that day. Why do Americans turn their pets into children?"

"Know what, Herman? You should—"

He kept talking. "And stores. In the old country, we have small shops where once you get in the door, you can see everything. Like here in my deli. Once you walk past the meats and cheeses, it's wide open and everything can be seen. But American stores? Big. Everything has to be big. Escalators, elevators, thirty different cash registers. You need a bicycle to get from the dairy to the deli section in one of these places. But here, no one rides bicycles. I suppose they are not big enough either."

"Herman, you should write about that. About the differences between your old country and the U.S. I bet people would be interested."

"I am a very good writer, Anna, but less good in English. Besides, who would read it?"

"Well, I would. And I bet other people would. I told you I didn't want to retire, so I decided to start a magazine. Something small and local, and now I'm trying to find articles to put in it. What you just told me would interest a lot of people. Especially people from foreign countries. Why not give it a try? I could help you write it if you want."

He put his chin on his fist and frowned. "I would have to think about this."

~ * ~

She took a ride that afternoon to the schoolhouse, just to stroll around and dream. It had one room big enough for half a dozen desks, a full kitchen, and a small pantry just off the kitchen. Tucked in the corner of the main room was small bathroom with a toilet designed for people with shorter legs and smaller rear ends. *Functional in a pinch, but not real comfortable,* Anna thought. She added 'new toilet and plumber' to the startup list.

The main room was carpeted, and recently painted with bright red, blue and yellow walls. She sat on the floor of the empty room, put her list of contacts on her lap, and dialed her cell phone.

Her first call was to Miriam, a writer (Anna was getting accustomed to thinking of them as 'content providers') who had left *Aplomb* a few years ago to test the waters as a freelance writer. As Anna remembered, she could afford to test the waters, being married to a lawyer.

"Miriam, hello, it's Anna. Anna Pennington from *Aplomb*."

It took a minute, but she said, "Oh, Anna! Of course! How nice to hear from you."

They chatted for a few minutes about people and old times. Bernard's health was a big topic, and co-workers who had changed jobs, retired, gotten married or passed away.

"Miriam," Anna said when the conversation flagged. "I hope you don't mind a call out of the blue, but I have a question for you."

"It's always good to hear from old friends, and I'm curious about the question."

"I retired recently. After Bernard got sick, I was kind of pushed into retirement, and it's not for me."

"No. I never thought you were the type to sit on a beach."

"Everyone seems to know that, except the guy that pushed me out. So, and I know this sounds odd, but I decided to start a magazine of my own."

A long silence. "Really? A magazine of your own? Wow, that's, uh, that's..."

"Ambitious. Maybe crazy. Maybe a death wish, but I'm doing it anyway. And I'm looking for staff writers. You are the first one I thought of."

"Nuts," Miriam said.

"No kidding, really. You are the first one I called, because I remember enjoying your short pieces in *Aplomb*."

"No, you misunderstand. I wasn't doubting you. I was saying that taking on something like a new magazine is kind of nuts."

"Oh."

She sighed heavily. "Words, Anna. Words are becoming a problem for me. I can still write okay, but when I'm talking, sometimes words don't cooperate. Or they come, but too late, after everyone else is talking about something else, you know?"

"Like senior moments."

"Sometimes it feels more like senior day-and-a-halves."

"I have them sometimes, more than I care to admit," Anna said. "We all do. It comes with the golden years."

Miriam sniffled a little. "But I can still write. Usually, as long as I can think for a minute, I get the words. Sometimes longer than a minute, but I get them right."

Anna said. "Then, what do you say? If you've still got it, then use it. Write for us."

"Oh," Miriam said. "I'm flattered, but, well...I would have to think. You're talking humor pieces, right? And human interest? Short, and um..."

"Yes, exactly. I'm not certain about the makeup of the magazine, but it will be a little local news, some cartoons and mostly humor. And you were always—"

Miriam interrupted. "Punchy. That's the right word. Short and punchy. "

"Yes. Short and punchy, which you were always good at."

"Well, give me some time to mull this over. I haven't worked much in a few years, just a piece or two here and there. I've gotten used to the retirement life, and I may be rusty. So, it's a lot to think about."

"Oh, I know. I won't pressure you and I don't want to take up too much of your time, I'd just like you to think about writing for us."

"Yes, of course I'll think about it. But I have a lot of questions, mostly about your plan, your business plan. Publishing a magazine is not as simple as doing the dishes or taking out the um, you know…

"Well, it will be a small, local publication, for sure. Certainly at the beginning. And you know, I have forty years' experience in magazines, and I'm good at my job. I think…"

"Garbage."

Anna was stunned. "I'm sorry, Miriam. Garbage?"

"Oh, no, no, no. I was finishing my other sentence. Not as easy as taking out the, um, garbage."

Anna laughed. "Oh, I see."

"You begin to understand my problem," Miriam said. "You begin to see why I like retirement."

"Yes, I'm getting it. But you said writing was different, and I still want you to write for us. Please. Have lunch with me, or better yet, meet me at the schoolhouse, and I'll tell you all about my plans, such as they are."

"The schoolhouse?"

"I'm renting a cottage that used to be a pre-school. That's going to be the office."

"Aha, a pre-school," Miriam said, uncertainly.

~ * ~

The next phone call, to an accountant who had worked for *Aplomb* more than ten years earlier, was a wrong number. The call after that, a copywriter, L.T., short for LaToya, only got as far as a generic voice message; "The person you are calling is not answering right now. Please leave a message after the tone." Which she did.

She called Jasmine, an illustrator who had left Aplomb a few years ago, and asked the boy that answered the phone to please have her call back. *What else, what else, what else? Time for another list,* she thought and wrote it in her memo book.

- *Writers: at least two, including me, if Miriam agrees. Robert and Carla are maybes, at best. Herman, I think is a non-starter.*
- *Copy editors: two, including me, if I can reach L.T. I'd love to have Chloe, but I can't pay her a full-time salary.*
- *Illustrators: one, maybe Jasmine. Probably need another. Maybe another just for cover art. If there's going to be a cover.*
- *Editor-in-Chief: She smiled when she thought, Oh, that's me, And then she laughed loud enough for the sound to echo in the empty room.*
- *Auxiliary people: a printer, an accountant, a web designer, an attorney, a marketing director. She got up to walk a bit and said to the empty kitchen, "That's way too long a list for a start-up operation. The auxiliary people will just have to wait. Oh, and we need a microwave and a coffee machine. Coffee machine goes to the top of the list. Well, no. A plumber and an adult toilet are the top of the list."*

On the drive home, she thought of one more important item for the list: A name for the magazine. *Yep, that would help a lot.*

Four

Miriam called the next evening to say she hadn't made up her mind, but wanted to hear more about the new magazine. They made a date for lunch the following week, and then a visit to the schoolhouse.

Jasmine called too, and said she might be interested but wanted to hear more. Anna invited her to lunch with her and Miriam, and then a trip to the schoolhouse. She wasn't thinking of it as an office yet.

Meanwhile, Anna kept busy with her setup plan. She had ordered office furniture, computers, and telephone service, and was a bit frustrated that it would take ten days to two weeks for all of it to be in place. "Rome wasn't built in a day," she said to herself, and then the Latin translation popped into her memory; *Romae non fuit dies*. It startled her that she remembered it, and then it struck her. Aloysius. Aloysius used to love to show off his Latin. She hadn't thought of him in years, and this was the second time in a week. *Stress*, she thought. *When things are more settled, he'll go away.*

She called L.T. again, and gave her answering machine a longer explanation of why she was calling. She mentioned the lunch, and the name of the restaurant, and hoped she would be able to make it, or at least call back.

Lunch was at a small restaurant and bar that Miriam suggested. Anna arrived a few minutes early, ordered a drink and looked at the menu. Jasmine found Anna and gave her a nervous smile as she draped her coat over a chair. "It was a real surprise to hear from you, Anna. To be honest, I always thought you didn't like me."

Anna's eyes widened. "Really? I didn't like you? I'm sorry if I gave you that impression, Jasmine. I was always impressed with your work. I'm sorry, really. Looking back, I think I may have been a little intimidated by you. People able to just draw something at will are an amazement to me. I am a complete cliché when it comes to drawing. With a number two pencil and a ruler, I can't draw a straight line. It comes out oval." They talked for a few minutes, the main topics being who had left the company, who got married, and Bernard's heart attack.

"Jasmine, let me just say it again. I never had bad feelings toward you. I don't, I never, I..."

"I shouldn't have said anything, Anna. I'm probably just being overly sensitive. Self-esteem issues growing up. A confidence kind of thing. We should just forget I said that, okay? I'm interested in what you said over the phone. You're really starting your own magazine?"

Anna smiled, happy to be back on solid ground. "Yes, that's the plan. I've been working on it for a couple of weeks and a few things have fallen into place. But I need people. Staff."

She spotted Miriam then and waved her over. She introduced Jasmine and Miriam but got a little uneasy because she could not remember either of their last names. Jasmine and Miriam hadn't worked at *Aplomb* at the same time but were familiar with each other's name.

"I subscribed to *Aplomb* for a few years after I left, and I think I remember a drawing you did," Miriam said. "Did you do that one with the birds flying over a bloody, vicious battle scene and one is saying to the other, 'I just don't get it, do you?'"

"I remember that one," Anna said.

"My take on the war in Afghanistan. Yeah, that was mine. I'm flattered you remember," Jasmine said, smiling.

"Well, as long as we're reminiscing, I recall a piece you did, a very short piece, about a stolen painting that was recently recovered. It was honest, and funny enough that I still remember it."

"Oh, yeah. The 'Blue Dog.'"

"I guess we can order," Anna said, "and I can talk about the magazine. Just one of you please tell me if I'm spitting or drooling while I eat."

When the food came, Anna jumped right in to her story. "Okay, from the beginning. You both know Bernard had a heart attack. His nephew, well, no one is really sure if he *is* a nephew, but he's the nephew of his third wife. Sebastian, that's his name, has a business degree and the PTB's felt..."

Miriam looked at Jasmine and then at Anna. "PTB's?"

"Oh, sorry. 'Powers That Be.' The empty suits in Corporate. They felt Sebastian would do a good job in spite of minimal magazine experience and a personality that is, in my father's description, pathologically at rest."

Jasmine said, "Lazy, right?"

"Profoundly," Anna told them. "He wasn't able to run things but resented the fact that I was keeping things running. He spoke to Human Resources, and they forced me into retirement. So, I'm starting my own magazine."

"Good, good," Jasmine said. "Now we're getting to it. Tell me more about the magazine you have in mind." Both she and Miriam stopped eating and leaned forward.

Anna took a forkful of her quiche, and said," It's still in the early stages, I'll be honest with you. But I have a place to work out of ..."

"A pre-school," Miriam said.

"Right. I leased a cottage," she said to Jasmine, "that used to house a pre-school. It's small, but the magazine is going to be small to start off with. I'm getting phones put in, and computers and desks, and a fax machine. I don't envision that you, or anyone, will be working full time, but people will be coming and going all day long. My early plan is to have a couple of writers and illustrators provide the content, and then advertise for submissions."

"Who is your audience, Anna? You're not going to be competing with the big guys."

"No. I'm picturing the target audience in terms of concentric circles. The center is local, and small. Very local people we can advertise with in the printed magazine and on social media. A limited-run print version for advertisements and Forest Hills community news, basically. The next circle is the borough of Queens, the next is New York City, and if there is room and an interesting piece comes in, something national. It will be online, too, so like everything now, occasionally something will be global."

Jasmine took a quick bite of her tuna salad. "So, as far as the print version, you're saying Forest Hills is the pond all of us frogs are squatting around,"

"I'm sorry, what?" both Anna and Miriam said.

Jasmine looked surprised. "You know. That thing Plato said? About those Greek guys being frogs around the pond?"

"Oh, yeah, I guess," Anna said. "Meaning Forest Hills will be our center. That's accurate for the print version."

"Oh, I see," Miriam said. "I didn't understand what you meant about, um..."

The waitress came by to fill water glasses and asked, "Do you ladies have everything you need?"

"...frogs." Miriam said.

The waitress stared at Miriam. "I'm sorry, I don't think we serve..."

"Oh, no, I'm sorry. Not you," Miriam said. "I wasn't speaking to you. I was referring to, you know, something else."

"We're all good here," Jasmine said with a broad grin. "Everything is copacetic."

"Ah," the waitress said. She smiled quickly and walked away.

They ate quietly for a few minutes. "What else can you tell us?" Miriam asked.

"I can't pay the same rate *Aplomb* was paying, and probably not what you were getting freelance. But I'm thinking seventy-five percent of *Aplomb's* rate for starters, and a review after six months. And, if we're doing well, or even doing okay, I think some form of profit sharing is possible. I'm not in this to be a millionaire. But please understand, the profit-sharing piece is not a promise, although I am optimistic."

They were quiet again until coffee, both Jasmine and Miriam glancing quickly at each other, and avoiding eye contact with Anna.

Anna was afraid the seventy-five percent rate may have turned them both off, but waited to hear something from either, or both of them. "On the plus side for you guys, you will have a market for whatever you write without much competition." When the bill came, she made sure to put the receipt in a safe place in her pocketbook. She smiled and said, "This will be the first business lunch I can take off my taxes."

Anna drove Jasmine to the schoolhouse and Miriam followed in her car. "You're probably curious about Miriam and saying 'frogs' to the waitress. That was kind of weird."

"No, I get it. It's age. Another gift of the golden years. My brother, a younger brother scarily enough, is in the early stages of Alzheimer's, and Lord, the problems he has saying the simplest things. If it weren't so horrible, it would be risible. We're all aware at home, and we're patient with him, so I can be patient with Miriam."

"Um, risible?"

"Yeah, risible. It's means laughable but doesn't sound as hurtful."

In the cottage, Miriam and Jasmine just strolled around quietly for a few moments. Miriam said, "The color on these walls reminds me of my granddaughter's pre-school. Every place I ever worked, the walls were either gray or beige. I prefer the bright."

"I know it isn't much now," Anna said, "but I have a different perspective than you. I see the desks and computers and hear the writers arguing about what's funny and struggling to put something good on paper. I have a vivid imagination, I guess. There's a little bit of Walter Mitty in my DNA, I guess."

"Itty bitty of Mitty," Miriam said. She strolled in to look at the kitchen.

Jasmine peeked into the bathroom and said, "Oh, it's a little potty."

Miriam came out of the kitchen looking angry and said, "What did you call me? Did you say I was a little potty? I'm not! I have trouble concentrating sometimes, that's all."

Anna said, "No, no, Miriam..."

Jasmine said quickly, "No, look Miriam, look here. It's a potty for the kids. It's a little potty, I didn't mean...I wasn't saying..."

Miriam looked at both of them with a grin and laughed. "I knew it, Jasmine. I was pulling your leg. I saw that little toilet when we first came in."

Anna laughed too, and whispered to herself, "Oh, boy, this is going to be a good group."

They stood in a small circle and talked for a few moments. Jasmine asked, "What kind of paperwork are we looking at here, Anna? I assume you don't have a Human Resources department."

"I have a lawyer working up a contract, Jasmine. It should be ready by the time the furniture arrives and we're ready to kick into gear."

"Which is when, Anna?" Miriam asked.

Anna thumbed through her phone for the message from the furniture company. "Next Thursday. And they were good enough to narrow it down, too. 'Delivery will be between eight a.m. and five p.m.' I suppose that's barring severe weather or any unforeseen circumstances like a tsunami or a plague of locusts. And as luck would have it, the computers are arriving the same day, at exactly, believe it or not, *exactly* the same time, between eight a.m. and five p.m."

Miriam fished in her pocket for her car keys and walked toward the door. "That's good in a way, I suppose. It gives me a few more days to make up my mind, and to talk to Art about it." She waved from the doorway and giggled softly. "Little potty."

Jasmine walked slowly around the large room again. "I think I'm with you, Anna," she said, "depending on how the contract reads. I've been doing a lot of freelancing, mostly fantasy and science fiction drawings, for video games and fan magazine covers and such. You won't believe what they're asking me to do. Vampires and werewolves I can manage, but the gory, mindless junk they want me to draw is something else. Everything is either dark or dripping. If it's not dark or dripping, then it has a misshapen head and is carrying a knife. Werewolves carrying guns riding on unicorns with fangs. They tell me it's creative, but it's all just variations on a theme. And the theme is ugly. Ugly, ugly, ugly. I have perfect twenty-twenty vison, but drawing this sludge is giving me esotropia."

"Esotropia, Jasmine? I don't know what that is."

"It's making me cross-eyed."

~ * ~

Thursday morning, Anna arrived at the pre-school at around 7:30. The computers, seven brand new Dells with flatscreen monitors, arrived at 11:00. Anna burst out with a "Yippee" as she yanked open the boxes and started to put things together. She had been an advocate, in the dark ages of the 1980s, of using computers in the office, and to a degree, had kept up her knowledge of current technology. She knew connecting power to the computer, and the computer to the printer, was the easy part. Installing the software and getting them to talk to each other in a common language was the real challenge. She had three of the seven operational by the time the truck pulled into the driveway with the furniture. The driver and his helper were good enough to place the desks and chairs where she asked. She slipped them each a ten-dollar bill and heard a familiar voice just outside the door. In what seemed to Anna like a miraculous white light, Jasmine appeared, volunteering in a voice that could make angels weep, to help with setup. Between the two of them, they got the other four computers on the desks and humming in time for Anna to breathe deeply and call for pizza.

"Onions and mushrooms on my half," Jasmine called.

"That works for me too," Anna said. "What to drink, though? Soda? Beer? Something else?"

"Well, with soda, the excess effervescence usually escapes orally. And with beer, if my husband is an example, the excess usually discharges in the contrary direction."

Anna scratched her head for a minute and translated, "Soda makes you belch and beer makes you fart, right?"

"Precisely. So, ladies and gentlemen, for your safety and comfort, how about we have ice tea?"

Halfway through lunch, Jasmine picked up her slice of pizza and moved to the far corner of the room.

Anna, surprised, said, "I just had the iced tea, like you, Jaz, so I don't think your safety and comfort have been compromised."

Jasmine laughed. "No, the atmosphere remains acceptable. I just wanted to get a different perspective. Illustrator talk, meaning I want to see if maybe this scene would be good to draw." She pulled a sketch pad and a pencil from her backpack.

Anna watched Jasmine's left hand move swiftly across the paper, and her eyes make small subtle movements. Within ten minutes she had sketched the room: windows, desks, computers and the outline of a small, happy woman, looking at all of it.

"Well, here's an idea, Anna. Maybe this can be the first illustration in our new magazine."

"'Our' magazine, huh?"

"Yeah, it's feeling that way. I like the room and the bright colors and the laid-back atmosphere. I've been doing this for a long time, and I'd like to enjoy where I'm doing it. I don't see a single alien, or even a werewolf riding a unicorn. I could get used to this. Of course, none of us is a size twelve anymore, so we *will* have to replace that potty."

Telephones came the next day, and on the Monday following, the conference table. For some reason Anna could not articulate, the conference table was the final and most important part of the startup puzzle. It was where, in her imagination, the real work of the editor-in-chief would take place. And once the table was in, turned and rotated through the narrow doorways into the middle of the room, the list that had bounced around in her head for weeks was complete. Anna realized how excited she was, and how nervous.

~ * ~

By Saturday afternoon, Miriam had signed the contract and emailed that she had already written something for the magazine. It was still 'the magazine' in Anna's mind, because she hadn't been able to come up with a name for it yet. Most of the good ones were taken, she felt. *Aplomb* itself was only barely acceptable, being in her not-so-humble opinion, too close to both 'a plumb' and 'a bomb.' At the end of a long day at *Aplomb*, she often imagined the magazine cover as a bomb—one of those cartoon round ones with a fuse—painted a shiny plum color.

Titles, she knew, needed to be both catchy and succinct, and illustrate what would be under the fancy, glossy cover. *Time* did that. *The New Yorker* did that. *People* did that. But the titles she conjured while tossing and turning at night did not. *The Forester, Trending, Oeuvre, Whimsey.* No, no, no again, and oh, hell no. The magazine was to be a combination of local color and humor, but humor in the context of the kinks and quirks of twenty-first century reality. 'Wit' was a front runner for an evening, later mutating into 'To Wit' but the shine on that one only lasted until the next morning. With a mouth foaming with toothpaste, she said to her mirror, "Wit is a stupid name. 'To Wit' is too close to 'Twit.'"

She thought of famous humorists that would be recognizable: Twain, Oscar Wilde, Dorothy Parker, or her favorite, James Thurber. She wondered if anyone would buy a magazine called *The Thurber*.

A group email to Miriam, Jasmine, the still missing-in-action LaToya, and Chloe, generated a few more ideas, none of which were blue ribbon winners. Checking her email one last time before bed, she saw a response from LaToya. "Honey, you are a small magazine in a small market and somehow you are thinking much too small. If you do it right, humor will be at the core, but you are providing much more than humor. You are *informing* that small market with your small magazine and also crafting an environment for independent thinking. And what, historically, is the origin of information? And what institution in this backassward world teaches us independent thinking? Schools, honey, schools. In light of where you're working, I think your magazine should be called '*The Schoolhouse.*' I think that will say it all."

Anna's last thought before falling asleep was, "*Nailed it, girl.*"

~*~

The next day, Anna strolled over to the game room and found Carla and Robert laughing over ping-pong. "I got winners," Anna said.

"There are no winners here," Carla said. "If you keep score in a marriage, you may as well keep a divorce lawyer on retainer. We just play until someone's arthritis acts up."

"Probably just as well," Anna said. "I slept wrong last night, and my shoulder is killing me. I really just want to talk anyway."

"Talking we can do," Robert said. "Arthritis doesn't seem to have an effect on that. Sometimes we talk all night."

"Sometimes *you* do," Carla said. "What did you want to talk about, Anna?"

They sat at a card table and Anna described her plans for the magazine. She told them their anecdote about a secret code that helps them avoid arguments could easily be turned into a short article.

"You want us to write for your newspaper?" Robert asked.

"Magazine, Robert. I call it *The Schoolhouse*, and I'm planning for the first issue to come out at the end of this month."

Robert looked uncertain, but thoughtful. Carla leaned forward on her elbows and said, "Tell me more."

~ * ~

Anna stepped into the warmth and savory odors of Herman's delicatessen and shook the rain off her plastic hat.

"I know it is probably not Saturday, because my calendar girl, Anna, who used to be so predictable, is here. I have looked for you the last two Saturdays without a trace, and therefore, I know today is not Saturday. Since I am closed on Sunday, that leaves a one-in-five chance that today is, um, let me see, Friday. Yes, I think today is Friday."

"Mathematics must be another gift of your German heritage," Anna said. "Yes, it is Friday. A glorious, getting-close-to-spring Friday where the rain is mixed with small droplets of ice, and the wind thoughtfully blows it in your face."

Herman, reigning from behind his counter, laughed. "Irony, Miss Anna. Do you know the definition of irony?"

"Yes, Herman, I do."

"Irony is when you say something by using words that mean the opposite. Kind of like one of those Yogi Bear sayings."

"Yogi, Yogi Bear? Oh, Yogi Berra, maybe?"

"That's the guy. 'Nobody goes there no more because it's too crowded,' he said one time. Irony. What you were saying, Miss Anna, without saying it, is that for you at least, this drizzly, dismal afternoon is a good day."

"It is. I think it truly is. I have something I want to ask you, Herman."

"Ah. I have been expecting this Anna, and I've been struggling with my answer, only because you are a long-time customer."

"You've been expecting this? Really?"

"It has happened before. A person retires and financial wobbles happen. It's not unusual."

"Wobbles? Oh, maybe you mean financial woes."

"Okay, that. Financial woes. I would like to be able to extend you credit, Miss Anna, because you have been a steady customer, and because I like you, but I just am not able." He walked around the counter and began to rearrange the loaves of bread.

"No, Herman, my friend. That's not…"

"If I do this for you," he said over his shoulder, "I would have to do it for others, and that just isn't—"

"No, I don't want credit. That's not what I'm asking. I want you to write something for me. Something for the magazine I'm starting."

He looked over at her. "Oh, yes. A magazine. We have spoken of this before."

"Yes, we have. I'm like you, Herman, I don't want to retire. I want to work, so I am starting a magazine. Right now, I am looking for articles to publish in it. What you were talking about last week, the differences between living in Germany and here in America, would make an excellent essay. I want you to write it, and if it's good, I'll pay you for it."

Herman walked slowly away, rubbing his chin. He turned and looked at her once, took a few more steps and squinted at her. "I have given this thought, but I am not a good English writer, Anna. Surely you know that. My English, although perfect, is not quite standard."

"I could help you with it, Herman. That's what I did for a living for many years. I could make your English more standard."

He looked at her for a long moment, still uncertain. "Really?"

"Yes. What you told me about the differences would be interesting to many people."

"I would have my name on this writing?"

"Oh, yes. We call it a byline."

"And it would be read by many people?" He was nodding his head, which Anna took as a good sign.

"The magazine is just beginning, Herman, so probably not a *lot* of people. But I have plans. I have plans for a bigger magazine with wider distribution. Your article will be in the first issue."

He smiled broadly, then laughed. "So, perhaps this will be a collector's item someday, and people will ask me to autograph it. It may even be placed behind glass somewhere in a museum?"

She smiled back at him. "Absolutely, Herman. No doubt in my mind."

~ * ~

That evening, L.T. left a message to say she wanted to see a copy of the contract, but didn't explain why she hadn't responded earlier. Anna spent the last half of the week shopping for office supplies, kitchen supplies, pictures to hang on the wall, anything to make the cottage a pleasant place to work. Evenings she ate bland meals, chewed antacids, and listened to soothing music with a warm cloth over her eyes.

She scheduled a meeting via group email for the following Tuesday morning at the school. All were expected to bring something written or drawn for the premier issue of *The Schoolhouse*. That issue of the magazine, only a twelve-page production, was, in Anna's optimism, to be edited by Thursday and delivered to the printer on Friday. She was a little disappointed that she didn't have a contract with a printer yet, but she would pay for the first edition out of pocket.

The first meeting, the maiden voyage around that brand new oval conference table, would be with Anna, Miriam, Jasmine, LaToya, Carla and Robert.

Five

"It was a small infarction at about three o'clock this morning. He says he didn't even feel it," Doctor Dasgupta was explaining to Sherilyn and Sebastian. "Structural damage to his heart was minimal, although it is concerning from a diagnostic perspective. It may be indicative of a larger problem."

"Well, he's had two heart attacks already," Sherilyn said. "And one of them while he was in *your* care. That seems like a pretty big problem to me."

The doctor leaned back in his chair, surprised at the volume of Sherilyn's comment. He wasn't sure if she was angry or not, but this didn't seem to be a situation where shouting was necessary. He looked over at the young man for some kind of reassurance, but he was just looking around the office like a prospective renter looking over a living room.

"What else are you doing for him?" Sherilyn asked, almost as loudly.

The doctor blinked a few times. "We have changed the dosage on two of his medications, and he is already being closely monitored day and night."

"Is he allowed visitors?"

"Yes, but with some additional restrictions. For the next week or so, only five minutes at a time, and only a maximum of two people at a time."

Sherilyn looked over at Sebastian. "I guess we should go and see him."

"I suppose," he said. He was distracted, admiring the doctor's telephone, impressed that it had video capability. Sebastian's didn't have that, and he was wondering who he could ask at Corporate to get one. The doctor shook hands with both of them and sneezed as they were leaving.

They took the elevator down to the third floor. Sebastian walked over to the nurse's station and said, "We're here for Bernard Holloway. I just spoke to his doctor. We're allowed a visit of five minutes."

The nurse checked something on the computer. "Are you a family member?"

"Yes," he said. "Of course I am."

"I remember her," she said, nodding at Sherilyn, "but I haven't seen you here before."

He frowned at her. "No, you haven't. I have an important and very high-pressure job, and this is the first time I have been able to get here to see my uncle."

"Yes," she said. "Of course."

At the door, just before they entered, Sebastian said, "I hate nurses. Always so snooty, so superior. And they don't really do that much. Take your temperature, give you a shot, that's about it."

Sherilyn nodded. "I hate doctors for the same reason. And I hate hospitals because, well, I don't really know why, but I hate them a lot." She took a step back and gestured for him to open the door.

"Ah, darling," Bernard said. "Somehow I sensed you were here."

"My spiritual advisor once told me I had an unusually encompassing aura," she said.

He smiled. "You have no idea."

"Hello, Uncle Bernard," Sebastian said, smiling, standing just inside the door.

"And you brought Seabass along," Bernard said. Sebastian scowled but said nothing.

"We've been worried about you," Sherilyn said, and brought a chair for herself close to the bed. Sebastian remained standing.

Bernard was more pale and drawn than when Sherilyn had last seen him, almost a week ago, and Sebastian was surprised by his appearance.

"How do you feel, Uncle?" Sebastian asked.

"Oh, probably just a little worse than I look," Bernard said. "I don't think I have one foot in the grave yet, but my big toe is beginning to burrow in the dirt."

"Well, it should cheer you up that things at *Aplomb* are going well. We're all anxious to have you back, of course, but you can rest easy about the magazine."

Bernard laughed weakly. "Not what I hear."

Sherilyn leaned over and looked through several 'get well' cards on the small table next to the bed. "I don't see one from Paula. Have you heard from her and just neglected to tell me?"

"I suppose it could have slipped my mind, as I haven't heard from you in a while, but no. No word. Did you think she may have slipped back into the country and I forgot about it?"

Sebastian asked, "Who's Paula?"

Sherilyn ignored the question. Bernard said, "My ex-wife, if she is my ex-wife."

"Oh right, yeah."

"Oh, stop it, Bernie," Sherilyn snapped. "She abandoned you. Took a powder. Hopped a flight. Flew the coop. How much more 'ex' could she be?" Bernard just smiled during the long and uncomfortable silence.

Sebastian finally asked the question that was on his mind. "What did you mean before, Uncle, when you said, 'Not what I hear'?"

Bernard frowned and drew a deep breath. "There's a guy, Simon, I think his name is, from HR. He called me, but couldn't get through, finally he wrote a note I had to bribe a nurse to show me."

"Simon? From HR?" Sebastian said. "I don't think I'm familiar."

"Right. Nor is he with you, apparently. But he has been getting some complaints."

"There's always one, Uncle."

"Three, Seabass. Three separate people, but all saying pretty much the same thing. And when Simon called you for clarification he couldn't get past what's-her-name."

"Probably Donna. She has been handling my calls."

Bernard looked over at Sherilyn. "I'm lying here wondering if that's all she's handling."

"Bernard, stop that. Seabass, I mean Sebastian, has a business degree. He's doing the best he can in a difficult situation. It's not easy to replace the boss." She smiled over at Sebastian.

"Well, Simon, who seems a conscientious sort, came to the office to see you. You were out at a dentist appointment according to Donna, on a Wednesday morning and again on a Thursday afternoon. Seems odd to have dental work twice in two days, but—"

A nurse stepped in and told them time was up, and for the patient's benefit, they should leave.

Sherilyn kissed Bernard on the forehead and he struggled not to sneeze. Sebastian just waved, and Bernard said to him, "If you visit again, you can fill me in about your fillings."

In the hallway, Sherilyn whispered, "You're blowing it, Sebastian. We worked hard to set you into that job, and you're going to lose it."

"He's exaggerating, Aunt Sher. I'll call this Simon guy on Monday and straighten it out. Things at the office are fine. Really."

They found signs directing them to the cafeteria. Sherilyn said, "I'm feeling a little weak, dear heart. It's my low blood sugar again. Would you get me coffee and something, I don't know, a sandwich or maybe just a donut? Yes, a donut would do, thank you, sweetheart."

He came back a few minutes later with coffee and a sugar donut for his aunt, and soda and a buttered roll for himself. He tilted his head and raised his eyes. There was something vaguely modern jazz-like coming over the speakers. "Listen to this tripe," he said. "This isn't music, this is only *derived* from real music. It's music-oid. The kind of people who like this stuff would chew gum at a job interview."

Sherilyn was eating her donut, nibbling delicately to avoid getting powdered sugar on her makeup. "So, who is this Donna that Bernie mentioned?"

"No one, really," Sebastian said. "Just one of the office staff."

"Is she pretty?"

"I haven't paid much attention to her, Aunt Sher. You know I'm in a relationship back home."

She dabbed at her mouth gently with a napkin. "'In a relationship.' Such a hollow, anemic little phrase. It seems to say something, and yet it doesn't really say anything."

"Well, anyway, I really don't think that Francine and I are working out as a couple. Besides, she's on the opposite coast."

"So much for being in a relationship."

Sebastian took a bite of his roll and said, "You never really told me about Paula. Sounds like a juicy backstory there. Did she really abandon Bernie?"

"He doesn't talk much about her. All he'll say is that she's in Europe. No one knows why, and he won't talk about it. She was married to Bernie for, I think less than a year, and was suddenly gone. He got a divorce before he married me, of course, but she is still out there somewhere. And she must have heard about his heart attack."

Sebastian shook his head. "I don't how she would have heard. It's not like it was in all the papers."

"I don't know for sure, but I suspect he's had lots of lady friends over the years. One of them could still be in touch with Paula."

"I would bet the farm it's Anna," he said.

Sherilyn curled her upper lip and mumbled, "Anna."

~ * ~

Chloe came to work at *Aplomb* a little earlier than usual on Monday. Her nose was red, and the tissue in her hand was balled up and soggy. She was working on a humor piece someone had submitted about the Bob Hope Golf Tournament from the sixties: practical jokes, celebrities wearing silly hats and checkered pants and women, for some reason, all wearing very short skirts. Chloe was struggling with some of the special vocabulary from the game of golf. She had watched

The Sound of Music, a favorite, the night before and began to sing to herself, "Mashies and niblicks and putters and drivers," to the tune of "My Favorite Things." Because of her allergies it came out as, "Bashies and diblicks and butters and dribers." There was no one in the office to notice.

By nine, the office was beginning to fill. Coats were hung up, computers turned on, bodies settled into chairs, agendas referred to. Chloe took a few minutes to make coffee, and when she got back, Donna was sitting next to her desk. Chloe was of the temperament that tried very hard to like everyone. With Donna, she found it was not possible. She was not overtly unpleasant, and brief, friendly conversations often happened, but there was a subtle aggression in Donna, and Chloe always had a nagging sense she was after something.

"Good morning, Miss Chloe. Thank you for making coffee."

"Good morning, Miss Donna. Glad to do it."

"We haven't chatted in a while. How are things with you?"

"Oh, fine, I guess. Except it's almost spring, there is a good breeze, and my nose is stuffed like Bob Cratchit's goose. How are you?"

She leaned forward and frowned. "I'm disappointed. Please don't mention this to anyone, but this job is getting on my very last nerve. I was never a big fan of Anna, but since she left, this whole operation has been swirling down the drain. People are taking advantage of Seb's easy-going management approach. There are too many inflated egos around here. Way too many."

Chloe was surprised. Donna rarely said a word about Sebastian, positive or negative. The relationship between them was a poorly kept secret. Donna denied it, Sebastian ignored it, everyone else gossiped about it.

Chloe sniffled and blew her nose. "I miss Anna too, but do you really think things are that bad?"

"You were at the 'Inter' meeting Wednesday," Donna whispered. "That whole thing was a joke. Just absurd."

"Well, sure, but the interdepartmental beatings are always contentious. Everyone wants their stuff in the latest issue." Donna hesitated a moment at 'interdepartmental beatings,' but quickly realized Chloe meant 'meetings.'

"Yeah, but those meetings usually keep going until there is some kind of agreement. Or until someone makes an executive decision. I've seen discussions on one drawing go on for an hour. But that one..." She looked around. "Sebastian walked out before it was over. And if you ask me, I think he's just fed up with all the squabbling."

Chloe said, "He was mad? I thought he looked confused about Marielle's cartoon, the Aristotle taking poison thing. No, not Aristotle, the other Greek guy. Alexander. No, Socrates. Socrates and the hemlock."

"You think he was confused? Why would Seb be confused? I think he was tired of Marielle and Ed bickering about that caption."

"He is the department manager. Couldn't he have just picked the caption he liked? I liked the one saying, 'No, thanks. One more cup and I'll be awake all night.'"

Donna nodded. "That was Marielle's original. Ed, of course, that pompous ass, had to come up with another one; 'Do you have this in decaf?' What a jerk."

"I actually thought both were pretty funny, and I kept looking over at Sebastian to see what he thought. He had this lost look. I think he didn't understand the joke."

Donna frowned. "Of course he understood the joke. He's the department manager, and he has a business degree. He gets jokes."

Chloe hesitated for a moment and then said, with a smile, "Of course, you're right. I must have misinterpreted his look. He was probably frustrated with people disagreeing all the time, and you're right, it's happening more and more. Makes me glad I don't contribute content, I just edit."

Half an hour later, Chloe went for more coffee and passed Donna sitting at Aaron's desk. She overheard the phrase again, 'swirling down the drain.'

Sebastian arrived around ten o'clock with his headphones on and carrying a cup of coffee. Donna slipped into his office for a few minutes before he shooed her out to make an important phone call. He found a Jordan Simon in the corporate directory, took a deep breath and dialed the number. "It was actually a root canal," he told him. "I had to go back the second day because they missed a piece of the nerve. I can confess without fear of contradiction, it was the worst pain I have ever experienced."

Simon, like Sebastian, was ambitious, and preferred not to rock the boat. If a situation could be ignored, or even glossed over, then it was no longer a situation.

"There have been some other irregularities reported, Mister Jenkins. Minor to be sure, but worth mentioning."

"May I ask who has been reporting these irregularities?"

"Obviously, sir, I can't tell you that. But if there are more complaints in the same vein, I may formally recommend a group discussion here at Corporate to clear the air. That seems confrontational, I know, but with minor matters of this sort it can often defuse a potential problem."

"Well, I'm sure those complaints were more in the nature of pranks, Mr. Simon. Can you tell me more specifically what they were they about?"

"Well, yes, in general. They were in reference to staff meetings. There was a concern on the part of two callers that meetings, I believe they were interdepartmental meetings, were somewhat disorganized and unproductive. I really don't think I can say more."

"I see. We have had a good deal of vigorous discussion about content lately, but that's very much standard procedure here at *Aplomb*. Humor is often in the eye, or ear, of the beholder. I allow more leeway in disputes than my predecessor, but with the final product of the magazine always uppermost in my mind. To me, a spirited debate is healthy, even fruitful, if kept within reasonable boundaries."

"It might be helpful to have that discussion with your employees, to let them know this is a strategy on your part, and not failure to apply appropriate guidance."

"That's sound advice, Mr. Simon. Perhaps I'll send around a memo to that effect."

"That would be a good first step, but it should be followed up with a face-to-face meeting. Perhaps with a few employees at a time, or perhaps as a preamble at your next interdepartmental meeting."

"Yes, a small face-to-face sounds right. If you would tell me who contacted you, I can start with them."

Simon laughed. "That would be against all of my training, Mr. Jenkins, and contrary to common sense. Why don't I contact you again in a few weeks and see what progress you've made? And then I can reach out to the employees who contacted me."

Sebastian frowned and reached for his coffee. "I look forward to hearing from you in a few weeks, then." He hung up the phone and called, "Donna!"

~ * ~

That evening after dinner, Chloe 'messaged' Anna from her social media account. She was surprised when Anna replied almost immediately.

SnowyChloe: "What did you do"?

AnnaBNana: "What? I didn't do anything. What's going on?"

SnowyChloe: "Your good friend Donna has gone undercover. I'm not sure what she's looking for, but she's sniffing around. Got her nose on the ground, and her butt in the air. She even mentioned your name. She said the whole operation is screwed up since Anna left. 'Swirling down the drain,' she said."

AnnaBNana: "I haven't spoken to Bernard in almost a week. I sure haven't talked to Sebaceous or to his aunt, either. I don't know what it's all about, but I'm sure it's not good."

SnowyChloe: "She caught me first thing in the morning and was really listening carefully to me, like trying to read between the lines. I wonder if someone called HR and got Sebaceous in trouble. I had a feeling that was going to happen."

AnnaBNana: "Are things getting crazy there? I was hoping that after I left he would straighten up."

SnowyChloe: "He hasn't. Things are pretty much status quo. In late, out early, headphones in the morning, stereo in the afternoon. But it seems to be the 'Inters' causing the problems. Lots of squabbling. Anyway, that's what Donna was focused on. But the heck with all that. How are you doing? How is your grand project going?"

AnnaBNana: "Moving along pretty well, I think. I have a loan, an office, and people willing to take a chance on a new venture. Tomorrow will be a big day. We're meeting to put together the first issue."

SnowyChloe: "Wow. Exciting. I envy you. Will you keep me in the loop?"

AnnaBNana: "Oh, for sure. And you please let me know of any developments with Detective Donna. Toodles."

SnowyChloe: "I will. TTFN."

~ * ~

The morning of the staff meeting Anna vacuumed the main room, made coffee, arranged chairs around the conference table and read over her final edit of Herman's essay. She felt a little like a hostess at the grand opening of a new restaurant, but reminded herself that she was now the boss, the editor-in-chief, the reincarnation of Perry White. "Great Caesar's Ghost!" she said to LaToya, the first to arrive. "Thank you for coming, L.T. I was concerned when I didn't hear from you."

"Oh, I'm sorry, Anna. I'm in mourning. I wasn't really communicating with anyone."

"Oh, my condolences. Someone close?"

"Well, Clarissa passed away suddenly. I missed an episode, and I never saw it coming. She was strangled by that bald Ukrainian government agent at the helicopter pad on top of her building. She thought she was being flown to Washington to tell the CIA what she knew about neodymium ion components for a—"

Anna stifled a laugh. "L.T., is this a show?"

"Yeah. *Quinlan; Insider.* Clarissa is the computer genius with low self-esteem that works for Bryce Quinlan at the Pentagon. She's moony for him, those cheekbones you know, but he only cares about her firewall. I guess he can forget about *that* now."

"Right. Her firewall. Anyway, I'm glad you made it. I have a copy of the contract for you to look at. I hope you can join us."

~ * ~

Anna had made copies of several documents to pass around:

- *-The 'code' article from Carla and Robert.*
- *-The article from Herman, edited by Anna, on the differences between European culture and American culture.*

- *-A short piece by Miriam called Through My Glasses Darkly.*
- *-A cartoon by Jasmine of frogs around a pond i.e., The Schoolhouse staff around a puddle, with the caption, "I'm not sure this is what Plato had in mind."*
- *-A sketch of The Schoolhouse building to be used as a header for all future issues.*

After everyone arrived, Anna sat at the head of the big table, feeling self-conscious, and made introductions. "I thought about name tags, but decided against it," she said. "Not for any aesthetic reason, but because I think they're stupid, and they get glue all over your blouse."

A few of them knew each other, or at least knew of each other: Anna, Jasmine, Miriam and LaToya were all alumni of *Aplomb*, and she told them about Herman. She felt sure Carla and Robert, the only other strangers, would not be shy.

"I've wanted to work in a place like this for a very long time," she said. "Casual, collegial and close to home. I'm hoping we can get to know each other and produce a product people can relate to. Something classy. So maybe that's what the subtitle for the magazine should be; 'Casual, Collegial and Classy.'"

She looked around the table slowly at all the faces. No one laughed, no one fainted, no one gave her the raspberry, so she decided she had made a good start, and continued.

"Today's meeting will be a dry run. I wasn't able to get the material to you on time, but I want your opinions on these articles, drawings and captions. What we'll do is have our staff discussion next Tuesday. I'll edit, compile everything and get it to the printer by Friday."

She passed around her written introduction to the new publication, which, with Jasmine's drawing of the schoolhouse and the sub-title printed below it, would take up most of the first page.

"This first document is my introduction to the publication. Back in the eighties, working for *Aplomb*, I came to loathe those 'mission statements,' chock full of swollen verbs ending with 'ize.' I have no desire to revolutionize anything. Or to incentivize anyone."

Robert said, "I was asked one time to write an ad for an air freshener company that wanted to 'ozonize' the work environment. Sounded a little like mass murder to me." No one felt comfortable enough to laugh, but everyone except Miriam smiled. She was concentrating.

"I can't stand that 'incentivize' one," LaToya agreed, "but the worst is 'reconceptualize.' I mean, why just think about a problem if you can go full tilt and reconceptualize it."

Miriam said, "I like, um,..."

Carla laughed and said, "My students always liked to use 'dematerialize,' you know, turn invisible. In my classroom, that's what a lot of them wanted to do."

Anna was laughing, but she said, "Okay, let's get back to the subject at hand."

Miriam said, a little too loud, "...moisturize!"

Everyone turned, startled, and looked at Miriam. Quickly, Anna passed out the next documents: the short, humor piece by Miriam, and in quick succession, the sketches from Jasmine, the article from Herman and the 'code' piece by the Bronners.

"I'd like you all to take some time and look over that material, and also take some time to get to know each other and what we have here at *The Schoolhouse*. Oh, in case I didn't tell you, that's the name of the magazine, *The Schoolhouse*. LaToya can take credit for coming up with that, and it fits with how I think of this adventure. A place to teach and also to learn. I know *I* have a lot to learn.

"You all have my email address, so please feel free to write with questions or comments, and, of course, award-winning essays are always welcome. That's my whole agenda for this morning," Anna said, "and thank you all for coming. There's coffee and cake in the kitchen, please help yourselves. I'm going to be around for most of the day if you want to talk, or, you can call 'dibs' on a computer or sit and read."

Miriam came over and said, "Sorry, Anna. I kind of stepped on my tongue there."

"Oh, no, Miriam. I'm not accepting 'sorry' from you. I read your *Through My Glasses, Darkly*, and I thought it was good. If you produce stuff like that, content like that, I will not hear the word 'sorry' from you."

"Thank you, Anna. Your confidence means a lot."

Miriam drifted into the kitchen and stood talking for a while with Jasmine. Carla came over with her coffee and said, "I liked your piece about the glasses. I agree, I'm pretty sure the little critters are screwin' around with us. I think we should form a posse and round 'em all up."

"When I was reading it," Jasmine said, "I was thinking of Mister Magoo. Remember him?"

"Oh, I used to love him when I was a kid."

"What would you think of a small drawing of Magoo at the bottom of your piece? With those squinty eyes of his. It seems to fit, I think. I could talk to Anna about it."

"I'd love it. I think Mister Magoo would be, you know, um...."

Both Carla and Jasmine waited patiently until Miriam said, "... perfect."

~ * ~

Late that afternoon, Anna took the subway to Presbyterian Hospital again to visit Bernie. She walked up to the third floor, never even thinking about the elevator, and poked her head in the door to be sure he was alone.

"Hey," Bernard said.

"Hey, back," Anna said.

He looked at her carefully for a minute. "You didn't bring me a newspaper."

"No, I brought you something better. A magazine. Well, not a magazine, but some of the building blocks."

He looked at her quizzically. "Building blocks?"

She handed him a manila envelope with the documents from this morning. "I held our first staff meeting today, Bern. It's starting slow, but I can see it developing. My feet haven't touched ground all day."

"You're still serious about a magazine? I thought you would get cold feet, on the ground or not, when you saw how much work there was."

"Oh, I get it about the work, Bern. I knew that going in, but my feet are still warm. Here, read some of this stuff. It's not *The New Yorker*. It's not *Aplomb*. But it's *The Schoolhouse*."

"*The Schoolhouse*. Huh. I think I like that. A whole lot less pretentious than *Aplomb*. I never did get used to that name, but it's what Meyer wanted. He thought it was sophisticated. I tried to tell him that sophistication want out of style in the sixties, but he didn't listen."

"I didn't know him as well as you, Bern, but I always thought Meyer could talk, but he didn't know how to listen."

"Yeah, true. But when you own three-quarters of a successful magazine, you can pay other people to listen." He opened the manila envelope and took out the first document. Anna pulled a chair up next to his bed and started jiggling her foot.

"Preface," he read. "That's a good start; 'Preface' rather than 'Introduction.' An introduction is part of a book, or magazine. A preface is external to it."

"Yes," Anna said, "I think you taught me that." She crossed her legs and started jiggling with the other foot. Bernard got silent, reading carefully. Anna crossed her legs to the other side, and kept jiggling.

Bernard stopped and looked at her. "Being nervous is not good for you, and very bad for me. I've never seen you fidget before."

"I've been working hard on this, Bern. I want it to be good."

"Well, just to keep us both healthy, why don't you go get coffee or dinner or a stiff drink, or something? Come back in a little while and I'll tell you what I think. And as long as you're going, bring me back a double cheeseburger."

"Oh, absolutely," she said. "You want fries with that?"

"No. Fries are bad for you. I read they clog the arteries. Just a side order of onion rings, if you would. Maybe a chocolate shake. A small one."

"Got it. Double cheese, onion rings, chocolate shake. That's the hospital value meal number one, I think. It comes with a ten percent discount for a bypass operation."

He laughed. She stood and walked to the door. "Your honest opinion, Bern. No pulling punches, right."

He nodded. "You know me better."

~ * ~

She had a light dinner in the hospital cafeteria: grilled cheese and a cup of Jell-O. *Eating Jell-O is a requirement in a hospital,* she thought. *The five food groups here are: Meat, dairy, fruits and vegetables, bread and grains, and most important, Jell-O.*

To give him more time to read, she found her way to the lobby and paged through yesterday's paper. She only read the funnies she liked years ago, so that didn't take long. The books in the gift shop were all about romance, or mindfulness, or the psychology of healing, which would have made Bernie gag. Flowers and stuffed animals weren't right for him either, so she bought him a balloon that said 'Get Well Soon.' *What else could it possible say?*

She found Bernie half asleep and with only two of the articles out of the envelope. A nurse came in right behind her and checked on the monitors and his pulse. Anna caught her out in the hall and asked about his progress.

"Are you family?" the nurse asked.

"No," she said. "I'm afraid not."

"I'm sorry, I can't tell you much. He has been improving, but slowly, since his last episode."

"Episode? What episode?"

"I'm sorry. I really can't tell you more."

Back in his room, she said, "Know what, Bernie, I'm just gonna go. You need some rest."

"She told you, right? I had another one. A small one. Didn't even wake me up, but they said it was one. Infarction. That sounds like passing gas, but I never heard of a heart fart before. One doctor said it was sort of an aftershock. Like a tremor after an earthquake."

Anna tied the balloon on the bed. "Well, you don't need me around here giving you work. I'll bring that stuff back when you're feeling better. Better yet, I'll bring you the finished product."

"I'm sorry, Anna. I did read two of them. Your preface was fine. A good overview of what the publication will be. The other piece, about losing your glasses...I thought that was soft. It can work, but it needs a re-write. One man's opinion."

"Okay, Bern. You just get your rest and I'll stay in touch. I know you're going to get better. I know it."

"You always were smarter than me."

~ * ~

For the rest of the week, Anna kept busy with the second tier of her startup list. She negotiated and signed a contract with a printer, hired someone to set up the website, advertised in two online databases for writers, and wrote advertisements for her magazine in a couple of monthlies dedicated to writers. She rewrote her preface twice, even though Bernie had said it was 'fine.' To Anna, the word 'fine' meant 'good enough,' which meant in reality, not quite good enough. Having told Miriam her piece was 'good,' she worried about editing it, and was relieved when Miriam emailed her a rewritten, and better, version. *This must be why editors-in-chief drink martinis.*

Finally, she got a post office box, realizing that most of the submissions would be electronic, but unwilling to miss anything at this early stage.

She got some suggestions on Herman's piece from the Bronners, mostly changing commas to semicolons or semicolons to commas, and a couple of vocabulary changes which Anna had already made. Their piece, *Hassle Hack*, was well written and funny, and except for a few stray semicolons, Anna didn't change a thing.

She printed everything out, stapled it, added a cover with Jasmine's sketch of the schoolhouse, and stared at it for a while.

She typed out a table of contents, arranged the essays, changed their sequence and retyped the table of contents. She read through each piece, thumbed through each page again, and wrote herself a note.

"An okay, but light, first effort. It needs more local content, more humor pieces, illustrations, and more general interest. Talk to Robert about local issues, talk to LaToya about arts and entertainment, talk to Jasmine about local drawings."

Six

THE SCHOOLHOUSE
Casual, Collegial and Classy

Preface

Even with so many magazines available, it is difficult to find one that strikes a balance between the informative and the sociable. *The Schoolhouse* restores us to a time when early education filled both of those needs. As children, schools provided stimulation for learning and an environment where friendships were a natural product of community. We hope to emulate that atmosphere in our staff and also in our publication.

Our central focus will be derived from quality-of-life concerns of the residents of our locale, Forest Hills, New York. The content will be lighthearted, but never frivolous. Humor will be at the core, and I hope, will radiate amiability and optimism among our readers. Larger concerns, that is, city-wide and national issues, will occasionally influence our publication, but only as they have bearing on our principal audience.

Our banner reflects that this magazine will strive to be 'casual, collegial and classy' and we hope, through your letters to the editor, to establish a discourse with you, the audience, to meet that goal with every issue.

We look forward to bringing you fresh, uplifting, and thought-provoking content with each publication of *The Schoolhouse.*

Anna Pennington, Editor-in-Chief

Through My Glasses, Darkly
by
Miriam Seeger Glasner

I have four pairs of glasses. Well, four that I know of. There may be others lurking in dark recesses, shirking their duties, probably even smirking. The two pair I can currently locate are prescription bifocals: one regular, and one with a coating that darkens the lenses in sunlight. So far, the 'polychromatic' lenses have proven useless because we haven't seen the sun around here since January. The other day I heard the song "Here Comes the Sun" and a government agency immediately condemned it as fake news.

The other two pairs currently in circulation are just readers, available at any drugstore, locksmith, dermatologist, or tree surgeon. I try to keep the readers in the house, conveniently placed so I can find them quickly, and read. Like chocolate chip cookies, the remote control, Zinfandel, and Tylenol, it's important to have immediate access to these crucial daily requirements.

For all the good it does me. Anyone over thirty living in the twenty-first century knows eyeglasses migrate. There is a theory they elope with the socks that go missing from your dryer, but I don't believe that. Clearly, socks are snobbish and would never share their alternate universe with something as nerdy as eyeglasses. Glasses simply sneak into shadowy, dust-filled corners and skulk. The naïve among us swear this is not true, but they don't even try to explain how they end up somewhere other than where they were put. I don't know if they flip, slide, swim, roll, slither, or call an Uber. I only know they relocate when no one is looking. Now you see me, but now you can't see through me.

Take this morning, for example. At least one pair of the bifocals is supposed to be in the car for distance vision when driving. I don't need the readers in the car because I don't usually read while I am driving. Almost never. The readers are supposed to be in the house so I can use them to read because I don't generally drive the car in the house. Again, almost never. So, I'm late for work this morning, and somehow both pairs of readers were in the car and both pairs of bifocals were in the house. I'm pretty sure they're just screwin' with me now.

Solutions abound, of course, and I have tried them all. I locked my specs in a pink box which somehow emptied itself within a few days. I tied a bunch of them together and, a week later I had one pair with a ribbon around it. I'm still working on that knot. For a while, I tried speaking lovingly, soothingly to them, but stopped so my plants wouldn't get jealous.

I'm going to try a high-tech solution next: nanny-cams equipped with motion detectors in every room, the garage, and the driveway. When those bony little rascals begin skittering into their secret lair, I'll be watching. I won't be able to see very clearly, but I'll be watching.

Hassle Hack
by
Robert and Carla Bronner

It's a common trope that money is the great equalizer. It's also said that music is the great equalizer, and that nature is as well. No, no, and you must be kidding. Stick around for a while, live a full life and you'll come to understand that marriage is the great equalizer. That's right, marriage. A few years after your 'I dos,' you may be faced with a double decker cargo ship chock full of 'I do nots.' People, well-meaning but oblivious people, will tell you with a straight face that communication is the cure.

No.

The real solution is to avoid communication. Not dodging it altogether but deflecting it strategically at critical moments. My bride and I, married for forty years and happy for fifteen of them, have perfected a system of deflection we apply whenever the specter of discord tippy-toes 'like a fog on catlike feet' into the conversation.

There are only a handful of subjects that trigger arguments between spouses. Money, of course; sex, or, more likely, the lack of it; chores and who does them; food choices; time management, or, more likely, the lack of that, too. Of course, children are another source, but the children argument is insolvable and always has been. Cicero said so, and so did Gandhi. I'm not sure, but I think there is a quote in the book of Proverbs: "The purpose of children is to make their parents old."

So, those are the foundational elements of strife between two shining examples of humanity that once happily traded rings, vows and saliva.

Here is our solution, in modern parlance, our 'life hack.' Let's say one of you, the one staring in her closet for half an hour to pick out shoes, is running late for a movie or a dinner reservation. The other one, who has been dressed and clutching his car keys for twenty minutes, could say, in a moment of cataclysmic pique, "We're going to be late, sweetheart." We'll let you imagine the response to that because this is a family magazine.

Instead, employ a code...a word or phrase with the same underlying meaning, but minus those blasting caps on the surface. Instead of "We're going to be late," the one dressed and clutching could say, "Time and tide, dear," to which the shoe enthusiast could reply, "Speaking of Tide, dear, it's your turn to do the wash."

You see? Deflected. A slight bump to the ego, but not one causing permanent injury. Within the hour, you may leave for that reservation with love in your hearts and dirty clothes still in the hamper.

Over the years we have developed several codes that work for us: 'Everything is better with a cup of coffee;' 'That front lawn is not going to mow itself;' and the most frequently used, 'Consign that one to the dustbin of history.' Of course, this is not one size fits all so, you'll need to create your own.

Try it. Fifteen happy years out of a total of forty, or thirty-seven percent. Seems like a pretty good return on investment.

Variations
by
Herman Becker

I was born in Germany, never mind when, and lived there for seven years. My father, a wise and practical man, brought our family to America, to New York, to reap the benefit of the culture and commercial potential of this country. I recall, soon after we arrived here, my father slipped and fell down a full flight of stairs, sending my mother scurrying to the medicine cabinet for a mustard plaster. He was unconscious for a few minutes, terrifying us children. But he awoke soon, pulled himself up to his full height, and the first words from his mouth were, "God bless America! Hot in the summer and cold in the winter!"

And we have prospered beyond the dreams of even my father. Many years later, I could stand on my deli counter and roar, "I am a proud American!" I don't do that, of course, for fear of frightening my customers, but if the need arose, I could.

In my years living and doing business here in Forest Hills, I have carefully observed my neighbors and noticed some peculiar differences between the lives of those good people and memories of my home country.

Size, of course. Germany could fit inside California, and still have room to squeeze in New Jersey. Of course, the Californians might object to the smell around Newark, so healthwise, it's maybe not a good idea. Size is a mania with Americans. Skyscrapers are an American invention; so are department stores with escalators, elevators, and restaurants. I read of one that was thirty stories tall. Thirty stories? How could you possibly fill a thirty-story market? Keeping the shelves stocked would be a miracle.

The Germany of my youth had shops. A customer could walk into a shop and, by just leaning to the side a little, see everything there was to see: all the shelves, all the racks, all the meats and cheeses hanging over the counters. What you could see is what you could get. Here, what you often see is a sign pointing you somewhere else.

There are other differences, too, like money. Germany and Europeans have always used many coins, whereas the U.S. uses more paper money. In northern Europe, this can be a positive thing. When a strong wind blows across the North Sea, the coins in their pockets often prevent citizens from being blown over. Ha, ha, my little joke.

Another difference is how we treat our pets, cats and dogs. As a boy in Germany, I had a small dog, a Bichon. I loved that creature and would never embarrass him as I see some Americans dishonor their pets. I have seen beautiful animals dressed as clowns, as ballerinas, as robots. Dogs must tremble at the approach of Halloween. Why would you have a birthday party for a dog? Do you think he counts and perhaps multiplies by seven?

There is also in the United States a certainty one can almost feel that what we do is always the right thing. It's more than optimism, it is a recognized certainty. The German people once had a similar certainty, but no more.

Of course, these are all trivial musings from a contented man, one who may not have all he wants, but has more than he needs. We are three proud generations in America now. This country has been very generous to me and my family. I speak in one voice with my father: God bless America!"

Seven

Anna emailed a reminder that the next meeting would be on Tuesday at 10 a.m., and all subsequent formal meetings would also be Tuesdays at 10 o'clock. Publication of *The Schoolhouse* would be monthly, for now, and all staff would be expected to submit something at least once a month. She also told them her hours would be 10 a.m. to 4 p.m. Monday through Thursday, and 10 a.m. to 2 p.m. on Fridays. All were welcome to stop in and talk about *The Schoolhouse* anytime during those hours.

The Bronners, Carla and Robert, were first to arrive, holding hands but silent. They sat at the conference table for a few minutes and quietly avoided each other. Carla coughed, stood, and went into the kitchen to make coffee. Robert looked blankly at Anna. Carla came back to the main room with the coffee pot and three cups and said to her husband, "Here's some coffee to go with that dead horse you're beating."

"I'm glad to have you both here," Anna said. "And thanks for coming early." Robert gave her a half smile and looked down at his papers.

"I feel like six out of seven dwarves," Carla said.

Anna poured coffee for herself and said, "Is that one of your codes?"

Quickly, Robert said, "Well, sort of. It means she's not Happy."

"Ha ha," Anna said. "Happy. I get it. Well anyway, everything *is* better with a cup of coffee." Carla looked away, but smiled. Robert coughed and poured himself a cup.

Miriam had given Jasmine a ride, and they came in together. "Greetings, pilgrims," Jasmine said. "We arrive on your planet in search of intellectual sustenance." She went to hang up their coats and Miriam whispered to Anna, "She talks like that all the time. It's weird, but I like it."

Anna poured coffee for Miriam and Jasmine just as L.T. came in. "I think I'm on time. Am I on time?"

Anna had put a Felix the Cat clock on the far wall. She glanced at it and said, "Yes, L.T., you're fine. Felix is telling me you're actually a few minutes early."

Robert put his coffee down and said, "Felix? Who is Felix? Is there another guy signed on to this enterprise?"

L.T. said, "Enterprise? You're a *Star Trek* fan?"

Robert wrinkled his brow. "Um, no. Not really. I've heard of it, though." L.T. frowned and nodded.

Anna passed out copies of her mock-up of the magazine and gave them a few minutes to look it over. Each went to his or her own contribution and smiled, chuckled, or at least nodded.

Anna said, "I think the rendering of *The Schoolhouse* on the cover is ideal." She nodded at Jasmine. "The humor pieces included are all solid quality. Jaz, I was thinking of some drawings of the Forest Hills neighborhoods. Maybe a building you think is interesting, or a landscape from Forest Park?"

"I sketched the stadium at a Brooklyn Cyclones game a few weeks ago. It's Brooklyn, but... what do you think?"

"Sure, that's the kind of thing I had in mind, Jaz."

"Oh, the Cyclones," Robert said. "The class of the New York-Penn League."

"Pen league?" Carla said, thinking. "Maybe we could sponsor a team. It's perfect, right? The Pen League for a bunch of writers."

There was a long silence until Anna said, "Oh, Carla, I'm glad you're thinking out of the box, but it's actually the New York-Pennsylvania League, so...maybe not."

"Oh, well," Paula sighed. "Another great notion consigned to the dustbin of history."

"Well, this one, yeah, but keep 'em coming. You all should know I have had a lump in the pit of my stomach for weeks," Anna said, "but I am thrilled at the way it's developing. I honestly didn't think it would come together as quickly as it has."

"When I was still working," Robert said, "and ambitious, I read some books on management theory. What it boils down to, as far as I could tell, is finding the right people, treating them right, and trying to stay out of their way while they work. 'Serve your family first,' was the title of a chapter I thought made good sense. A sense of community, a sense of shared purpose can go a long way. I was going to use it for a Thanksgiving ad, but you know, copyright."

"Sounds a little cannibalistic, doesn't it?" L.T said.

Robert thought for a minute. "Yes, I suppose copyright could be considered somewhat cannibalistic."

"No," L.T laughed. "I mean 'Serve Your Family.'"

"That's cannibalistic? How?" asked Robert

"Well, what else does 'Serve Your Family' mean?"

"It doesn't mean *eat* them. It was Thanksgiving, for cryin' out loud."

"Well, I know what you *meant*," L.T. said, "but the way it sounds..."

"No, no, no." Robert said. "You got it all wrong. It's just a sales thing—"

Anna interrupted. "I love it that you guys are talking shop, but we should probably move along here. I have some other things to talk about, including the next issue."

"Good, good," L.T. said. "Robert and I can talk later."

"Okay," Anna said. "Then let me just unload on you. You don't really need to know any of this, but I'd like to keep everyone in the know as much as possible. I spent too many years as a victim of the 'Mushroom Theory of Management'."

"That's a new one on me," Miriam said.

Anna nodded. "The Mushroom Theory of Management has one major principle: 'Keep them in the dark and feed them a lot of, um, let's call it fertilizer.'"

"Ah," Carla said. "That principle has proponents in education as well. And it's safe to say the higher up you go, the darker it is, and the deeper the fertilizer."

"So," Anna continued, "As I said, the plan is to keep you all in the loop. Here's where we are." She spent the next fifteen minutes describing the nuts and bolts of the business plan she was developing. The printing was taking longer than she anticipated but would be on track soon. She had contracted with several small shops, markets, grocery stores, and candy stores to display *The Schoolhouse*. Her plan was to make the first two issues free in order to stimulate some business, load them up with advertisements, then decide how much to charge. There would be a six-month and a yearly subscription price as well, once she felt *The Schoolhouse* had been established. Distribution would be local, primarily Forest Hills, but pockets in a few areas as far east as Queens Village.

"As you can see, it is still very much a work in progress. My biggest misstep, at least so far, is that I didn't look for a web manager soon enough. *Aplomb* resisted the digital world longer than most magazines, and I made the same mistake. I corrected it, though. Last week I hired a webmaster..."

"Web...*master*," Jasmine said under her breath. "Kinky."

"I do truly hope not, Jaz. I don't want to see someone walking around here in latex. Plus, Sam is not your typical—"

"Plus, I heard latex bunches up and squeaks when you move," Jasmine interrupted.

"And getting it on is a day's work," L.T. added.

"Not to mention how much you sweat in something like that," Jasmine agreed.

"Good to know, Jaz. I will mention all of that to Sam. But seriously, it's not a secret the internet is a prime source of business. Probably *the* prime source of business in a shrinking world. It may force us to branch out a little, past the local scene, but as the saying goes, 'we'll cross that bridge when we get around to it.'"

"It's a brave new world out there, Anna," Miriam said.

"Oh, I remember that show," L.T. said.

"What show?" Miriam asked.

"*Brave New World*. It's all about life in the future. Babies manufactured in laboratories, the government passing out drugs to keep people calm and happy. There is a rule for everything. *Everything*. Makes me glad I'm old and won't live to see that."

"Okay," Anna said quickly. "Who has questions or comments before we move on? I want to talk about the next issue."

Carla, the teacher, put her hand up. "Anna, are we doing any literary reviews? I was thinking the other day about that book, *Let's Eat Grandma*."

"Oh, no. More cannibalism?" L.T. said.

"Oh god, no," Carla said. "It's a book about grammar and punctuation."

"About eating somebody's Gammy?"

"It's a joke. It's really a very funny book. See, if you leave the comma out, it means...It's easier to see when it's written down. I'll show you later."

Anna said, "Oh, I read that book, Carla. I think a review would make a good piece. I was thinking also of a review section of classic books. Everything new gets ink, but where can you get an honest review of, say, *Wuthering Heights?*"

"That could be my thing, Anna. I can easily pop out a review every month. And I think I can make the reviews, well maybe not funny, but at least relevant. Hemingway, Faulkner, Steinbeck. I love those books."

"Why don't you write up something for next issue, and we'll see what it looks like."

"I had an idea," Robert said, "sort of based on our last submission. I want to call it *Hacks for Mental Health*, or something like that. There are so many good ideas hung out on the internet that make life a little smoother, I would like to write about some of them. Publicize them a little, choose good ones, and maybe make fun of the bad ones."

"I'm glad you are coming up with ideas, Robert, but you'll have to be careful," Anna said. "Copyright could be an issue. Also, a lot of that stuff is pretty trashy."

"'As seen on television,'" Miriam said.

"Guaranteed to break when exposed to air," LaToya said.

"Recrement," Jasmine said.

"Recrement?" Anna asked.

"What is, um...?" Miriam said.

"It means the stuff that's left after all the good stuff is taken out," Jasmine said. "Like grapefruit rinds."

"Or the stuff at the Salvation Army," LaToya said.

"Or, actually, digestion, if you know what I mean." Jasmine said.

"That sounds very biological," LaToya said.

A long silence around the table until Anna said, "I'm writing a note to myself, 'Buy...a...dictionary.'"

"A big one," Carla said. "Maybe the one that comes with a magnifying glass."

"Anyway, Robert," Anna said. "I'm not sure that idea could work, but you ought to look into it. Why don't you give us an update at our next meeting?" Robert smiled and nodded.

"Other ideas, comments, complaints?" Anna said.

"Ooh, me," Jasmine said. "An idea. I would like to draw each of you, just head shots, to include with your articles, next to your byline."

"You mean sit for a portrait? Like a model?" Anna asked.

"More like a sketch at a street fair. I'm not talking about a full color portrait of an emperor, just a sketch. Twenty minutes of your time, thirty at most. Maybe a little longer for you, Anna, because you have a certain regal aura about you. It's difficult to capture."

Anna laughed. "You're so kind to me, Jasmine, and yet, somehow, so full of it. But it's such a great idea, I wish I had thought of it. I'll sit for you, but please do me last. I'll need to schedule a few days' reconstruction work at my salon."

"I have an idea for an article," Miriam said. "I'll work on it and bring it next time. Or email it to you. Is emailing still a good way to send you written work?"

"Yeah, oh yeah, Miriam. And everyone, email is best. Snail mail if you really want to, and there is time. And I'll be shopping for a fax machine over the weekend. You can text me, too, or since I'm a lonesome senior, just drop by. I'll be here every day, and there will always be coffee. "Oh, almost forgot," Anna said. "I think we're not paying enough attention to the local interests. Not news, exactly, that stuff is covered by local newspapers. I'm thinking about narrower interests, the kind of thing that might fall between the cracks. Robert, I'm hoping I can rely on you to check through government websites, state and local I guess, and tease out anything of special interest for Forest Hills. I'm thinking of changes in zoning restrictions, local construction plans, maybe even city council meetings; that kind of thing. I appreciate that local government can be a 'rabbit hole,' but I'm hoping you'll agree to be our Alice."

"I never watched that movie," LaToya said. "Or my kids, either. That psychedelic stuff is all wrong. Just all wrong."

"I get what you're after, Anna, and I'm happy to do it," Robert said. "I generally keep an eye on that stuff anyway."

"He does," Carla said. "I can always tell when he's on the New York State website. There's a distinctive tone to the way he growls."

"And Jaz," Anna added, "I had an idea for you as well. Would you survey the local art and entertainment scene? Again, the kind of things that would be of interest to locals but might fall between the cracks."

"Yes, that's a good idea. In fact, I have a couple of pieces I'm working on now I think will fit in *The Schoolhouse*."

The meeting broke up and everyone either paired up to talk or opened up a computer to write something. Carla and Latoya sat at a desk and got into a conversation about the difference between commas and semicolons.

"It's sort of the difference between a yield sign and a stop sign," LaToya said.

"Or between, "'Kids, please settle down' and 'I'm handing out detentions on the count of three,' Carla said.

L.T said, "In the world of magazines, they got people like me to pore over it and take care of punctuation and grammar and 'i before e', and all that stuff."

"But that doesn't work for everyone," Carla said. "If a student writes a resume, who's gonna check it before it goes to an employer? I studied grammar years ago, I guess it was high school English. It actually made sense for a couple of months, but then when I tried to teach it to tenth grade kids, oh, man, it gets complicated. Past perfect? Future perfect? And please don't even start with me about 'who' and 'whom.'"

Robert came over and said, "I thought about what you said, LaToya, and you're right. 'Serve your family' could be interpreted as something creepy."

Carla scratched her head and said, "Wasn't there an old, really old *Twilight Zone* episode like that? 'Serving Man,' or something like that."

LaToya smiled. "Yeah, I remember that one. Gave me nightmares."

"To Serve Mankind" was the name of the episode," Miriam said. "Just like me to remember something so esoteric."

"Esoteric, yeah, probably. Gonna have to look that one up, too."

Anna and Jasmine were drinking coffee and watching Carla, Robert and LaToya from the entrance to the kitchen. "Poor Robert is outnumbered, and I don't think Felix the Cat counts," Anna said. "One guy in the whole group. Hope that doesn't turn into a problem."

"And yet, somehow I don't feel sorry for him."

"Not him so much, Jaz, as all of this." She swept her arm across the whole room. "This project, this magazine. I don't want it turning into *Ms.* magazine."

"What about the other guy, Herman? Is he gonna jump in?"

"Doubtful. He has a whole other life, and I don't think writing is his strength. I had to do a fair amount of reconstruction on his piece."

"You mentioned the webmaster guy, Sam. What about him?"

Anna shook her head. "No, Sam is Samantha. Also, not a writer, and also she's only fluent in techno-speak. Five minutes of Sam waxing poetic about bandwidth and TCP-IP, and you'll all be doing cartwheels out the door."

"Five old babes and one old dude doing cartwheels," Jasmine said. "That would be something to write about. Or draw. Maybe I will."

"There you go again, making lemons into lemonade," Anna joked.

"Well, we're still in the early stages here, Anna. Maybe some bearded, undiscovered literary genius will come stumbling through the door, eager to work with a bunch of old ladies."

"That could happen," Anna said, looking up and stroking her chin. "Yes, I see a tall man, smoking a pipe, wearing a herringbone jacket with patches on the elbows. and dazzling us all with his smile and his erudition."

"Yeah, that wouldn't surprise me at all," Jasmine said.

~ * ~

Anna picked up fifty copies of the first edition from the printer on Friday, saved a dozen for her staff, and distributed the rest: libraries, grocery stores, supermarkets, bookstores, anywhere a newspaper or magazine could be found, she left a few copies of *The Schoolhouse* with a prominent email address and sparkling new web address. This was not the fully realized product of her vision, but an overture prior to the beginning of the symphony. She made sure to send a copy to Keith Dannell, the Forest Hills School Superintendent, with a note reiterating her promise to publish the winners of the high school's writing competition.

Before going to *The Schoolhouse* next morning, Anna stopped at Herman's Deli for coffee and to drop off a copy of the first edition. The store was almost empty. She found him, his glasses halfway down his nose, behind the counter going through receipts.

"Ah, here is my friend and literature colleague, Anna. Coffee, a bagel and a schmear, all on the house for Anna. I am celebrating today the work we did together."

"That's why I'm here, Herman. I want to show you the complete product. Please understand that when we get really rolling, it will look better. It will have a glossy cover and better quality paper, more content, and I hope more advertising. But I wanted you to get a sense of what it will look like." He looked around quickly to be sure there were no customers, and then paged slowly through the magazine.

"Is this copy for me?" he asked.

"Yes. And I will get you the next copy when it comes out. The printing has been a little delayed, but certainly within a few weeks."

"I am very proud of being a contributor to your magazine, Anna. Thank you for the opportunity. But I don't think the life of a writer is what I am cut out on."

"Oh, not what you're cut out for?"

"Yes. That. I believe this world is made of both people who think and people who do. I could easily be a thinker if I chose the writer's life, but at the bottom of my heart, I am a doer. I love what I do here. I don't want to change."

"I can certainly respect that decision, Herman, as well as agree with it. You are a doer."

"But you still get your bagel and schmear."

"Thank you, that is very kind. But I do have another request to make of you. Actually, two requests."

He looked at her suspiciously. "A request? Are we talking about credit again?"

She laughed. "No, my friend. Credit is not necessary. I would like you to display my magazine for the next few weeks. The copies will be free."

"Certainly. You bring them, and I'll put them on the rack by the newspapers. And the second request?"

"That one is more of a business arrangement. How would you feel about advertising in my magazine?"

He looked down again at his receipts. "I have advertising. I have signs all over my front window. I have my nephew change them every week."

"Yes, Herman, but for a customer to see the advertising on the window, he has to walk by the store. In my magazine, a customer on the other side of town can see what you're selling and what your prices are. Why am I telling you this? You're a smart businessman, you know about advertising."

He walked around the counter to the middle aisle very quietly, looking down at the ground. "I do know about my business, Miss Anna, and I know how I like it. I like my customers. I know what they want and what they need, and how I should treat them. A customer from miles away, what do I know?" He was looking at her now, and he was looking daggers.

"I'm sorry, Herman. I should not have said anything. You're right. You know your business." She started toward the door. "Please, just forget I said anything. Thank you for the coffee and bagel."

She walked half-way out, but turned quickly and came back in. "Herman, please forget what I said about advertising. The magazine is important to me, but I would not want anything to affect our friendship. That's more important."

He looked at her, with a half-smile. "Yes. I will think about what you said, Miss Anna. I will think on it. Please come back on Saturday, or a different day, for your coffee, and I will see you then."

~ * ~

Anna knew fifty copies of a thin magazine was paltry, almost embarrassing, but it was a start. She had already realized, belatedly, that unlike *Aplomb*, printed hard copies were not going to be *The Schoolhouse's* primary form. She was going digital.

Anna brought Eleanor Roosevelt along to meet with Sam, the 'webmistress,' at *The Schoolhouse*. She still hesitated when she thought of that term, imagining a spider wearing leather boots and brandishing a whip. "I was born at the end of the World War Two," she told Eleanor. "It was not only a different millennium, it was a different world. The word 'web' had only one meaning, and the word 'mistress' had only one meaning. No one, genius or otherwise, could think far enough ahead to combine those two words. And no one could possibly imagine what the combination would mean."

Eleanor, Mrs. Roosevelt, sat on her haunches staring at Anna and then licked her paws. Her meaning was clear: *It's the twenty-first century, lady. Get over it.*

~ * ~

Anna was not easily intimidated, but Sam was formidable in more ways than one. Her skill with computers was daunting, and she was also physically imposing, looming over Anna at over six feet tall, large boned but not fat, with an attractive face and bright smile under short blonde hair. She shook Anna's hand and went immediately to work setting up the website. Anna said, "It's my policy to leave people alone when they're working, but would you mind if I looked over your shoulder for a little while? This is all like sorcery to me. I want to know enough to at least read the directions. I promise I'll be quiet."

Sam, named Samantha Josephine after both her mother and her father, smiled. "Oh, please, stay and watch. I'll talk through what I'm doing, and you can stop me at any time and ask questions. I love talking about this stuff."

She used a flash drive to install something, and as the computer was humming, flashing and asking yes/no questions, she explained, or at least tried to explain, what was happening in the secret conclaves of the internet. She spoke slowly, checking once or twice to see if Anna was still listening, and used terms like bandwidth, router, domain, firewall, FTP, SEO—"

Anna said quickly, "Wait, I've heard of SEO. That stands for, wait, I know this one... oh, never mind, I don't know what it is."

Sam just smiled. "It's a big deal for business, and it will be important for your business. It stands for Search Engine Optimization. SEO helps a user out there find your website, this website, which is competing with a gazillion other websites."

"Oh, right," Anna said. "Search Engines. Google and like that."

"Exactly. Oh, hang on, running into a snag here. Oh, I may need to update your SSL certificate. Well, maybe there's a way to work around that, but it may take a little time. "

"Well, yeah, of course you need to update my Cecil certificate. I could have told you that without even looking. You need to SEO my firewall so it's compatible with my bandwidth transfer protocol."

"Oh, wow, you *do* understand!" Sam laughed. "That's it exactly."

"I will let you get to it then, while I demonstrate my technological acumen by programming the coffee maker. I often refer to it as a COE, a Caffeine Optimization Engine."

A few minutes later, Anna called from the kitchen, "Seems like a good time to take a break. Coffee is ready, and there is some pound cake left over."

"Um, yeah, just, let me, um...okay, give me a minute," Sam muttered. Anna brought the coffee and cake out to the conference table. Sam stared at the monitor for a minute longer and said, "That ought to do it." She went over and poured herself coffee.

"Is there a problem?" Anna asked. "Are those computers up to the task? I bought what I thought was more than adequate."

"Oh, yeah, they're fine. It's just, you know, technology. It's tough to keep up with all the changes. If you really want to know, the web host software I installed wasn't compatible with the security software because the security software was too secure, not for the software, but for the certificate that was required for the...oh, I know that look. I should shut up now, shouldn't I, or I won't get any cake?"

Anna said, "I just want people to be able to get to the site and submit articles. Can you make it do that?"

"Wait for it," Sam said with a half-smile and then had a forkful of cake. They both were quiet, listening to the barely audible hum of the computer.

Before they finished their cake, they heard, 'ding.'

"Music to my ears," Sam said.

"What?" Anna said, nervously. Sam gave her that same half-smile.

Anna walked to the computer and read the screen. "Hee-hee," she giggled. "Arkang101 just submitted a short story. *The Unicorn Learns to Swim.*

Eight

During the afternoon, the computer made her jump with that 'ding' sound a half dozen times before Anna found the way to turn the volume down. When she had placed an advertisement in the online databases for writers, she made sure to specify she was looking for humor and general interest pieces. "We do not accept fantasy, horror, science fiction, mystery or romance stories. We appreciate your interest in our publication, but we print exclusively humor and general interest pieces."

The title of *The Unicorn Learns to Swim* seemed, at first glance, offbeat enough to have some humor potential. After a few paragraphs detailing a heroic unicorn's struggle to find water on a desert planet and escape from a band of government-appointed vampires by climbing a magic tree, it was clear that it did not. The next offering that went 'ding' took place on a jungle planet where talking trees were nobility, singing flowers were damsels in distress, and the grass, although not very bright, had organized itself into townships with a mayor and a town council. Another 'ding' was about a series of brutal murders, graphically described, on a spaceship slipping between alternate realities.

The next two offered sanity and hope. Anna printed them out, to be reviewed by the full group, and added them to a book review by Carla, and a short piece by Robert.

THE SCHOOLHOUSE
Casual, Collegial and Classy

The Once and Future King–T. H. White
A Review
by
Carla Bronner

In this periodical, I will be recommending those books which I find most rewarding, most entertaining, and most worthy of your time. It will be a long list, but at the top of this list will be *The Once and Future King*, by T. H. White. Yes, it is the basis for the Disney animated classic *The Sword in The Stone*, but that is the tip of the iceberg, the moat around the castle for this rich, sparkling novel.

I have known since youth, like most people, the legends of King Arthur and the Round Table. Or at least I thought I did. What I knew, I realize now, were unconnected fragments of the adventures of knights and damsels. This book, in clear, engaging prose, connects these fragments into a cohesive and fascinating epic. It narrates the story of Wart, the hero of *Sword in the Stone*, right through the final battle with his malevolent son, Mordred. Along the way, White weaves a tale of forbidden love, betrayal, magic, family loyalty, and above all, tragedy.

It was written in the 1950s, and a sequel called *The Book of Merlyn* was added twenty years later. The main characters are the stuff of legend: Arthur, Merlyn, Lancelot, Guinevere. But it's the secondary characters, those I have always known of but knew little about, that make the story live: Morgause, Galahad, Gawain, Mordred. This is a book in which fantasy and romance are knit into classic literature. Without reservation, I recommend this book to anyone who loves epic literature and gets swept away by romance.

Biker Geese from Heck
by
Thomas Barone

A motley gang of leather-clad geese is heading south on the sky highway. There are about thirty of them; most have tattoos, a few have their bills pierced. Some have knives, some guns, and a few have guitars strapped to their backs. All scowl as if they really mean it. They are all humming, rrrrrRUMRUMRUMrrrrr rrrrrRUMRUMRUMrrrrr as they fly along the empty skyway. They aren't looking for trouble, not really, but they won't mind if they come across it, either.

Their leader, Rip, aka Shred, aka Slash, and lately known as 'Lou,' scans the marshes below for a good place to rest and find some food. Night is coming, too, and he is proud that of his band of thirty hardened biker geese, only a few are afraid of the dark. He signals a turn, and banks down to a marshy area where he comes to a running stop, but trips and gets his bill stuck in the mud. With one eye he can see that the others in his ragged band have all landed safely.

His second in command, Claw, aka Talon, aka Mangle, lately known as 'Ed,' waddles over and peers down at him.

"Are you all right?"

"Nnn. Ah junee uh iddle heh," Lou replies, just needing a little help.

"Um, 'June in January'? Is that what you said? You want me to sing 'June in January?'"

"Nuh. Nuh, nuh. Heh. A junee heh." Lou says, wriggling a little bit in the mud, and asking again for a little help.

"A jaunty hat? You want a jaunty hat?"

Lou shrieks, but the shriek comes out sounding like 'aspidistra, applesauce and argyle socks!'

"Pull!" he shouts. And this sounds enough like 'pull' for even Ed to understand. Ed pulls Lou's face out of the mud and backs away a few feet.

Lou sits up, trying to regain his alpha-male dignity, and scowls at Ed for a moment.

He points at him angrily. "'June in January,' really? 'June in January,' Ed?"

Ed says nothing but keeps a wary eye on his leader.

"Everyone get down, okay?" Lou asks, wiping his bill with his wing.

"Yeah, they're all down. A few are out scouting the area. I think there are a few locals living on the other side of the marsh. Maybe we can have some fun with them."

Lou adjusts his eye patch and checks to be sure his penknife is still in the sheath attached to his leg. "Okay, let's check it out."

They walk across the muddy marsh, Lou in the lead, Ed a few paces behind him, and both saying, 'rrrrrrRUMRUMRUM rrrrrrrRUMRUMRUMrrrrrr' softly as they walk. From the top of a small hill, they see a few of their gang laughing and squawking at an older goose. One, with an American flag bandana on his head, runs up behind the old gander and kicks him.

"What? What was that for?" the old goose bellows.

"That's for being old, and not giving us any food," his tormentor replied.

"But I have no food to give you!" shouts the old timer.

"Just another reason to kick you." One of the others in the crowd laughs.

Lou and Ed stride into the middle of the group. "We're hungry, *mon ami*. We need food, *comprendre vous*?" asks Lou.

'rrrrrrrrRUMRUMRUMrrrrrrrrrrrrrrrrRUMRUMRUMrrrrrr' Ed mumbles behind Lou.

"Turn your engine off!" Lou yells at him. "Trying to make me deaf?"

"We have only enough for my little family," the old gander replies. "We got a late start this season, and most of the grass and good vegetation is all dried up. We have barely enough for ourselves."

"Not our problem, old man," Lou yells. "We're badass biker geese, and we take what we want. We're rebels, you know."

The old gander looks confused. "What are you rebelling against?" he asked.

"Whadda ya got?" Lou says with a sneer.

Just then, another goose came running, sort of, up the hill and squawking, "Don't hurt him! Please don't hurt him." She is a young goose, a light, blondish gray, with a trim waist, a kissable beak, a long neck perfect for nibbling, and extra feathers where they would do the most good.

"Please, please don't hurt my grandfather," she pants when she reached the tableau. "He's all I've got."

Lou scowls. "Apparently, you're all he's got, too, which is a problem. We need to eat, sister, and if you and this old bird here can't point us to some good grassland, you're no good to us. Except maybe as entertainment, if you know what I mean."

"No," Mehitable says, for that was her name. She was given this awful name by a vindictive mother, who married for money and then found out her husband didn't have any. When Mehitable was a small child, her mother always forced her to play the duck in 'duck, duck, goose' and as a result, her daughter developed a crippling identity crisis. That's the reason she was now living with her grandfather, even though he often smelled funny, especially after a big meal.

Lou, who sometimes repeated himself just for emphasis, said again, "You're no good to us. Except maybe as entertainment, if you know what I mean."

"No," the young goose said. "I don't know what you mean."

"He means 'if you're gonna dance, you have to pay the fiddler.' Do you understand now?" Ed growled.

"Uh, no. Not really," Mehitable says nervously.

"We mean," says Lou glaring at her, "'all that glitters is not gold.' If you know what I mean."

"I'm, I'm sorry," she stammers, "but I don't. I don't understand what you mean."

"We mean," Ed says, "'sauce for the goose is sauce for the gander.' Do you understand now?"

"Oh. Oh, yes, I think I...no. No, I still don't understand."

"Oh, never mind!" shouts Lou. "If we don't get something to eat soon, I won't be responsible for my men. That's what I mean!"

"Oh, food. Why didn't you say so? I can help you there," Mehitable said. "I know a spot less than a mile from here, tucked in a valley, where the grass is green and fresh all year long. I can take you there."

"So, how come the old granddad here didn't tell us about this valley, eh?" asked Ed.

"Well, he is old," Mehitable said. "And almost blind. And his daughter, my mother, makes anyone in a hundred-kilometer radius insane. Besides, he's a gander. Since when do males know anything about food?"

"Lead on, sister," Lou said, darkly.

They walked down the road, two of them humming 'rrrrrrRUMRUMRUMrrrrrrrrrrrRUMRUMRUMrrr' very softly, and Mehitable wondering where the sound was coming from. When they reached the top of a ridge, they could see the small valley below filled with grass, and seeds, and even a little pond with mosquitoes buzzing around on top. Everything a goose with an attitude problem could possibly want.

Later, after the whole gang had eaten their fill, they sat on the grass, resting. Some strummed guitars softly. Very softly, because it's hard to make a lot of noise on a guitar with a wing made of feathers. Some are playing mumblety-peg with their penknives, and others are taking bets that Ed will be the first to spear his own foot.

Lou was lying in the grass with his head in Mehitable's lap. "I guess we'll have to be on our way soon. I'm a traveling goose, you know. An adventurer. A rolling stone. Born under a wandering star."

"Will you take me with you?" she asked. "I can hum as well as anyone in your gang."

"Oh, I don't know," said Lou. "It's a tough life. Bar fights, bugs in our beak, and cops on our tail, and sometimes, a serious head wind. No, not a life for a nice country goose like you."

"Well, will you come back this way sometime? I could wait for you. I'd be glad to wait for a goose like you."

"Sure kid, sure we'll come back," he said with an artful smile. Then he whistled, which is a difficult thing for a goose to do and tells you something about why he was the leader.

He made a wing signal to his gang, and within minutes they were all lined up in formation, ready for take-off. Lou nodded to Mehitable, gave Ed a high five, and stepped in front of the group. He started running for his take off, but tripped and landed beak first in the road. No one dared to laugh. He soon was airborne once again at the head of his ragged band of misfits and troublemakers. He waved once at Mehitable, then banked majestically and headed north for the winter.

Alarm Clock Time Machine
by
Anita Blankenship

The alarm clock in my room is set twenty minutes ahead, and has been for several years, with good reason. A moment of early morning math and I can safely bury myself again in the deep and dark paradise of my bedclothes. For those fleeting twenty minutes I can, in semi-consciousness, feel that I am in control of my life. The operative word being 'fleeting.' When the snooze button time runs out and the alarm rings again, I groan out that math again, and the real world invades.

Later in the day, that clock becomes a primitive and interactive time machine. Outside the bedroom door, the world tick-tocks in that mysterious and all-inclusive process that Einstein and Newton only understood dimly. Inside the bedroom it is always twenty minutes earlier, life is still waiting for me, and so I'm never late. Well, sometimes I'm late anyway.

It grants me power in some small measure...very small measure. I have, in frivolous moments, fiddled with the clock to turn back time, but it just won't go back far enough to vote for Hillary, or allow me to ask Plato what the heck he was talking about. And it won't go ahead far enough to develop a winning stock portfolio. So I settle, reluctantly, for that respite under the bedclothes, and the fantasy of what I can do with an extra twenty minutes.

A Beautiful Machine
by
Robert Bronner

I was driving to the hardware store today, and I pulled up next to a Corvette. A well-kept, vintage, blue beauty. I usually get jealous for a moment or two when I see a car like that. This time though, not so much.

I looked over at the driver, and he had a finger so far up his nose I thought he was going to pull a muscle. He looked over at me, paused for a second, and then dug a little deeper. When the light turned green, he drove off with a squeal of his tires, one handed.

There is often a wide, wide gap between money and class. Certainly, it is possible to have both, but it's also possible to have one, and profoundly, tragically, lack the other.

~ * ~

"Oh, that one *is* snarky," Jasmine said. "I love snarky."

"I'm working on a piece, a short one," Miriam said, "but I'm going to need LaToya's..."

Five people around the table held their pose for a five count until Miriam finished her sentence. "...expertise," she said.

"Sure, Miriam," LaToya said. "Glad to help."

"It's kind of a medical, whiny, humor piece about rheumatologists. If we look at it today, it could be ready for our next meeting."

All five people immediately looked over at Jasmine for clarification. "A rheumatologist is a doctor who specializes in diseases of the joints," she said, casually.

"Right," said Anna. "I have to remember to get that dictionary."

Before the meeting broke into groups, Jasmine asked for volunteers to sit and have their sketch done. Anna put her head down and walked quietly into the kitchen. Carla said, "Not yet," and sat at a computer to print off her review. LaToya and Miriam started editing Miriam's rheumatologist piece.

"Looks like you're up first, Robert."

"Okay, I'm ready, Jaz. Got my ears lowered last week, and I'm wearing my best turquoise string tie."

"That should really capture your reader's attention, Robert."

"Got it in Flagstaff, Arizona a few years back when Carla and I were..."

"Just pull up a chair there, Robert, and face toward the door. I'm gonna do you in a three-quarter view."

"That's fine, just don't ask which is my best side, because I don't have one. Even as a child, the doctors were amazed."

"Ha. Good one."

"Three-quarters is fine, whatever you think best. But let me tell you, Arizona was fantastic. We were traveling Route sixty-six, just before we swung over to Grand Canyon National Park."

"Uh, huh."

"You ever been out that way? Beautiful country."

"No."

"Oh, the Painted Desert alone…"

"I'm sorry to interrupt, Robert, but are you familiar with Picasso's paintings? Where he put crazy things, like an extra nose on a face or an eye on the side of the head? Do you know why he did that?"

"Artistic license, I guess. Cubism and all that."

"No. It was because his model kept distracting him by talking."

"Oh." And that was Robert's last word.

~ * ~

They had all brown-bagged lunch, and afterwards, they met again at the conference table to talk about the next issue.

"We have a fair number of submissions coming in by computer, but a lot of them are non-starters."

"Non-starters meaning 'wack,'" Jasmine said.

"Wrong-headed," LaToya said.

"Egregiously imprudent," Miriam said, with a big smile.

Anna laughed. "And I think first prize for the memorable phrase of the week goes to Miriam."

"Anyway," Anna continued, "buried among all of the egregiously imprudent are some winners, I think. I hope. I am going to be digging them out and asking for your opinions. I believe much of what gets published will be generated by you folks, but some of it will come in through the website. Collectively, we will decide what we leave in, and what we leave out."

"Well," said Robert, "As far as these pieces, I think the *Alarm Clock* and the *Geese* stories fit the profile pretty well. The *Geese* one

93

is just for entertainment; it's really just a giggle about a gaggle. The *Alarm Clock* will certainly ring a bell, pun intended, with a lot of folks out there who love to just smack that alarm and settle back under the covers."

Jasmine said, "I agree with Robert. Both of those stories are good fits. I felt a little sad that Mehitable got left behind, but such is often the fate of a goose with a perfect neck for nibbling."

Carla said, "I actually spit out my coffee at that line about the jaunty hat."

Anna was lost in thought. That phrase she had used, 'What we leave in, and what we leave out?' was stuck in her head, but she could not recall where she heard it. *Bernard, maybe? No, not Bernie. His predecessor perhaps, Mr. Wexler, who would never let anyone use his first name? No, it wasn't him either.*

It dawned on her suddenly, like a rain squall on a sunny day, that it was Aloysius. She put it out of her head immediately, and she would not let it back in.

"Okay, my brain is turning the page to the next issue, and if you have something to work on, please stay, or dig through some of the submissions, and we'll start the process. Thank you all."

~ * ~

Anna stopped off that evening to do her grocery shopping and when she got home, she found a message from Chloe on her social media program.

SnowyChloe: "Help, Anna! I'm getting it from both sides!"

AnnaBnana: "Oh, boy. Sebaceous again?"

SnowyChloe: "He's only on one side. Detective Donna is on the other."

AnnaBnana: "What? What's going on?"

SnowyChloe: "The worst-case scenario. Imagine a guy you don't like hitting on you and his girlfriend, who you don't like either, finds out about it."

AnnaBnana: "Sebaceous is hitting on you? Get out, really?"

SnowyChloe: "He asked me out twice, for drinks the first time and for lunch the second. Donna is spitting nails. I put him off both times, but eventually I'm gonna have to say either yes or no."

AnnaBnana: "Have you talked to Human Resources? He's your boss, so it sounds like harassment."

SnowyChloe: "I don't want to do that, because then it really hits he fan. I think Donna has him convinced I'm the one calling HR about him. I think that's why he wants to go out, to weasel something out of me."

AnnaBnana: "Someone's been talking to HR about him? Oh, yeah, you told me that."

SnowyChloe: "A guy from HR has been over here a couple of times. Simmons, I think? Simpson maybe? Short guy, blond combover. I don't know what's going on, but I had nothing to do with it."

AnnaBnana: "Simmons? Simon maybe? I know of a Simon. Justin, no, Jordan. Jordan Simon. Yeah, blond combover. He has a stick up his fundament, but he's not the worst of them."

SnowyChloe: "I don't know what to do, Anna. On top of everything, Mike is ticked off and wants to punch out Sebastian. He would lose his job for sure."

AnnaBnana: "Mike? How'd he get into this?"

SnowyChloe: "Mike, um, I've gone out with him a couple of times. Nothing serious, but I like him. He really is kind of a nice guy."

AnnaBnana: "Yeah, I know he's kind of sweet, but you know, that other problem."

SnowyChloe: "Yeah, I'm gonna be working on that. I'm starting allergy shots soon, and if they work, you know what that means."

AnnaBnana: "I guess, if your nasal blockages are gone, it could turn into a relationship problem."

SnowyChloe: "The shots take a while to work, so, well, we're gonna work on it in the meantime."

AnnaBnana: "Yeah, okay. Well, let me talk to Bernie about the Simon guy. He may have an idea, or may know someone over in HR. I'll let you know."

SnowyChloe: "Is that a good idea, Anna? Bernie might say the wrong thing to his wife, if she is his wife, or to his nephew, if he is his nephew. Then I'm really in deep water."

AnnaBnana: "I trust Bernie. He knows how much he can say to Sebaceous. Have faith, Chloe."

SnowyChloe: "Okay. I'll talk to you soon. TTFN."

While making dinner, and watching Mrs. Roosevelt eat hers, Anna told her, "When I get more time, I'm going to teach you an old Bing Crosby song; *Ac-cent-tchu-Ate-the-Positive*. When you deal with a couple of dim-bulb humans like Sebaceous and Donna, that's just what you need to do."

~ * ~

She called the hospital first thing in the morning. Bernard did not have a phone in his room, but a nurse told her he had had a good night and remained stable. She planned to visit that evening but got caught up with work; work was now, as much as anything, at *The Schoolhouse*, poring over submissions and trying to separate the wheat from the chaff, sometimes just by the titles. Chaff was outperforming wheat by about a two-to-one margin. When she looked up from the computer it was almost eleven o'clock, so she packed up and drove home. Visiting hours were well over, her sciatic nerve was beginning to hum a familiar tune, and Mrs. Roosevelt was looking for some attention. "Tomorrow" was the last word Anna whispered to her pillow.

~ * ~

She called Chloe from The Schoolhouse next morning and asked if she wanted to visit Bernie at Presbyterian that evening. They could have a bite to eat at the hospital cafeteria, and maybe a drink on the way home.

"Yeah, that sounds good. Give me the address of the hospital and I'll meet you in the lobby."

They met around six, both of them feeling hungry, and went first to the cafeteria before going upstairs to see Bernie. "I hope this is okay, Anna. He doesn't really know me very well. This seems like an intrusion."

"Oh, he knows who you are. I'm quite sure he knows who you are. And I don't think anyone else goes to see him, Chloe. Just me and Sherilyn. He'll be glad to see a friendly face."

They walked into his room, and there was a different patient there. Anna had a horrible moment when she was afraid Bernie had passed away. She went quickly to the nurses' station and asked.

"He was transferred this morning," a young nurse with a 'Rob' nametag told them. Anna had asked the question, but Rob, tall and dark, was focused on Chloe.

"Where? Why?" Anna asked.

He paged through some papers on the desk. "Yes, transferred. First thing this morning, he was brought to cardiac rehab up in White Plains. That's actually a good sign. He must be improving, or he would still be here."

Anna got the name and address of the rehab center. "Can he get telephone calls up there?" she asked.

"I don't think he can," Rob said to Chloe, who smiled. "They work hard to keep the atmosphere toned down, and I think they request the families to hold on to the cell phones. But maybe try calling the nurses' station. Wait, I'll give you the direct number." Anna nodded, and Chloe looked over her shoulder as they walked away.

"Wedding ring, Chloe," Anna said.

"Oh, damn. I was afraid of that. I really need to pay more attention."

They stopped at a small restaurant on Broadway for a glass of wine. The place was just beginning to fill up, but they found a booth in the corner away from the noise of the bar. "I'm sorry, Chloe," Anna said. "I wish they had told me on the phone yesterday he was being transferred. I feel like I dragged you up here for nothing."

"It's okay, Anna, it's really fine. It's nice just to get out and talk with someone. You and I don't see much of each other since you, rreee, rreee, you know. But can we not talk about *Aplomb,* please? I am sick of thinking about Sebastian and just sick of Donna altogether. Tell me about your magazine. How's all that going?"

"Oh, Chloe. I don't know what to say. It's been...it's been so—"

"That doesn't sound so good, Anna."

"No, it's been great! I'm not making any money yet, but that always takes some time. The staff I have is amazing. A couple of them are alumni from *Aplomb,* before your time, I think, but everyone seems invested. They all want to make *The Schoolhouse* work. I'm working hard, maybe too hard, but I am *really* enjoying it. The attitude of the people and the atmosphere at the meetings is terrific. It's energizing."

"*The Schoolhouse?*"

"That's what we call it. The office is what used to be a pre-school, a little red schoolhouse. So we named the magazine *The Schoolhouse*"

"I'd love to see it."

"Oh, yeah, I brought you a copy. It's thin, but we just started getting online submissions." She reached into her pocketbook and handed Chloe a copy. We've finished two editions, but the second hasn't been printed yet." Chloe flipped through it quickly and put it in her coat pocket.

"I'm a little jealous, Anna, especially now that Donna has drawn a bead on me."

"I wish I could hire you, Chloe, but I don't think I can afford you. Everybody but me is part-time and working for peanuts."

"Oh, I know, Anna. I'm probably overreacting to all this. It will work out. I have faith."

They walked down Broadway to the subway station and parted at Times Square; Anna for the 'R' train to Forest Hills, and Chloe for the Number Seven to Flushing.

Nine

Chloe was late for work the next day. In her haste, and thinking about Donna, she spilled a glass of orange juice on herself. She washed the floor, and went to the bedroom to change. She had no clean pants to wear, so opted for a skirt, but had no stockings. She pulled a pair of pants out of the wash and ironed them quickly, and afterwards realized her shoes and socks were wet too. She almost decided to call in sick and spend the rest of the day with her head under the covers, but at the last minute found a pair of sneakers and pink socks.

Donna, of course, was standing near Mike's desk and watched her as she walked in. The clock near Sebastian's office was at almost nine-forty.

"We were beginning to worry about you, Chloe," Donna said with a smile.

"One of those mornings, Donna. I'll stay later to make up for it."

"It's just a surprise, you know. You're usually such a conscientious worker. And loyal, too."

Mike came over and said, "Let me get you coffee, Chloe."

Donna smiled. "By all means, Mike. Help out your friend. You two seem to be all about teamwork."

"What do you mean, Donna? What kind of teamwork?" Chloe asked.

"Oh, it's just that Mike talks a lot about you, and I see you having lunch together sometimes, and leaving together."

"Is there a problem with that?" Mike asked.

"No, no, not at all. It just makes me wonder. Oh, and Chloe, Sebastian would like to speak with you this afternoon. I'm not really sure what it's about. I believe he said four o'clock." Chloe smiled and nodded. Donna smiled and nodded and walked back to her desk.

Mike brought her the coffee and said, "That was really weird, even for Donna. I get it that she's playing Bonnie to his Clyde, but I don't get why it involves you. He's been hanging around you, and she's working you like you're a suspect in a heist. What is her problem?"

"It's not something I want to talk about right here, right now, Mike."

"Okay, then have lunch with me."

She was about to agree, but thought better of it. "Do you want her to see us having lunch together?"

"Yeah, right. I see what you mean."

"Can you meet me after work? How about Allesandro's, the coffee shop over on Third?"

"Okay, sure. Let me buy you a cuppa."

"Oh, shoot, I told her I would work late. Can you come at a little before six? Would that work for you?"

Mike, who had a six o'clock finance class at a school downtown and really hated to be late, said, "Sure, that works."

He left the office after five, walked a couple of blocks out of his way, and was in Allesandro's Delectable Deli and Restaurant by quarter to six with a clear view of the door. Chloe came in about twenty minutes later with her head down and a tissue at her nose. Mike thought her allergies were acting up, but when she got closer, he could see the tears.

"Maybe I should just go home, Mike. I don't feel much like talking." It sounded like "Baybe I should just go hobe, Bike."

"Come on, Chloe, it's me. What did that bastard say to you?" A waitress stopped at the booth and Chloe ordered a cup of tea. She looked up at Mike and then added, "I'd like a piece of cheesecake too, please."

She was quiet for a while, fussing with her pocketbook, getting new tissues, checking her watch. "Don't you have a class tonight? Oh, please tell me you didn't skip class for me."

Mike shook his head. "Chloe, please tell me what happened. Was it Donna?"

"No. Donna sat in the corner of the office like a garden gnome. Sebastian did all the talking, and me, like a mouse, said nothing. Exactly nothing."

The waitress brought her order. Chloe took a few minutes, stalling, to squeeze the tea bag and add milk to the tea.

"Come on, Chloe, you're killing me here."

She began telling the story, pausing to take small forkfuls of cheesecake without looking at him. Sebastian had been, as Chloe spooled out the account, purely Sebaceous. He let her fret for a minute while he adjusted his stereo and then turned it off. He looked at her blankly and told her he was concerned about her career at *Aplomb*. The quality of her work had fallen off lately. Donna had noticed several errors, both in fact-checking and grammar, and also a noticeable lack of seriousness about her job...leaving early, coming in late, etc. He had wanted to address these sensitive issues privately, that's why he had asked her to lunch, but her resistance had made it necessary to have this formal meeting.

"Sounds like a lot of crap to me," Mike said. "You never leave early. Today was the first time I ever saw you come in late. And I *know* you're careful at your job."

"It got worse," she said. "He said there's been some grumbling about the way the interdepartmental meetings are managed, and he and Donna are concerned that I may be one of those employees, he stressed the word 'employees,' that's doing the grumbling."

"What a complete shmuck. How does he even walk upright?"

"And I still didn't say anything. Not a peep. I was too stunned. And I never say anything at those meetings. I don't think that's my place. That's pretty much for the content people."

"Did he mention the guy from HR? I know him a little, by the way. He's not a bad guy. We've had a couple of conversations about my college hoops bracket. He hates Duke, so we have something in common."

She looked at him, the first time since she sat down. "I don't know what that bracket thing is. And who's Duke?"

"Doesn't matter, it's beside the point. Do you want more tea? Or we could do dinner if you want?"

"I don't know, Mike. I don't know, I don't know, I don't know."

"Okay, sorry. Just take your time. Did he say anything else?"

"Yeah. That's when Donna cleared her throat, like a loud stagy cough, and he asked me about you."

"Me? Really, me?"

"Yeah, sorry. You. Kind of like that 'teamwork' thing she said this morning."

"I guess that explains it. She thinks you and I are talking to Jordan. Jordan Simon. That's the HR guy."

"I never talked to anybody in HR. I never talk to anybody about work. Not even you."

He dropped his head and focused on stirring the dregs in his empty cup of coffee. He made a face she could not interpret.

It took a moment to dawn on her. "You?" she asked. "You're the one?"

He hesitated, tried to speak and stopped. Tried again and just said, "Yes."

"Oh, man, Mike. That's like, like, I don't know what that is, but he pulled *me* into his office. He thinks *I'm* the grumbler."

"Yeah, I know, but I never thought they would point a finger at you. And besides, I had to do it. It's my job. And besides *that*, I'm not the only one that talked to Simon. Sebastian has been screwing up royally, and knives are out."

"It's your job? How is it your job? I'm not even sure what your job is."

"My job title is Purchasing and Customer Service Administrator. You clever folks create a product, and I get to deal with the fallout when somebody screws up."

"I'm not sure what all that means."

He took a deep breath. "I keep tabs on the minions that buy the paper and ink and glue for the magazine. I deal with the shipping department when the magazine is late or too early, or they don't have the trucks, or bad weather prevents a delivery from Mom and Pop's tiny little candy store, where by the way, Mom has my phone number. Also, I have to..."

"Okay, okay, I get it. I don't really get it, but I get enough of it. So, you're hearing from a lot of unhappy people—"

"From across the whole country."

"—because Sebastian is not doing his job."

"My phone actually sizzles. Seriously, the paint is peeling off. I may have to start using an oven mitt."

She laughed, but very briefly, and took another small bite of her cheesecake. "I don't want to get fired, Mike. I can't get fired. I need this job. And I don't want you to get fired either."

They sat without talking for a few minutes, listening to the buzz of conversation around them, the scraping of utensils, the polite chatter of the waitress giving someone a check.

Mike said, "I hate to seem selfish, Chloe, but there is a more immediate problem that needs attention."

"Of course, there is. Because I currently don't have enough problems."

"This problem is mine, but you're probably the only person who can help. I mean, if you want."

She looked at him suspiciously. "What?" she said.

"It's a physical thing. A craving, actually."

"Mike...Mike."

"The thing is, I'm hungry. I won't be able to think straight until I have dinner. But afterwards, we can work up some great ideas. We can brainstorm all night long if you want. So, have dinner with me..."

She smiled at him, shook her head, and asked the waitress to bring two menus.

~ * ~

On Friday afternoon, after reading through a few submissions and replying to emails from Robert and Miriam, Anna drove up to

White Plains to see Bernard. She was a little nervous about running into Sherilyn or Sebastian, so she looked carefully down hallways and around corners, and asked a nurse if Bernard had any visitors. The halls were empty, and she pushed the door open a crack to peek in his room.

She found him, dressed in jeans and a sport shirt, sitting up in a chair reading a paperback book.

"Wow," she said. "You look like a different man."

"Looks can be deceiving, it's the same old me. But come in, Anna, please come in, don't stay out there in the hall."

"They told us at Presbyterian that you had been transferred to this place. Sorry, this is the first chance I've had to drive up here."

"Presbyterian told you? Not Sherilyn or Seabass?"

Anna shook her head. "No. Chloe and I came to talk to you, and they told us at the nurses' station."

"Oh, Chloe, too? I'm sorry you made the trip for nothing."

"It scared the hell out me. I thought you were maybe, you know, but seeing you upright and in civilian clothes kind of makes up for it."

"You're looking chipper yourself. The aggravation and long hours of an editor-in-chief must appeal to you."

"Yeah, I feel like I'm changing from a caterpillar into a butterfly. Maybe more like changing from a nail into a hammer."

He hesitated, with a look on his face she could not place. "Ah, well, I wish you had called first. Thing is, I have to go to therapy in a little while, and then an education session on nutrition, and then dinner, and then I think visiting hours are about over."

"It's only three o'clock, Bern. The sign in the lobby says visitation hours are until seven. I can wait while your do your therapy. What is it with 'visitation,' anyway? Isn't than an angel thing? Do you have cherubim and seraphim dropping by for a chat?"

"Oh, they drop in regularly. Every time one of us codgers does fifteen minutes on a treadmill, another angel gets his wings."

"Ha. You must be getting better. Your jokes are getting worse."

"Really, Anna it's different up here. You know I love chatting with you, but there's stuff I need to do. Wait, did you say Chloe went with you to Presbyterian?"

"She wanted to talk to you about something going on at *Aplomb*."

"Well, I could maybe give her a call. Or better yet, I hope to be out of here in a week or two, I could talk to her then."

"Bernard, what's going on? You're nervous and jumpy, and I think you're trying to get rid of me. Wait, are you expecting Sherilyn? Or Sebastian? Oh, no, don't tell me they're both coming."

"Yes, that's it. They should be here any minute. Why don't I give Chloe a call? Or you? There is a phone by the nurses' desk I can use. I can call next week, or tomorrow."

Anna turned to the door but hesitated. "So, you're expecting them, and you have a therapy appointment? Come on, Bern, what's going on?"

"It's just that I'm trying really hard to stick to the rules. I want to get better and get out of here. If Sher or Seabass sees you, I'm gonna hear about it, and you know I don't need that."

She frowned and moved toward the door, but then walked back and stood next to him. "You're playing at something here, Bernie. I don't know what it is, but it's not like you at all."

She stared. He stared. He shrugged. She nodded and said, "Okay, but call for sure. Call me, and I'll give you Chloe's number. But just understand, Bern, things are getting really squirrely at *Aplomb*."

"Okay. I'll call, I promise." He looked behind her at the door. "Oh, and when you go, take a left. There's an exit right down the hall. If you go toward the cafeteria, it gets really, you know, busy. Wheelchairs and stuff."

"I see," she said. "You'll call, right?" she said and left the room.

She turned left as he suggested, but when she saw the exit, she turned and headed the opposite way. The entrance to the cafeteria was to the right and a patient was walking slowly about fifteen feet ahead of her. She only caught a glimpse of his face, but thought she recognized him. *No, just someone that looks like him*, she thought. She hoped.

She followed him and stood just inside the cafeteria entrance. He turned to talk to someone and she got a good look at his face. He had a little less hair, a lot more flesh around the cheeks, and a sprinkling of grey in what used to be fiery red hair, but she knew it was him.

A cold shock went through her. "Bernie," she whispered. "Why didn't you tell me he was here?"

She stood at the entrance and watched him sit quietly at a table and look at a menu. He looked up at her briefly. It took a minute, but he looked again and his eyes widened. She smiled and walked slowly over to his table and sat across from him.

"Hello, Anna," he said.

"Hello, Aloysius."

"When I saw Bernard here, I figured you would visit sooner or later."

"He didn't say anything to me. I thought you were still out West."

"I wasn't ever out West. And I've been back for a while. Kind of at sixes and sevens right now, though."

"Hmmm. 'Sixes and sevens.' I forgot that one. What does it mean?"

"Lost," he said. Another patient came over and sat at their table.

"Hey, Al, am I interrupting?"

Anna smiled at the man and said, "No, it's fine. I need to go yell at someone." She looked briefly at Aloysius and walked away. This time, she didn't look carefully around corners, and she didn't carefully open his door to peek in. She pushed it open with a bang. "Why didn't you tell me?"

He stood up. "I, Anna, I..."

"You got here a week ago. 'There's a phone at the nurses' station,' you said. It's *Aloysius*, Bernie, and you knew. You've known for a week, and you could have called me."

"I saw him the second day I was here. Couldn't believe it. Could barely talk to him, and he could barely talk to me. I didn't know you'd be coming up here, Anna."

"You didn't think I would come?"

"Okay, okay, I knew you would, but I thought I had a little time, you being so busy and all. And I didn't know what to do. I didn't know how to tell you. I knew it would..."

Anna grunted, turned and left, and walked to the nurses' station at the end of the hall. "I'm a friend of Mr. Holloway. Can you tell me how he's doing? I know you can't say much, so, you know, just in general." The guy behind the counter was wearing blue scrubs and had a stethoscope around his neck.

"Bernard?" the guy said.

"Yeah, Bernard. I think he's in room one-fourteen. Can you tell me if he's improving?"

"You're asking the right guy. I'm his physical therapist, and I'm glad to tell you he's doing pretty well. I'll tell you what I'm allowed to tell. His stamina has increased, even in the last week, and his BP remains steady at a good level. A lot of recovery depends on attitude, and Mr. Holloway, Bernard, has a very positive attitude about things."

"So, is he out of the woods?"

"Oh, it's too soon to say that. He's better, but he has a ways to go. He still needs to be here."

"So, he still needs rest, peace and quiet, no excitement, no one yelling at him, all that stuff."

"Yes. Exactly."

"Ah, too bad," She thanked him and walked slowly back to Bernie's room. He looked at her, embarrassed, wordless.

She took her time, careful of what she said to him. "I don't think it's a good idea to say what I would like to say to you, but I guess you're able to figure it out. I'm leaving now, Bern, going straight home. I want to go and talk to him, but I can't. Not now. You know I can't." At the door, she pointed at him and said, "You should have told me."

The drive home was miserable, a combination of early rush hour, construction delays, and a light drizzle. Worse though, was the stream of memories, disconnected and disorganized, cataloging and fragmenting the collision between her past and Aloysius.' The news on the radio didn't help, being only the groans and squeals of a world gone mad long ago. Music was almost as bad. The kind she liked were mostly love songs, but what she heard only reminded her that romance is fragile, and dreams burst without warning.

She sat in the parking lot outside her apartment, churning up images of a younger and happier Anna, and a younger and healthier Aloysius. She wondered when the tears would start to flow. Suddenly, in a torrent, they did.

~ * ~

"Did you know adult cats are lactose intolerant?" LaToya asked the group. Anna had brought Mrs. Roosevelt for company and had propped her on her lap for the meeting.

"Hypolactasia," Jasmine said.

"That can't be true. Everyone knows cats love milk," Carla said.

"That sounds like that movie," Miriam said to Jasmine. "The Disney movie with the dancing alligators and hippos wearing skirts. What was the name of that movie?"

"Kittens love milk," LaToya said. "Grown cats don't. I don't know how old Mrs. Roosevelt is, but at a certain age, she will turn up her little button nose if you put a bowl of milk out for her. "

Miriam, still thinking out loud, said, "Was it *Anastasia*? No, that's not it. Southeast Asia? Hmmm, no."

"Hypolactasia is a biological failure where the milk doesn't get digested all the way, and they fart a lot," Jasmine said.

"I think I have a cat like that at home," Carla said.

Robert gave her a funny look. "Sweetheart, we don't have any pets."

"I didn't say it was a pet, dear," Carl said, deadpan.

"I remember it was one of their older movies," Miriam said. "Like maybe from the sixties."

Anna looked closely at her cat. "Mrs. R. is only five, L.T, so I don't think I need to worry about it yet. But to move on, I am looking for some more help. I'm spending most of my nights and weekends reading the stuff that comes in online. And also, I'm trying to find a reasonable attorney."

"'Reasonable attorney' is an oxymoron," Robert said. "And I don't need Jasmine's dictionary to know what 'oxymoron' means."

"If life made sense, or if language did," Jasmine said, 'an oxymoron would be an ox that couldn't get past third grade."

"I need help," Anna said, over the laughter. "I need a clerical assistant."

"*Fantasia!*" Miriam said.

"Oh, great movie," LaToya said. "The part where that wizard..."

Anna interrupted, a little too loudly "Come on folks, help me out here. Does anyone know someone who might be willing to work part time?" No one answered. "Well, think about it, please. I can really use a break."

Mrs. Roosevelt jumped off Anna's lap and stalked slowly under the table, sniffing everyone and everything, but being very careful. Carla took the opportunity to go into the kitchen and get the pot of coffee and a cake.

"Is that what I think it is?" Miriam asked. "Is that a pineapple upside down cake? I thought they were a myth."

"Yes, it is, Miriam. We're celebrating coming together as a team, and the cake represents a theme."

"A theme," Latoya said. "The pineapple is a dead giveaway. Anna is taking us all to Hawaii!"

Anna smiled for the first time that morning.

"I would if I could, L.T, but no."

"Carla thought long and hard about this theme," Robert said.

Carla beamed. "It's an upside-down cake because we are turning the magazine world upside down!" she said. "I can be so corny. My students used to call me Mrs. Groaner."

Robert laughed, LaToya smiled, Jasmine reached down and petted Mrs. Roosevelt. Anna, both out of sorts and a little embarrassed, just said, "Thank you for the enthusiastic sentiment, Carla. And for the cake."

With cake in front of everyone, Anna passed around a couple of articles recently submitted over the internet. "We have Carla's review of *All the King's Men*, by Robert Penn Warren, a book I was not able to get through. We have Miriam's *Rheumatologist*, Robert's piece on his barber, which I think is charming. And we have a long piece that was submitted last week. That one is a little quirky, but I think the humor fits in with our overall approach. So please, finish your cake, give Mrs. Roosevelt a rub behind the ear, and take a look at these pieces. As always, your comments and opinions are valuable and respected."

THE SCHOOLHOUSE
Casual, Collegial and Classy

All the King's Men— Robert Penn Warren
Review
by
Carla Bronner

All the King's Men, by Robert Penn Warren, is a Thanksgiving feast of a book, with meat, veggies, dessert, and enough leftovers to snack on for days. It's often considered a political novel, but it's much more. A romance in spots, a coming of age for a quartet of main characters, and a multi-generational family tragedy wedged in to help tie everything together. There is even a chapter, almost gratuitous, that William Faulkner could have written.

The ending, unexpected, and yet inevitable, is Greek tragedy infused with modern soap opera. Sorry, no spoilers here, but unlike many novels, all characters are given an ending.

So, I am stuffed with a writing style that's rich and deep and difficult to digest. Robert Penn Warren, being from the South, spins a yarn that is complex and multi-layered. Being a poet, he reinforces that yarn with elegant and erudite descriptions of people, places, things, and what his narrator thinks about them all. It is all impressively crafted, but becomes tedious, and for me his erudition bogs down the progress of what becomes a political and personal tragedy.

It is a six-hundred-page classic and Pulitzer winner that could have been a three-hundred-page classic and Pulitzer winner. But that's picking nits, of course. I am generally very stingy with superlatives, but it is easy to recommend this book. If you have some time to devote, a fair amount of time, it is a compelling and satisfying book.

Procrasti
by
George Franklin Robertson

I'll finish the title later, but first I want to get started on the, you know, main event. Just as soon as I get a drink of water and trim my armpits. Should only take a minute.

~ * ~

There, I'm back. Ready to get to work. This is going to be a story, or maybe an essay, or perhaps a full novel about wasting time. Maybe a screenplay, or perhaps just a blog entry. I'll think about that later. But anyway, this is about wasting time, a skill of mine since I was young and forced to do homework. My mom, who resented me because I was born about two weeks late, used to tell me I would be late for my own funeral. I always wondered why that would be a bad thing.

So, procrastination. Dawdling. Vegging. What James Thurber called 'wool gathering.' It's a terrible thing and robs the world of the fruit of human labor. And speaking of fruit, just hang on one minute while I acquire a quince, or maybe commandeer a cumquat. Won't be a minute.

~ * ~

Sorry for the delay. While I was quartering my quince and corralling my kumquat, my neighbor came by to yell at me for not returning his snow blower, and we got into a long conversation about what he can do with a snow blower in April, anyway, and while we were leaning on my car talking I noticed the inspection was about four months overdue, so I went to take care of that and, by the time I got back home, there was a game on, and they went into extra innings, but now I'm all ready to go.

The History of Procrastination

If you think about it, history *is* procrastination. Consider this: the universe arrived after the big bang, about 14 billion years ago. Earth is about 4 billion years old. What do you think was happening during those missing 10 billion years? Procrastination on a massive scale, that's what. Those tiny building blocks of atoms, now known to be leptons, quarks, and bosons, just kind of leaned on astrophysical lampposts for a couple of billion years waiting for the right girl lepton, quark, or boson to float by so they could whistle and ask for her atomic number, or whatever.

And later, when the first organisms had congealed and were about to climb out of the primordial ooze, guess how long that took! No one really knows. But we do know it rained a lot in those days, so the theory is that we could have crawled onto the primordial ooze eons earlier, if the squishy beasts hadn't been afraid of the rain. Precambrian procrastination at its worst. I can just imagine the conversation:

Squishy Organism #1: Well, Beatrice, it looks perfectly lovely up there on land, but I just had the extensions on my tentacles done, and you know how kinky and knotted they get in the rain.

Squishy Organism #2: Oh, mine too, Sylvie. Maybe we should wait a few millennia until it stops. By then, we may have grown penumbrellas, or whatever.

Eventually, they made it to land, and from the land into the trees. Then it took almost forever to come back down out of the trees to start civilization. Imagine your ancestors, probably on your father's side from the looks of his eyebrows, gibbering, and picking nits off each other's backs. Not a care on Gaia about the future of civilization. Irresponsible, I call it. Irresponsible and procrastinatious. And a waste of the fruits of the labor of billions of quarks, bosons, and squishy organisms. Hang on a minute, I have an itch.

~ * ~

Here I am, and sorry about that. I took off my shirt to scratch my shoulder and noticed I've put on a few pounds, so I went to the gym and, on the way back, stopped and met the Mrs. for a quick bite then hit a bucket of balls at the driving range, but I'm back now. I'm back and we're talking about...

The History of Procrastination

When man evolved, finally, and started rocking out from the cradle of civilization, it was the ancient Egyptians who first grabbed the Sphinx by the horns, or whatever. By doing some complicated math, stolen from the Mesopotamians (Mesopotamia; a Hindu word meaning, literally, 'middle size vitamin pill') the Egyptians figured out that the Nile River overflowed its banks every 132 days, or thereabouts. They also figured out, procrastinatiously, that there was no sense doing any kind of farming work until it did, so they just kind of hung around waiting. In time, the Pharaoh got wind of what was going on and made them build the pyramids, but that came later. Meanwhile, at the risk of being repetitious, or even redundant by saying the same thing twice, they were wasting the fruits of labor on a semi-annual basis. (I just realized my semi-annual checkup is a year and a half late. Note to self: make appointment for check-up. Second note to self: buy appointment book so you can write down your notes to self).

After that, things started to move along at a pace, although procrastination was, and still is, our planetary pastime. The Greeks took over from the Egyptians and invented sundials so they could figure out exactly how much time they were wasting. The Romans took over from the Greeks, and every school child knows that Nero fiddled around while Rome was adjourned, or whatever. The Christians took over from the Romans and refused to believe that the sun was the center of the universe. That's because a heliocentric universe (heliocentric; a Latin word meaning, literally 'one hundred helicopters') would have completely screwed up their Julian calendar. The Julian calendar, much beloved by popes, cardinals, and stockbrokers, had a four-hour work day and a couple of three day weekends every month.

Once Henry VIII took over the Reformation the calendar did change, although people were not happy about it. They had much less time for woolgathering, and so they begged the king to please lighten up. This was, of course, not only the fundamental principle behind the Enlightenment, but also the beginning of Daylight Saving Time.

Wow, look at the time. Yawn.

~ * ~

Well, good morning and welcome back. I've been waiting for you. Let's wrap this up before my second cup of coffee wears off.

Let's see. Henry VIII, Enlightenment, Daylight Saving...okay, we're in the home stretch.

Here at home, the Western Hemisphere, we had that Yankee Doodle, can-do attitude about procrastination. Basically, we were out to prove we could do nothing better than anyone else. The American Revolution took seven years to win. Our Constitution has a "preamble," literally, a short stroll before getting down to business. The Battle of New Orleans was fought two weeks after the end of the War of 1812. Why? Because no one bothered to read their email.

Old Fashioned Wooden Computer in Andrew Jackson's command tent: "You've got Mail!!"

Andrew Jackson: "Oh, shut up."

And of course, there is controversy about what the 'D' stands for in 'D-Day.' It's either 'Delay-Day' or 'Dawdle-Day. Personally, I am certain it stands for Dawdle because Dawdle Day sounds so much more like Doris Day when spoken by Elmer Fudd with a mouth full of caramel. But I digress. And procrastinate, or whatever. I'll be right back. There's a rerun of *Cheers* on where Coach says something really funny, but I can't remember what it was.

~ * ~

Sorry, turns out Coach wasn't in that one, but there was a *Star Trek* marathon on, so I boldly went 'where no man has gone before.' But it took me all day.

Procrastination is as American as apple pie. As human as flatulence. As natural as tooth decay. It's nothing to be ashamed of, but rather something to be accepted, embraced, and perhaps even celebrated. There should surely be a National Procrastination Day, where everyone makes a list of things to do and then totally ignores it. Hallmark could sell cards for people to address and never send. It could be held on February 29th — that way anyone who actually wanted to celebrate a holiday this stupid would be able to procrastinate for four years. Or whatever.

A Sage with Scissors
by
Robert Bronner

My barber is a true sage. After every haircut he says something to me that is profound and should be carved into a monument and taught in every school.

I hate getting my hair cut, but he takes the angst out of the process by the unaffected and buoyant approach to his vocation. In a less sensitive, less politically correct age, I could refer to him as that cliché, an Italian barber. He is an immigrant, been here for a few decades, and still speaks with a classic, stereotypical Italian accent.

"Hello dere," he says to every customer that comes into his one room, one man shop. In that less sensitive, less politically correct age, I could compare his speech patterns to Mister Bacciagalupe from Abbott and Costello, or even Stromboli, the villain from *Pinocchio*. The greeting is loud and definite and sincere and reminds me of when I needed a booster seat to get a haircut. It is not an 'Oh good, here comes another eighteen bucks plus tip for twenty minutes work' kind of greeting. It is a 'hail fellow well met, we're all in this together, everything is gonna be fine' kind of greeting.

No appointment is required, thank you very much. Just come in, grab a magazine, and wait your turn. And it doesn't really matter what kind of haircut you want, either. You come out looking the same every time. Well groomed, but the same. He will say, allegedly as a question when you first settle into the chair, "As usual?" but it doesn't matter how you respond. You can ask for a mohawk, or a shaved head, or a Dorothy Hamill wedge, you will get the same haircut. And it will be just what you need.

Once in the chair, he reads you. Emotionally, I mean. If you are in a quiet mood, he will not disturb it. If you are feeling garrulous, he is a champion at charming chinwag. Kids today... the election... crime... taxes... terrorism... his daughter's neighbor who is a slob... and, of course, Italy.

More specifically, Sicily, where he grew up. He is from Italy, yes, but he is an American, and happy to be here. Not an 'Italian-American,' not him. He is an American.

But he knows Italy like I know Queens, and likes to talk about it, both good and bad. There is crime, there are guns, there is poverty, there are crooked politicians. All of which sounds eerily, and warily, familiar in any election year. It isn't really a conversation, more like a guided monologue. I can toss-up a topic, say, double parking, and then return to my *People* magazine while he educates me. An occasional verbal nudge, like, 'Oh yeah, people these days,' is sufficient to keep him going until the haircut is done, and he can exclaim with well-earned pride, "Good for another ten thousand miles."

He can get a little frothy expressing some of these heartfelt opinions, which makes me sit up straight and be very still. Nothing improves your posture more than a frothy man with a sharp instrument near your jugular vein.

I over-tip when I pay him, or it would be an over-tipping if it were just a haircut, and I wait for his final pronouncement, which ties the whole adventure together. It's that profound statement, the 'carved in a monument and should be taught in school' statement.

He says, somehow without sounding corny or sanctimonious, "This is the best country on earth, and we should all be glad we are living here."

He's right, of course. And the only response possible is, "See you next time."

Rheumatologist
by
Miriam Seeger Glasner

I was watching TV the other day, and an ad for an arthritis medicine suggested I discuss my symptoms with my rheumatologist. I was shocked and embarrassed to realize I don't have one. Worse, I have never had one.

I know what you're thinking. "Did you just stumble out of your cave to club a wooly mammoth for breakfast? Do you even belong to this geological epoch, much less this century? You don't have a rheumatologist? Horrors!!"

But wait. Maybe it's not as bad as all that. I have always tried to pull my weight. I have an endocrinologist and a periodontist. I used to have an orthopedist, but I had to give him up when my foot healed. My husband has an allergist, and we are deeply in debt to my kids' orthodontist.

I wonder sometimes if there should be some kind of point system applicable to all of this. I think an allergist plus an orthodontist should equal one rheumatologist, at least a short one. So maybe I'm not so far behind in the 'edist' vs. 'ologist' vs. 'ontist' race. But just to be sure I'm holding up my end, I'm going to go find a rheumatologist of my very own.

If I'm lucky, maybe I can find one who shares an office with another rheumatologist. I think I can get bonus points for having a rheumatologist with a rheum-mate.

Ten

Chloe called on Saturday evening to ask Anna how she made out with Bernie. She was chipper, and a little breathless, having spent the afternoon on a bike path with Mike.

"I wish I could give you better news, Chloe, but we didn't get to talk much about you, or Sebaceous or *Aplomb*. Something unexpected happened that kind of blew everything up."

"Is Mister Holloway all right? Did he have another attack?"

"No, nothing like that. It was me. I blew everything up. Or everything got blown up around me. I don't even know. I don't even remember driving home."

"Well, are you all right?"

"Um, yeah, I guess. Actually, no. Maybe not. All in all, I'd have to say no. I've been thinking a lot about old times. Not a good idea at my age. It can dredge up a lot of, um...." she stopped when she felt a tear roll down her cheek.

"Anna? Anna, are you alone? Is there someone I can call?"

"No, no, I'm fine," she sniffled. "I have Mrs. Roosevelt here for company, so we're fine. Aren't we fine, Mrs. R?"

"Have you had dinner yet?" Chloe asked.

"No, I was just about to scour the fridge and see what I could put together. Can't say I'm really hungry."

"I haven't eaten either, Anna."

Anna took the hint. "Why don't you come over. I guess I can use the company. Mrs. Roosevelt is good to talk to, but her advice on matters of the heart is a little thin."

"Ah, I think I understand. Why don't I pick up something, soup or something, and we can have a 'girls night in?'"

She was at the door an hour later with salad, sandwiches, and a bottle of red wine.

"Thank you, Chloe. I didn't want to ask but thank you for coming. I feel foolish. I'm way too old for this stuff, and I don't want to burden you, but thank you for coming."

Chloe sat on the couch and petted the cat. Anna set the table and poured wine. "What you must think of me, Chloe, falling apart like this."

"Oh, come on, Anna, give yourself a break. I've known you for how many years and have never seen you this upset. Knowing you, it's not a trivial thing. You usually have the ability to swat trivial things out of the air."

Anna smiled. "You are always good for my ego. Maybe we should just eat. I'll have to work my way up to talking, if at all."

Anna didn't realize how hungry she was, and didn't realize how much the wine would help. They sat across from each other at a small kitchen table, Chloe sneaking a peek at Anna every few minutes, and Anna pretending not to notice. After they finished and cleaned up, they sat in the living room, each with a full glass of wine.

"Right," said Anna. "This is the talking part."

"Only if you want, Anna. And only if you think it will help. You know me, I'm not the gossipy type."

Anna just nodded. "It was just such a surprise," she said. "Out of the blue."

"Was it Bernie? I have heard buzz, probably from Donna, that Bernie used to mean something to you."

"No, that's just office blather. I love Bernie because he believed in me. But he was always just a friend. This was something else. Someone else."

"Before my time, probably. I missed all the good stuff."

"It was good stuff for a while, but it turned sour. Quickly."

She took a long drink of her wine and sat back on the couch. "He was an illustrator, and a good one. A broad, rambling, rumbling, Irishman with a smile that could turn your day around, and a sense of humor that just kept coming. Oh, god, listen to me. Like a goofy schoolgirl talking about Elvis."

"What was his name? *Is* his name?"

"Aloysius. Aloysius, oh, never mind his last name.

"Oh," Chloe said, with an odd look on her face. "Aloysius."

Anna looked at her and nodded slowly. "Bernie interviewed him and hired him, I don't even want to tell you how long ago. He liked him in part because he could come up with good, funny captions for what he drew. I always thought it was odd that more illustrators weren't good at that."

"I never realized it, but that's what most of the arguments are about at the interdepartmental meetings."

Anna stared for a while, then said, "We dated for months before, you know, anything serious. We weren't exactly senior citizens, but definitely on the cusp. Oh, god, that's one of his. 'On the cusp.' It sounds so much better with a brogue."

"Oh, he had an Irish brogue. I love them."

"He turned it on and off as he needed it. I loved it too, then. Can't stand it now." Mrs. Roosevelt jumped into her lap, startling them both and giving Anna a moment.

"Life is better with a cat on your lap," Chloe said. "I think maybe Confucius said that."

For a few minutes, Anna just petted Mrs. R. and sipped her wine. Chloe was thinking about the name Aloysius, scratching through memories of conversations with her father and her aunt Charlie. She was uncertain if she should ask more questions, so she looked straight ahead and waited. Finally, Anna went on. "We went slowly, as romances go, I think. Movies, dinner, walks in the park, and the Chorus."

"The Chorus." Chloe whispered.

"Yes, Chloe. The same one. I don't think I should say any more. I don't want to…"

"Anna, please. You need to get it out. I can handle it."

Another long pause, another long cat petting session. Mrs. Roosevelt was having a good night. "Aloysius was musical. One of the few facts he ever shared about his family was they were all musical. 'When I go', he would say, 'It'll be with a shillelagh in me hand and a song in me heart.' The man could really BS. He found a couple of women who liked to sing, a trio, and managed them, just as a sideline, an informal thing. They all had other careers: a nurse, a teacher," she hesitated and took a deep breath. "One had a little girl."

"Oh, god Anna. Aloysius managed The Chorus."

"I'm sorry, Chloe, I don't want to hurt you. You are the last person I should be telling this to."

"No. I think I *am* the right person to tell it to. I just wish…I just wish…" She stopped. They both stopped for a long pause.

Anna went on. "The Chorus. They went to schools and fairs and charity events and did a lot of traditional songs. Irish songs, American folk songs, and anything else that fit."

Chloe, sniffling now, on the verge of tears, said, "Wow, that's different. Kind of cool."

"Oh, it was. I can't sing worth beans, but a couple of times he talked me into being on stage with them and, what do you call it when you're faking?"

"Oh, yeah, lip synching, I think."

"Yeah, I did that. It was great fun. And the three singers were just such nice people. All just beautiful women, Chloe. We had so much fun. I miss them. I still remember some of the lyrics, and I sing in the shower. The neighbors haven't complained yet." Chloe didn't smile at the joke.

"And then something happened."

Anna glanced at her quickly, and then watched Mrs. Roosevelt for a little while and said, "Yes. Something happened." She stood, put

Mrs. Roosevelt on Chloe's lap, and walked into the bedroom. Chloe sat for a few minutes, unsure of what to do. Holding back tears, she said, "Oh, Aunt Charlie," a few times and then carried the cat into the bedroom.

Anna was sitting on the bed, head in hands, crying. "I'm sorry, Chloe, that was rude. You deserve better."

"Anna, really, whatever you need. If you want to just sit here, I'll go back into the living room."

"No, no, just give me a few minutes. I think talking about this is helping, but it's just not easy, you know. There's so much...and it was so...and you're..."

"I'm okay, though. Whatever you need, Anna. Mrs. Roosevelt and I will be inside. You take your time." Anna just nodded.

Chloe sat on the couch and played with the cat until Anna came back, eyes red from crying. She sat on the couch and Chloe put Mrs. R. on her lap.

"I'm sorry," Anna said. "I haven't thought about any of this for a long time. Blocked it out, I guess."

"I'm not sure how to help you, Anna," Chloe said. "You say talking is helping, but it's tearing you up. Why don't we play cards or read something, and maybe get back to it tomorrow? I want to hear it, but I don't like what it's doing to you."

"Yeah, but no. I need to talk it out. And eventually I need to go talk to him."

"Are you sure that's a good idea? It sounds like he hurt you pretty badly."

Anna took another sip of her wine, and then another. "We were good for so long. Humming along, actually. I think we were in love, whatever that means. And then he threw a wrench in the works."

"He cheated on you."

That surprised Anna. "Cheated? No. Even worse. He asked me to marry him."

"Threw a wrench in the works by proposing? Huh?"

"We were having fun, you know, dating, movies and holding hands and boy-girl stuff, and then he got serious. Did the whole scene...a ring, down on one knee, 'make me the happiest man.' All of it."

"And you said no."

"I didn't even think about it. I said yes. The word sprang out of my mouth, and we were doomed."

"You got engaged to Aloysius. That's the wrench, Anna? That's the doom?"

"I wanted to give him a wedding present, something really special. He was not a U.S citizen, but was here on a green card, a temporary resident card, which turned out to be expired, not to mention had been issued in the name of Aloysius McCaffrey who died in Carrickfergus, Northern Ireland, in 1956. I didn't know any of that, so I filled out an application for permanent status, and got a very carefully worded letter from the U.S Immigration Service, or whoever they are. They were a bit curious about how a resident of Northern Ireland was applying for citizenship thirty years after his death. Aloysius turned white when I told him. I thought full citizenship would be a great wedding present, but clearly not. Aloysius, or whoever he really is, was gone the next morning. I never heard another word from him until he said hello yesterday. He never asked for his ring back, he just left me a note full of regret and charming phrases. I read it so many times I have it fully memorized, but I will never show it to another human being."

Chloe moved next to a sobbing Anna on the couch and put her arm around her. She tried several times to say something soothing, something helpful, but there didn't seem to be anything. She stayed over that night, sleeping in the second bedroom where Anna's mother used to be.

In the morning, over grapefruit and cereal, Chloe asked softly, "Was he on the boat when the accident happened?"

Anna thought first about running back into the bedroom but controlled the impulse. After a minute she said, "Yes. He was in the back, the stern, and wasn't seriously hurt. The women, your mother, were all up in the front."

Chloe sat quietly for a few minutes. "I want to meet him, Anna. I want to..." That's all she was able to say.

~ * ~

Since Chloe's meeting with Sebastian, she and Mike had been on their best behavior at *Aplomb*, acting like two cordial-but-distant-

ships passing in the night. Chloe was in early every morning and kept copies of her work in case she needed to defend herself. Mike stayed late every night except when he had class, and they barely acknowledged the other's existence. Mike brought a sandwich or went to a hot dog truck for lunch. Chloe had a salad at her desk. They weathered the sidelong looks from Donna and the pointed stares from Sebastian. At the interdepartmental meeting, Chloe brought a pad and took notes, mostly to avoid eye contact with either of them. There was one disagreement, between Marielle and Ed again, about a caption for a cartoon Marielle had drawn. It showed a man in a gorilla suit with the head of the gorilla under his arm. He is explaining the outfit to his wife. Marielle's caption was "Well, I know we don't need one, honey, but it was twenty-five percent off." Ed wanted it to read, "Look, sweetheart, a job is a job."

Sebastian listened for a minute to the discussion and made up his mind. "Leave Marielle's caption. It's funnier." Ed frowned and grunted but said nothing.

At the end of the meeting, Chloe gave Donna the handwritten notes, more proof she was trustworthy. Donna frowned and said, "Right."

~ * ~

Mike had placed three calls to Jordan Simon, and one email asking about his *Final Four* picks, without response.

On Saturday, they were sitting in Chloe's kitchen having an early lunch and Mike said, "I don't know. I asked around a little, trying not to be obvious, but no one seems to know where he is. Someone told me he's taking long weekends, but really, who takes long weekends in March?"

"You really don't know him very well, do you?" she asked. She was at the sink, energetic, trimming the stems of the flowers Mike had brought. The dishwasher was empty, the counters had been wiped, Mike was working on his second sandwich, and his beer glass was frosted and full. "I hope he's not, you know, on their side," she said, "and waiting for something to happen. I need this job."

"Yeah, me too. And I don't want Sebastian to get away with being a lazy, conniving pissant."

"What exactly is a pissant, anyway?"

"Well, it's either an ant with a weak bladder, or a small-minded, insignificant excuse for a human being, probably also with a weak bladder. It could go either way with Sebastian." She laughed.

He ate the rest of his sandwich slowly, watching her from behind and smiling. *I'm in her kitchen,* he thought, *and she's laughing at my jokes. I never thought she would give me the time of day, and here she is making me lunch.*

"So, you never heard from Mister Holloway?" he asked. "I thought he was supposed to call you."

"I don't think Anna ever gave him my number. She was so upset that night. You know Anna, always in control, but not about this. You should have seen her."

"An old boyfriend, you said. But *old*, old, as in lots of years."

"Yeah, but age doesn't always matter. She still, you know, still... has feelings."

He ate some more sandwich. She had called it a cheese sandwich, which for him meant a couple of slices of swiss between two pieces of bread. She had loaded it up with lettuce, tomato, turkey, mustard and mayo, cut it into thirds, and poured him a beer. *This woman,* he thought. *This woman.*

"Maybe you and I should take a ride up there and talk to Mister Holloway. Why not? He always liked me, I think. I don't think Anna did, but Mister Holloway was always cool."

Still nervous, she was twisting a dishtowel and sat down across from him. "I feel," she began, "like we know each other well enough for me to ask you about this."

"I know where you're going with this," he sighed. "I know. You're embarrassed to ask about it and I'm embarrassed to talk about it."

"Yeah. It's, um, I guess the best word is hygiene."

"Yes," he nodded. "That would be the best word if hygiene were really the problem."

"Oh, come on, Mike. It's me. You can be honest."

He pushed his plate away. "Hyperhidrosis."

"Hyper hid what?"

"It's a skin condition, Chloe. Or kind of a combination skin and hormone deal. I've had it since I was a kid. Actually, I've been waiting for you to ask me about it."

"A condition? So, it's not just…"

"Not just being too lazy or stupid to wash myself? No. It's not that."

"I'm sorry. I didn't mean to insult you."

"It's okay. I'm used to it. It started when I was about fifteen. Now that I think about it, I never got acne. I think I would rather have gotten pimples."

"You've had this since you were a teenager?"

"Yeah, but for a couple of years, I had it under control. There are shots I took for it."

"Oh, kind of like what I'm taking for allergies."

"I guess like that. I got shots for a couple years in high school, and it seemed to take care of it. I didn't sweat much, and didn't, you know, smell."

"But you stopped? Why would you stop?"

"I broke out in hives. All over my arms, chest, legs…everywhere. Really itchy, really ugly. When I stopped the shots, the hives cleared up, but the other problem came back. I was in college by then, so I would try to cover it up by exercising a lot. Basketball, mostly, and running a lot. Anything to break a sweat. It didn't fool anybody for very long. As soon as people got close to me, well, you know, mostly they didn't."

"Oh, Mike. I didn't know. You never told anybody?"

"Kind of a difficult topic to broach, don't you think? 'By the way, I don't really smell bad, I have a condition.' That would go over big."

"Is there anything else you can do? Other treatments? Other, I don't know, really strong deodorants?"

He grinned at her. "I was depressed about it for a while, but I've been inspired lately by a friend at work. I found an endocrinologist, a hormone doctor this time, who thinks he can help me. Different kind of shots than before, maybe only a couple of months of them. He thinks it may do the trick. I'm stoked about it."

"That's great!" She grinned back at him. "I can't imagine what inspired you, or who, but that's great!"

They smiled at each other quietly for a few moments until he broke the silence. "There's also a historical connection to hyperhidrosis that's kind of interesting."

"Historical? How so?"

"They call it 'Descartes' Disease.' He was the most famous person to suffer from it."

"The philosopher guy? Really? Descartes had it?"

"Yes, and it really bothered him, too. He was very embarrassed by it. In fact, he mentioned it in his famous book of philosophy, but it's usually misquoted. What he actually wrote was, "I stink, therefore I am. Everyone gets that wrong."

She opened her mouth and stared at him, and then started laughing. She laughed so hard she almost fell off her chair. Mike was quick enough to catch her, and smart enough not to let her go.

~ * ~

Sunday morning, Mike picked her up and they drove up to visit Bernie. He got lost near the rehab center, but just kept driving, making an occasional random turn and muttering, until he found the right street. The Northeast Rehabilitation and Wellness Center was only a few miles from the Bronx River Parkway and tucked away from the traffic noise of the main streets. It was a new looking brick building, with large windows and automatic doors everywhere. Chloe signed the register, "Chloe and Mike," and liked the looks of it, but wondered briefly if it would be better as 'Mike and Chloe.' A smiling woman at the reception desk gave them visitors' badges and directions to Mr. Holloway, Room one-fourteen.

He had a private room, most of them were private rooms, and Mike knocked softly before going in. Bernard didn't recognize him until Chloe came around from behind him.

Bernie was in pajamas and a robe, sitting in a chair with his feet up, thumbing through a copy of *Travel and Leisure* magazine. "Ah, Chloe! How nice. I was wondering if you were going to show up."

"Hi, Mister Holloway."

"And, um, Mike? Yes, Mike. How are you both? It's nice of you to drive all the way up here to visit an old codger."

"Hello, Mr. Holloway," Mike said. "It's good to see you looking so well."

"They take great care of us up here," he said, "providing your insurance is paid up."

"Anna gave me the name and address here," Chloe said. "I was going to call, but I'm not sure if they allow phone calls. Anyway, it's a beautiful day for a ride, and it's nice country up here, so we took a chance. I'm glad to see you so well, too. Anna told me you were doing okay, but it's hard to credit that when you haven't seen the person in question even though, you know it's Anna that said so, and she's always so honest and straightforward about everything, but even so, I felt like we might be..."

Mike took her hand, and she stopped talking. "Chloe, easy Chloe," he said softly.

Bernard smiled. "I know there is something you want to talk to me about, and I'm sorry I didn't get in touch with you before. What's going on?"

"This guy from Human Relations has been coming around, talking mostly to Sebastian," Mike said.

"Yeah, I heard about that. A guy named Simon, right? I thought Seabass would have cleared that up by now."

"Seabass?" Mike said.

Chloe laughed. "Sometimes Mike calls him a pissant, pardon my language, but Seabass is better."

"Well sure," Bernard said. "'Seabass' is a name. 'Pissant' is just a description, although in his case an accurate one."

Mike laughed. "He did take care of the problem, sort of, by shifting it onto Chloe and me. He told Chloe her job is in jeopardy, and my name was mentioned as well."

Chloe said, "We've been waiting for the axe to fall, or the other shoe to drop, or whatever."

Bernard sat quietly for a few moments, and then tossed his magazine onto the bed. "I'm not sure what I can do for you. I know only a couple of people in HR, mostly because I never bothered them.

I settled my own problems. I know Simon, but only that he's an okay guy. He's no Sir Galahad, but an okay kind of guy."

"Mike knows him too, Mister Holloway. He's called a few times but never gets a call back."

Bernie said sadly. "I'm pretty much out of the pecking order now. I don't know if I'll go back to *Aplomb*, and I don't imagine I'm expected back. I guess I could call Atlee, I'm pretty sure he's still the Grand Poohbah over there, but I don't know what he would do for me. In HR, they don't like interfering if another guy is dealing with it."

There was a knock at the door, and another patient stepped carefully into the room. He was a big man, or at least one who used to be big, but seemed as if he had collapsed in on himself. A broad face grinned under red hair, sprinkled with gray. "Oh, Bernard, I'm sorry, boyo. Didn't realize you had visitors. I'll come back later." He backed out the door, moving slowly, still showing that big smile.

Chloe and Bernard shared a look. She knew who it was, and she was sure Bernard *knew* she knew who it was.

"That was just a neighbor from down the hall, Mike," Bernard said. "Probably wanted to borrow a cup of sugar or something."

"I think we should be going, Mr. Holloway," Chloe said. "You probably have things to do here. Therapy and such. Medicine, maybe."

"Yes," Bernard said. "That's probably right. Tomorrow I'll call Atlee, what's his first name? Oh, Tom, I think. I'll call him and try to sound out the situation. At the very least, I can get him to nudge this Simon guy."

Mike was a little puzzled. He thought Chloe would want to stay for a little while at least. "We're not in a hurry. We can hang out for a little while, Chloe," he said.

"Oh, I think Mr. Holloway needs to get back to his rehab schedule, Mike, and we need to let him." They both shook hands, told Bernard to get well soon, and left.

Halfway down the hall, Mike took her by the elbow and said, "What was that?"

She stopped and pulled him to the side of the corridor. "That was Anna's old, old boyfriend."

Part Two

Eleven

A few weeks before his coronary, Bernie was putting the key in his front door lock and thinking *I'm Home. God's in his heaven and all's right with the world.* Inside, the flowers he had sent were on the table, something in the kitchen smelled wonderful, and his easy chair was just a few steps away. *Ozzie and Harriet?* he thought. *Father Knows Best?*

Reality quickly crashed through his domestic pipedream. His new wife, Paula, came out of the living room, not smiling, not with a plate of cookies or a martini, but with an uncharacteristic frown. "We need to talk, Bern. Something serious has happened to Lyle."

"Lyle? Ex-husband Lyle?" Ozzie, Harriet and his easy chair vaporized and blew away.

"I got a call from the State Department today. They still have me listed as next-of-kin."

"Next of kin? Lyle is dead?"

"They aren't sure."

"It's usually not difficult to be sure about that kind of thing. Have they looked at him really, really closely?"

"Very funny. He's missing, Bern. They think he was kidnapped, maybe for ransom or god knows what, with those crazy people over there."

"He's missing, and they called you? You've been divorced for almost a year, and they still have you as next-of-kin? Oh, boy. Bureaucracy at its finest. Your tax dollars at work."

Paula was an attractive woman in her mid-fifties: trim, energetic, well-dressed, and usually smiling. She had separated from her first husband, Lyle, about six months before she met Bernie and had been working through the legal steps toward divorce. Bernie had only met his predecessor one time and could barely remember him. The man didn't make much of an impression. Bernard's only memory was of someone in a rumpled suit with a feeble handshake. He had been posted somewhere in Eastern Europe, Greece maybe, or Serbia, and Paula rarely talked about him. Oddly, she walked away from conversations the few times his name came up.

She stood at the far end of the room wringing her hands with a panicky look on her face. "I need to help him," she said.

He went over to the bar, poured himself a scotch, and shook his head slowly. She was a beautiful woman, only fifty, and a companion he could talk to, listen to, and laugh with. *Lucky*, he thought. *I'm a lucky man.* But he had never seen her so distraught. "You need to help him? Why? He works for the Unites States government. They can help."

"No, Bernie, please understand. I need to find him. I need to see him."

"Paula, what? I'm sorry if he's in trouble, but why you? And why do you think you can help him if the State Department can't?"

"He has something I need. Some papers he was supposed to mail to me. Please, Bernie. Don't ask questions, please just understand." She began to cry.

Papers, he thought. *What papers could he have, and why would she need them now? It's been almost six months.*

"Paula, you know I love you and would do anything for you, but I don't understand this. What..." He suddenly remembered something from the time when they decided to get married.

"Think back, Bern," she said. "The lawyer's office? I told him I would have the—"

"The divorce papers? Are you talking about the divorce papers from Lyle? You never got them?" He heard his voice rising.

"Please, Bernie, I tried. I called him. I wrote to him, emailed, texted, wrote to the State Department to get in touch with him. I tried everything."

He breathed slowly for a minute, feeling the heat rising to his face, and then poured himself another drink. Two was his limit, but it looked like a long night. With a conscious effort to keep his voice calm, he said. "So, you aren't legally divorced? And then you and I aren't…"

She sat on the couch, hands folded in her lap, and looked down at the ground. She didn't make any sound, but tears rolled down her cheeks.

He walked into the bedroom and changed into jeans and a sweatshirt. "How could you let this happen?" he yelled. She walked into the kitchen just for sake of moving. Tears still trailed down her face.

He came out of the bedroom, red-faced. "Do you realize we've been living together all this time unmarried? Cohabiting! Shacking up like hippies! How could you let that happen?"

Paula had spent the afternoon worrying about this since the phone call, trying to imagine his reaction, which ranged from tender forgiveness to this red-faced disbelief.

"I didn't let it happen," she said. "I did everything I could to fix it. And you're the one who wanted to get married right away. I wanted to wait. And you didn't want to hear a word about Lyle. I could ask you, how could *you* let this happen."

"Oh, no. You're not turning this around on me. I'm not the one who was married to that puffed-up, third-rate gofer."

"He was far from a perfect husband," she said, "but he didn't yell at me. He supported me when I needed it. I hoped you would, too. Oh, well. So much for that."

They both realized a major storm was gathering around them and turned away from each other. He walked back to the living room, and she stayed in the kitchen. The tears had stopped now, replaced by anger, confusion, and fear. He pretended to read a magazine; she re-arranged the glassware in the cabinet, and the silence grew like a shadow. Both of them realized, if not consciously, that anything spoken, whether neutral, loving, or completely irrelevant, would be an explosive opening salvo to the next skirmish.

He paged through another magazine without seeing anything. She decided the dishes in the cabinet needed to be rinsed off and dried.

"Paula," he said, the silence broken, the conflict resumed. She turned and looked at him without speaking. "You know I love you. I know you love me. Let's keep that in perspective."

She breathed deeply. "I feel there is a 'but' coming."

"We both know you are not the most organized person in the world. If the papers are lost we can—"

"Lost? Lost? You think I would lose something so important? Do you really think I'm—" The plate she threw landed two feet in front of him and smashed with the unmistakable sound of a broken marriage. Wide eyed, he glared at her, flung a magazine across the room, put on a jacket and left. When he came home the next evening, late, and smelling like cigars and scotch, she was gone.

She booked a room at the Best Western at Kennedy airport and began calling the State Department in Washington, D.C. She ran into one brick wall after another for two days as she doggedly made her way through voice mail, receptionists, secretaries, assistants to the Office of Whatever, and some functionaries without titles before she got to someone who would comment on Lyle's situation. He was a Mister Rogers, of all things. He knew nothing of the situation, but he had spent a little time in North Macedonia a few years ago and was willing to help.

Mister Rogers promised, in a very kindly voice, to speak to someone at the Embassy and call her back tomorrow with whatever information he had gathered. It took him two more days, but true to his word, he called and surprised her with his initiative. He read from an official notification based on the police report with the date and location of Lyle's disappearance, with the name and phone number of the police in Skopje, and he emailed her a copy of that report. Paula hoped the report would answer a lot of her questions, but it proved to be heavily redacted for security reasons. It was a two-page report, surprisingly in English. The top section referenced the date and location, but the rest was so filled with black marks that his name, the city of Skopje, 'the,' 'and,' 'or,' and three examples of 'however' were readable. Mister Rogers also found her a contact person at the embassy in the capital city of Skopje, and arranged for him, an assistant to the secretary for international outreach, to meet her at the airport in Athens and accompany her to North Macedonia. Paula made the reservations, New York to Paris, Paris to Athens, and nervous to the point of nausea, left two days later.

The flight to Paris was not as bad as she expected. The plane was cramped and stuffy, but she was able to sleep for a good part of the trip. Orly Airport in Paris was a very different story.

The plane landed right on time, but she had only an hour to find the gate for her flight to Athens. She made a wrong turn, ended up on an escalator, and got lost. After scrambling around and trying to read signs with her French cuisine vocabulary, she saw the correct gate on the first floor, overlooking it from the second floor, and missed her flight. She spent the night in a chair in the airport lounge leaning against her pocketbook. In the morning, she found a clerk with English, and managed to get a flight the next evening to Athens but couldn't figure out how phones work in Europe to get in touch with her Embassy contact. But, *mirabile dictu*, as she would learn to say, her contact was standing at the arrivals gate holding a "Mrs. Gervais" sign.

He introduced himself as Hercule, she didn't get his last name, and told her he was a friend of Lyle's. Paula learned, for he was a great talker, that Hercule, pronounced 'hair-kyule' was fifty-eight years old, five-foot-six inches tall, and had a lower back problem that frequently made him stoop. He loved his country he said, and he loved his job. He spoke both French and Greek fluently, and had a functioning knowledge of the Latin-based Romanian still spoken in North Macedonia.

"We'll have to drive from here to Skopje," Hercule told her. "There is a flight, but in a very small aircraft, and I am not a confident flier.

The air is thin in the Carpathian mountains and the pilots are not always careful of flight safety regulations."

"It's a lovely day for a drive," Paula said, gratefully.

His car was a compact Ford Focus, the American name of which gave her a feeling of security which didn't last long. Her luggage would barely fit in the trunk, and she barely fit in the passenger seat. For the next eleven hours, driving the narrow, curving mountain roads through northern Greece and southwestern North Macedonia, she found she could barely cross her legs, until she badly needed to cross her legs.

For much of the long journey, Hercule talked about North Macedonia, sounding like a tour guide with a microphone at the front of a bus. Because of his language skills, much of his job at the embassy had been to escort dignitaries and educate them about his country. It sounded rehearsed to Paula, and she didn't recognize many of the names, but found herself impressed by the beauty of the countryside, and the richness of its history.

"We are neither a rich country nor a celebrated one," he said, "and are recognized mostly for who has conquered us in the past. That list is long and illustrious: Darius of Persia, Phillip of Macedon, Alexander the Great, after him the Romans, Basil the Second, and the Ottoman Turks. We have been a part of Serbia, Yugoslavia and, during wartime, occupied by Bulgaria. We were familiar to both Homer and Hesiod in ancient times. History, wars and dynasties have often swept harshly across our land, and still we remain proud, free and happy." Rehearsed or not, Paula found it stirring.

He also told her a little about himself and about being raised in what was then called Macedonia by his grandparents, who were now approaching ninety years old. He talked briefly about Lyle, and admitted his friendship was partially because he was intimidated by Americans, and partially because he felt sorry for them. Paula, cramped and cranky after a few hours in the car, didn't ask him to clarify what he meant.

When they approached the capital city, Skopje, the gently rising hills turned into mountains overlooking deep valleys. In the little

Focus, Paula found herself leaning forward when the car slowed on a steep hill, and leaning, almost shoulder to shoulder with Hercule, when rounding a curve.

She found Skopje to be an appealing, old European city on a plateau surrounded by scenic mountains. At the first café they came to at the edge of the city, she ran to the ladies' room, *toeleta*, Hercule explained, and let Hercule order a dish of lamb wrapped in grape leaves for her.

She hadn't spoken much to him during the long drive, but now, close to their destination, she was filled with questions.

He held his hand up with a smile and explained. "You have been very patient, but your long journey ends soon. I will take you to the apartment of your husband and we will talk."

"And in the morning, I can find the police station. You can direct me, right?"

"*Politie*? You need police? Madame Gervais, I am *embrouillie*... um, confused."

She thought they were having confusion with the language. "Kidnapped, Hercule. Taken away. My husband was kidnapped, wasn't he? And the police are involved. Isn't the government looking for him? That's what I was told by the State Department."

Hercule's eyes widened and his face blanched. He looked at her, down at his moussaka, and then back at her with a look she could not interpret.

"You were told this by whom?" he asked.

"I got a call from a woman at the State Department in Washington, about five days ago. Her name was...it was, oh, I don't think I asked her name. But she told me he was missing and possibly kidnapped. Because of the trouble over the naming of the country. Weren't they fighting about the name Macedonia?"

"Yes, there was a bitter disagreement, but it was settled a few years ago. Things have been very peaceful here."

It was Paula's turn to look stunned and to stare down at her meal and then back at Hercule.

He said, quietly, "Talbot?"

"What do you...oh, yes...Mrs. Talbot! That was her name! The one who called me."

"Oh, Madame Gervais, I think we are both victims here. Talbot, Anita Talbot, was an embassy clerk who retired and went home to Atlanta about two weeks ago. She was friendly with Lyle, although she was very much older, and I fear he enlisted her to call you with a story."

After their meal, which Paula was uncertain about eating, but found delicious, Hercule drove her to Lyle's apartment and let her in. Through the meal and dessert, he had deflected all of her questions, kept his head down and focused on eating. "I will explain all I know when I deliver you to Monsieur Gervais' apartment." That was his first reference to 'Monsieur Gervais.' Up to then he had been 'Lyle,' or 'Monsieur Lyle.' His demeanor had done a complete reversal. Where he had been talkative during the trip, after she mentioned the police he became reticent, speaking in one-word sentences. Where he had been polite and deferential, he became brusque and unpleasant. She struggled with her own luggage from the car to the elevator and into the apartment. Inside, he silently opened drapes and windows and handed her the key.

"Hercule," she said. "Have I said something or done something to offend you? You seem irritated. You seem suddenly uncomfortable with me."

He pointed to the couch. "Please, Madame Gervais, sit. I have much to tell you."

He sat on the footstool and leaned forward to speak. "We, you and I both, have had a hoke played on us, I believe."

"A joke?" Paula said. "This is not funny."

"No, I do not mean joke. Hoax, I mean hoax. I mean we were made fools of. He used me to bring you here. I am not, uh, uncomfortable with you, Madame Gervais, but only with your husband. I think he has played both of us false. There is much to explain."

"Tell me first, Hercule, where is my...where is he? Where is Lyle?"

"He travels now. He is on an excursion with an American golfer on a *bonne volante*, eh, a good-will mission. They will talk about golf, and show about golf, and work to sell us the game of golf to play here in our country. Also, in Serbia and also in Romania, maybe. Good for business, our embassy thinks, and good for relations. He is with an American golfer professional, Russell is his name. Russell will play, Lyle will escort him and his wife. He has been gone one week only, and I think he did not know you would be here until his excursion was finished."

He leaned forward, eyes focused on her and told the whole story. On the road, talking about the history of his country, Hercule was smiling and animated, and sometimes amused by the folklore of his ancestors. Now, there was little facial expression and no humor.

"Lyle still loves you," he began, "and wants to win you back." He outlined Lyle's scheme, much of which he had been unaware of, but could now reconstruct.

"Does he have my divorce papers?" Paula asked. Her marriage to Bernard was still her main focus.

His eyes widened. "I do not know about this," Hercule answered. "He has not spoken of any papers to me, only to win your affection again."

The key to the hoax, as Hercule related, was Anita Talbot and her return to the States. Lyle had scripted her phone call to Paula telling her it was just an elaborate practical joke he would soon explain to his wife. They would have a good laugh about it later, he told her.

"She must be a very naïve woman to believe something that horrible," Paula said, angrily. "A stupid woman."

"*Oui. Certainment*," Hercule said, a bit embarrassed. For a while, he had believed it to be a joke as well.

The phony, redacted police report was an easy matter to arrange, with just some American folding money slipped into the right hands. The phone number she was given for the Skopje police department was actually the fax number of a cocktail lounge in the neighboring city of Kumanovo.

She leaned back on the couch, watching and listening to him carefully, but with no reaction. She was dumbfounded, but somehow not surprised, understanding after eight years of marriage that Lyle was capable of this degree of selfish duplicity. Hercule dropped his eyes to the floor and quickly told the rest of his story. Over lunch one day, Lyle had told him he had already confessed about the phone call to Paula, and that she was coming to North Macedonia to see him, possibly to reconcile. Until Paula mentioned the police and kidnapping, Hercule thought he was just doing a friend a favor by transporting his wife from the airport with the hope of repairing their marriage. Now he was angry and felt foolish. He burst into a flood of French and another language, most of which was lost on her. '*Stupide,*' fairly obvious, was a frequent choice, and '*stultus,*' which she later learned was a Latin form of 'stupid.' When he calmed down a little, he paced back and forth from the couch to the door and promised her he would help her as much as he was able. He made a quick, courtly half-bow, and left.

Paula felt completely abandoned, but Hercule proved to be as good as his word. He visited once or twice a week and arranged a 'spousal entitlement' allowance from the Embassy, enough to keep her in food and clothing until Lyle returned. He showed her where to shop for groceries, and wrote out a list of food items, common words and phrases. He found her a walking map of the city, and marked some places to visit. He apologized over and over again. "*Stupide,*" he would say, and again, "*Stupide.*"

~ * ~

She didn't sleep the first few nights in Skopje. She was alone in a strange apartment in a foreign city, waiting for either a husband or, she hoped, ex-husband, at whom she was furious. She didn't speak the language, and until the 'spousal entitlement' was approved, she had only the American cash she brought with her. She wasn't sure her credit card would be accepted there, and was afraid to try. *This is eastern Europe,* she thought. *Secret police, political trials, informers, interrogations. Probably better not to chance it.*

Out of boredom, she began going for long walks, and soon was enthralled with Skopje. "It's a small city," she wrote in her diary, "and the downtown area is walkable within an hour or two. The people seem to be always busy, and I think, friendly. They are consistently patient and smile and laugh at this babbling, gesticulating creature, but I can usually get my point across."

One morning, she took a new route and found herself on the edge of the city. A grassy plain opened ahead of her and descended to a wide-open mountain vista. The Carpathian Mountains rose majestically in the distance, but huge and seemed near enough to touch. She dubbed the place 'Maria Park' after the dramatic opening scene in *The Sound of Music*. She went there when she became anxious or depressed, which was often.

On the tenth day of her sojourn in Skopje, Lyle came home. She was at the breakfast table, and suddenly he was there, standing inside the door. He beamed at her, ran over, and tried to kiss her. She pushed him away so hard he almost fell. "What have you done?" she screamed.

"I just wanted to see you," he said.

"See me? *See* me? You had a stranger call and scare me half to death; you manipulated the hell out of me! You lied to your friend and you dragged me across an ocean because you want to see me? What is wrong with you, Lyle?"

"Paula, let me..."

"I'm four thousand miles from home, Lyle. I have no money, no friends here, and I'm afraid to call my husband for help."

"I'm your husband," he said. That stopped her for a moment.

She blinked a few times and walked away from him. "No. You're not. We're divorced."

"I never signed. I still have the papers. I'm still in love with you, Paula. I want you back."

"You told me you signed them. You were supposed to give them to me for *my* lawyer."

"I want to be with you. I want to try again. That's why I did all this. That's why I brought you here."

"That's crazy, Lyle. I'm married to someone else now."

"I don't care about that, and you know you don't love him. You're here now. We're together, far from crazy New York, far from all the stress and fighting and unhappiness. You'll like it here, I know you will. We can be happy again. I knew you would look for me. I knew you would come."

"No," she said, glaring at him. "No, not a chance. I divorced you because you were cheating on me. You were lying, sleeping around, and for years, everyone knew it but me."

"Paula, I never loved anyone but you."

She laughed at him. "So, of all those women you didn't love, how many did you sleep with?"

"Paula, please."

"Please, nothing, Lyle, If you want to show you care about me, give me the papers. Signed. Let me go back to my life and *my husband.*"

"No. No chance. I will not do that. In time, you will realize you belong here with me. Just give me some time."

He had brought a bouquet of flowers for her. She threw it at him. He offered to take her to dinner, she said she would rather go hungry. He pleaded, she closed the bedroom door and ignored him. Eventually, late, he told her he was staying the night, and would sleep on the couch. She pulled a small bottle from her pocketbook and pointed it at him. "Pepper spray, Lyle. American made, top of the line. Guaranteed not to cause permanent eye damage, but you never know. It will be under my pillow with my finger on the sprayer. Don't you come near me, you scheming snake."

In the morning he was gone. He left a long note, with an itinerary, explaining that his assignment was to escort a golf pro and his wife through several cities in North Macedonia, Albania, and perhaps as far east as Bulgaria. He mentioned a few cities, 'just in case I want to visit him.' If his schedule didn't change, he said, they would have plenty of time together. She didn't see him again for three weeks, and she was never given warning of his visits.

She spoke with his supervisor at the embassy, who welcomed her to North Macedonia but declined to interfere in a marital squabble. Hercule, honorable Hercule, visited when he could, always bringing something exotic sounding from a local restaurant, and although a welcome visitor, was not much comfort.

She asked him why this golfer, Russell, needed to be escorted everywhere. Hercule smiled. "He has an elbow problem, Madame Gervais. Someone nearby must be always aware of his elbow problem."

"Elbow problem? You mean with his golf game?"

"Oh, no, pardon me. Not with his golf. I mean he bends his elbow too often. Drinks much, much too much, and causes too much trouble. The Embassy has learned to be careful with American citizens who bend their elbows too much."

With his help, she managed a call to Bernard in New York, but she could only say 'hello' before someone hung up. She tried twice more in the coming weeks, and only got the answering machine. With Hercule's encouragement, she tried her credit card, but it was rejected. She realized that Bernard, angry at her, had probably closed her account and was screening his calls. She didn't have enough cash for a flight back to New York, could not ask Hercule for a loan of that size, nor did she want to leave without the divorce papers. She began putting away small amounts from her entitlement, but knew it would take months to save enough.

Evenings she would look through the window at Skopje in twilight. The lights went out early in this small city and she spent evenings looking at the stars, trying and failing to pick out constellations. Beyond the big dipper, she had no idea. On cloudy nights, the darkness came early. The blackness was total, enveloping, and intimidating for a woman alone. She taught herself to cook some of the more common Greek dishes: souvlaki, moussaka, baklava and Greek coffee for dessert. She was thrilled when Hercule referred to her meals as *Ellinika kouzina,* or Greek cuisine. She spent much of her time at Maria Park, teary-eyed, looking at the mountains. Lyle would show up every few weeks and they would re-hash the same conversation as that first night:

"I want you back," he would start with.

"Give me the papers," she would answer.

"You'll change your mind about me, you'll see."

"Pepper spray, Lyle. A full bottle."

The visits were random and not even connected to the schedule he had given her. They were generally short, always tense and frequently loud. He would be calm, patient, cajoling. She would start off composed and end up shouting and calling him names. He never tried to touch her, or even get near, but his dark aura and unnerving confidence permeated the apartment for days after.

His resolve to reunite was maddeningly consistent until the last time he came, almost four months after she had arrived in Skopje. He was unsettled and distracted, looking at her with a sad, hangdog look. He was a little unsteady on his feet, and she had never seen Lyle drunk.

"I won't wait for you forever, Paula," he said.

That surprised her but gave her a ray of optimism. "Good, Lyle," she said. "I don't want you to." She had figured out that in another two months she would have the money for a return to the U.S. *But still, the papers.*

"I'm not the worst guy in the world," he said. "You could do much worse than me. This guy I'm working with, this...ugly American..." he trailed off and was quiet for a minute and then said, "Paula, please."

"Oh, Lyle, you're not going to complain about work, are you? You lied to me and conned me into looking for you on another continent. And now I should give you sympathy? Oh, please."

"I've done everything I can," he said. "I don't know what else to do."

"Yes, you do. You know exactly what to do. It's simple, Lyle. Sign the papers and let me go home."

He looked at the ceiling and shook his head. She was getting used to that gesture. "You really think I'm a monster, don't you?

She walked away and sat at the small table in the kitchen without answering.

"You don't think I can change," he said.

"It no longer matters to me if you can change, Lyle. I'm out of your life. I am no longer married to you. I just want to go home."

"This is my home now."

"It will never be my home."

"Not everyone feels the way you do," he said. "There are people here who care about me."

"Then go stay with someone else," she said. He slammed the door on the way out.

Two weeks later, Hercule came to the door, smiling and bearing a manila envelope for her.

"He," Hercule now would only call Lyle 'he,' "was at the Embassy yesterday and gave this to me. He said it will make you very happy, and I am certain it will."

She opened the envelope quickly. Inside were the divorce papers, signed and notarized months before, and airline tickets leaving in two days...Athens to London, and London to Kennedy Airport in New York.

"I don't understand," she said. "What happened? What changed his mind."

"It is the old story, Madame Gervais, although I may now call you Madame, um..."

"Holloway," she said with a grin and a giggle.

"The old story, Madame Holloway, '*Cherchez la femme.*' 'Look for the woman.'"

She shook her head, confused.

"He has fallen in love with the wife of his golf associate. His affections are no longer focused on you."

She burst out laughing. "He is sleeping with the golfer's wife? Oh, that is too delicious, but who cares? I can go home, Hercule! I can go home!"

He grinned again. "There is more to tell, Madame. Firstly, I have received authorization to drive you back again to Athens Airport. We can easily make it in time for your flight. And secondly, perhaps even more satisfying for you, I delivered to *him* a message from both you *and* me."

"A message, Hercule?"

"I punched him on the nose. It was magnificent."

Twelve

Three long, anxious days later, Paula Gervais Holloway, nee Schultz, tossed and turned in her sleep and got tangled in the bed sheets. She had checked in at the familiar Best Western Hotel at Kennedy Airport after a torturous flight and had fallen asleep in her room about three in the morning. She unraveled herself, stumbled to the bathroom and managed to interpret the shower controls well enough to avoid being scalded. Dressed and reasonably awake, she went into the main room and groaned at the clock on the dresser.

"It's two? How can it be two o'clock if it's still dark? I cannot have slept around the clock. Can I?" She checked her phone but remembered she had lost the adapter for European outlets, and her phone hadn't worked for two days. She called room service and, embarrassed, asked, "Can you tell me what time it is? And actually what day it is? I had a horrendous trip and I'm a little confused."

As it turned out, she *had* slept for twenty-three hours. She fumbled through her pocketbook for her calendar to check the date but couldn't find it. With a start she realized it was in her hand. She laughed, fell back on the bed and slept for another four hours.

When she awoke this time, she was refreshed, clear headed, and very hungry. After a room service breakfast and several deep breaths, she tried her home number again. A groggy woman answered and told her it was only seven-thirty in the morning, for god's sakes, and I don't want whatever the hell it is you're selling anyway and hung up. Paula double checked the number and called back, but only got a busy signal. She called room service and got another pot of coffee sent up and wondered how she was going to get in touch with Bernie, or who she could call, or where she could go to find out. She had a phone number for Anna, but only got her answering machine with an odd message. "I'm at *The Schoolhouse* with Eleanor Roosevelt. Call me over there, or email me, or stop by, and we can talk about your piece."

What the heck? The Schoolhouse? What Schoolhouse? Eleanor Roosevelt? Piece of what? Could she be doing a quilt for a school?

She walked around the room a few times, and then told her reflection, "Not today. Too many airplanes, too many airports, not enough sleep. I'm going to stretch out on this lovely double bed and watch a trashy movie. I'll think about it tomorrow. Scarlett O'Hara, look to your laurels."

She woke late the next morning, had a leisurely breakfast, relishing the comfort of being in her home country where things worked as she remembered, people understood her, and information flooded in without pause. She flipped on the TV and got the time, the weather in six different metropolitan areas around the country, the news, the basketball scores, and the stock market report. She wondered how she ever got along without all of that, forgetting how glad she had been to get away from it all four months ago.

She called home again and got an answering machine with a voice that sounded like the same rude woman last night. "Sorry, darling," the voice said, "You have found me either out adventuring, or more likely, simply *dishabille*. You know I would love to chat with you, so please, please try me again later."

God, who talks like that? Paula thought. She tried Anna again and got the same message about a schoolhouse and was as baffled by it as she had been yesterday. *I'm beginning to wonder if I slipped into an alternate reality. Maybe at Heathrow Airport. That place was surreal enough.*

"Okay, Big Apple, here I come again," she told the mirror, which despite the fatigue around her eyes, had become her confidant. She found a cab and rode to the midtown office of *Aplomb*.

She expected the cab driver to have an unpronounceable name, to possess an uncertain command of the English language, and to drive too fast. Instead, she looked over the front seat at a handsome, white-haired, smiling Caucasian who was whistling softly. His hack license identified him as Steve Martin.

"You're not that Steve Martin, are you? The 'wild and crazy guy' Steve Martin? I haven't been away that long."

The cabbie looked at his license and then leaned over and wiped a smudge off it. It now read, 'Steve Martini.'

He turned to her with a big grin. "Don't I wish I was," he said. He drove carefully, stayed in his lane, didn't yell at other drivers, and never blew his horn. "I think I had the right idea before," Paula said, mostly to herself. "This is an alternate reality." Steve Martini smiled at her and waved at a guy on roller skates that had just cut him off.

She had been married to Bernard for only a few months when that horrible phony phone call had come from the State Department about Lyle. She had met Anna and a few of the other people at *Aplomb*, and had gone to dinner with Anna once, but much of Bernard's life was *terra incognita* for her. She was not a nervous woman, or easily intimidated, but the hassle of the last few days, actually the last several months, had her very much off balance. She remembered the office was on the fourth floor but checked the building directory and saw it was actually on the fourteenth. There was no receptionist, and the first desk she came to was Chloe's. "Is Mister Holloway in this afternoon?" she asked.

Chloe had seen her once or twice before. She recognized her from the wedding picture on Bernard's desk and didn't know what to say. "No, I don't think he is in today. Let me get Donna. She may know more."

Donna came over, slightly annoyed that Chloe could not handle a visitor, and said pleasantly, "Hello, I'm Donna. May I help you?"

"Yes, I hope so. I'm looking for my husband, Mr. Holloway. Isn't that his office back there?"

Donna paused, open-mouthed and staring, for a full five seconds before she was able to clear her throat and say, "Um, let me get the department manager for you," and trotted into Sebastian's office.

Paula looked to the young and kind-faced Chloe for help. "I just got back to the states," she said, "and things are a little disconcerting, you know? Confusing. Like someone rearranged all your furniture and moved your pots and pans into the bedroom. Everything just seems off."

"Sounds like my standard Monday morning," Chloe joked. Paula tried to smile.

Donna had run into Sebastian's office. "Mrs. Holloway is here."

"What? My aunt is here? She told me she was doing a spa day out on Long Island with a friend."

"No," Donna said. "Not your aunt. The Mrs. Holloway that's not your aunt."

Sebastian looked at her. "The Mrs. Holloway that's *not* my aunt. Donna, were you drinking at lunch?"

Donna waited; her head cocked to one side. It took a minute, but he got it. "Her? She's here?"

"Yes, and she's asking for Bernard."

"Get rid of her. Tell her I'm not here."

"She's not asking for you, Seb. She's asking for Bernard. Does she even know you? And she saw me come in here, so she knows someone is in Mister Holloway's office."

"Right. That was a mistake, letting her know I'm in here. I guess I'll have to see her, tell her something." He moved over to the corner of the office so he could see her through the opening in the blinds. "Oh, no. She's talking to that Chloe. Damn! She's talking to Chloe!"

"You could simply tell her the truth, Seb. You haven't done anything wrong."

He walked slowly back to his desk and sat. "You're right, I haven't. I was appointed to this job. I didn't give her husband a heart attack.

I didn't abandon him for months like she did and then just show up unannounced. Huh. Yeah, show her in. I'll think of something to say."

Donna opened the door and waved to Paula. Sebastian turned his stereo off and scattered a few papers on his desk.

When Paula came in, she looked quizzically at Donna, "Oh, maybe I'm in the wrong place. Didn't this used to be Bernard Holloway's office? I'm his wife."

"That remains to be seen," Sebastian said, with his hands folded on top of the desk. "This used to be Bernard's office, but it's mine now." He leaned back in his swivel chair.

"So, he moved? I don't want to be a bother, but I've been out of the country for a while. Can you tell me where he is now?"

"I can," he said. "But please sit for a few moments. Donna will get you some water, and we'll talk."

"Talk? I don't understand. I just want to see my husband."

"Yes, please just sit. I'll explain. About six or eight weeks ago, Bernard, Uncle Bernard ..."

"Uncle Bernard? He's your uncle? He never mentioned you to me."

"Long story but let me continue. Bernard had a medical episode." He looked at her expectantly.

"A medical episode? What is that? It sounds like some kind of a television show."

He shook his head. "No, you misunderstand. He suffered an untimely health crisis. A medical episode of the cardiac variety."

Paula frowned and took a little time to absorb this. "Can you just be clear, please? Are you saying my husband had a heart attack?"

"Yes," Sebastian said, and breathed deeply. "That's it exactly."

"Oh, god," she said. "When did it happen? Where? Where is he now? Is he all right? I wrote to him. I emailed. I never heard anything back. I thought he was still angry. Oh, god, he had a heart attack. Is he...he didn't...did he...?" Donna came back in with a cup of water and stood quietly near the door.

"No, yes. He's all right, yes. I saw him just a few weeks ago at Presbyterian, and he seemed much better."

"Presbyterian? That's a hospital, right? Is that where he is now?"

"Yes, it's a hospital uptown. And yes, no. He's not there anymore. He was greatly improved, and they moved him to a rehab facility upstate somewhere. I don't know exactly where."

"Rehab? You mean he has a drug problem, too?"

"Oh, no, no. Cardiac rehabilitation," Donna said. "Exercise and health lectures and like that."

"Oh. Good. Where? Where was he taken? Can I call him?"

"I don't..." Donna said.

"I don't exactly know," Sebastian said. "They didn't inform me. We were just told it was upstate somewhere."

"Who would know? Who informed you? I need to find him as soon as possible."

Sebastian thought for a minute. "Probably corporate headquarters would..."

Donna said quickly, "Anna. Anna would know." Sebastian glared at her at the mention of Anna's name.

Paula said, "Anna, yes, Anna Pennington. I've met Anna. Yes. I tried calling her, but it must have been a wrong number. Do you have her number? I'll call her as soon as I get back."

A quick look between Donna and Sebastian. Donna said, "Anna retired several weeks ago, Mrs. Holloway. May I call you Mrs. Holloway?"

"Um, sure. Why *wouldn't* you call me Mrs. Holloway?"

"Anna retired a while ago, and she was thinking about Florida, or maybe Arizona. We aren't sure where she is now."

Donna said, "Why don't you leave us the number where we can reach you, and we'll try to track her down for you." Sebastian looked at her, not angrily this time.

Paula nodded. "You could try some place called The Schoolhouse. That's where her answering machine said she would be. I just hope it's not a bar. Oh god, Bernard, oh god."

Paula gave them the hotel phone number on her keycard and stood to leave. "Thank you. Thank both of you for leveling with me.

Everything has been so off kilter since I got back. I just want to find Bernard. Then it will be okay."

"We will call you as soon as we know something," Sebastian said.

Paula said, "Thank you," again at the door, but then turned around and asked, "What did you mean before when you said, 'Uncle Bernard'?"

"Oh, just a term of endearment, you know? He's so well thought of here, and he's been so generous to me." Paula nodded, smiled and walked out.

As she was walking toward the elevators, Chloe said to her, "Don't turn, Mrs. Holloway. Don't respond to me. But please call Anna this evening. I know she'll be home then." She pointed to a sticky note on her desk with Anna's phone number.

Paula, completely confused, said, "That's the same number...oh, never mind, I'll try tonight."

~ * ~

After a bland dinner in the hotel coffee shop, Paula took out the sticky note and called Anna. She said a brief prayer she wouldn't get the same message, but Anna picked up on the second ring.

"Hello, Anna Pennington? This is Paula Holloway. You and I met—"

"Paula? Really? You're back?"

"I got in yesterday, I think. Maybe it was the day before yesterday. Anna, where is Bernard? Is he okay? Some guy at *Aplomb* told me he had a heart attack."

"Oh, Paula, you have a lot...Bernie is okay. I saw him just a couple of days ago, and he's okay. He had a heart attack, yes, but he is recovering. He's at a facility upstate, Northeast Rehab, for care after a coronary. He's recovering and he's going to be okay, Paula. He is."

Paula was silent, sobbing on her end of the call. Anna heard nothing and thought she had lost the connection. After a minute of silence, she heard sniffling. "Oh, thank you," Paula said. "A straight answer, at last. It has been so weird. I called my apartment and some woman answered, I called you and got some message about a schoolhouse, and Eleanor Roosevelt. Then I went to *Aplomb* and they told me he was in a hospital, but couldn't tell me where. I've been worried sick. Thank you so much."

"Paula, where are you? You're back in New York? You have so much to catch up on."

"I can see that; it's been so weird! And I have so much to tell Bernie. Oh, Anna thank you so much. It has just been *so weird.*"

"Paula, I need to see you. I can't tell you this crazy stuff over the phone. Where are you? Can I meet you? Can you come here?"

"I'm at a hotel at Kennedy, but I don't have a car. Can you come here?"

~ * ~

Forty minutes later, Anna spotted Paula waiting for her at the entrance to the Best Western at JFK airport. The two women didn't know each other well, had only met a few times, but neither felt any embarrassment when Paula ran up and hugged Anna. They sat in the lobby, leaning together and talking rapidly, Paula crying.

"I don't know where to start," Anna said.

"The heart attack. When did it happen? Where? How serious is it? When can I see him? How does he look? Can I call him?" She lowered her head and sobbed.

Anna held her hand and waited until Paula was calm. "The last time I saw him he was smiling and talking about getting out of there. He was sick, Paula, but he is definitely Bernie again. He's going to be okay."

They talked for half an hour, laughing, crying a little, taking turns being stunned at what the other had to say. Paula said, "I'm so glad that girl told me to call you. The 'Mrs. Roosevelt' thing had me hearing the 'dodo-doo-doo-doo' music from *Twilight Zone.*"

"Which girl? Oh, please not Donna."

"A cute little girl, maybe late twenties, brownish, sort of blondish hair, shoulder length. Talked like her nose was all stuffed up."

"Oh, good, that's Chloe. She told you to call me?"

"Yes, and what was weird, sorry to keep using that word, she didn't want anyone to know she was giving me your number. I think she was worried about those other two. I don't know their names."

"Sebastian would be the chubby one with his shirt sticking out, sitting in Bernie's office. The other would be Donna. Frosted hair, vermillion lipstick, kind of wide-hipped?"

"Yes. She was okay, but he was wei... no, creepy."

"Oh, Paula, you have no idea."

~ * ~

They went to Paula's room for some privacy, and she called down for a pot of coffee.

They sat on the two beds, across from each other, sipping coffee.

"Maybe we should have gotten drinks," Anna said. "This may be a long conversation. And, you know, complicated, too."

"I'm a little afraid to drink, Anna. I'm so stressed right now, but I'm so happy to be home. If I start drinking, I don't know if I'll be able to stop."

"Paula, no one, not anyone, understood why you disappeared, and Bernie seemed to be too embarrassed to talk about it. He said the word 'Europe' as if it explained everything, and that's all he would say."

"Yes," Paula said. "I really did a number on him, I know, but I didn't have a choice. I had to go." She told Anna about the phone call from 'the State Department,' the argument she had with Bernie, the trip to North Macedonia, Hercule, her prolonged battle with Lyle, getting the papers she needed, the trip home and finally her visit to *Aplomb*.

"It was really all about divorce papers?"

"That's why Bernie was so freaked out. He was afraid we weren't legally married."

"But you are, right? You got the papers from Lance."

"Yeah, Lyle. He had them all the time, that snake. He had signed them before he went to Europe, months before Bernie and I got married. A real snake."

Anna said. "Oh, Paula, you have really been dragged through it. I never even heard of North Macedonia. Eastern Europe, right? Like 'Iron Curtain.' It sounds ghastly."

"Oh, no. it was lovely. In different circumstances, I would love to go back. For a vacation, I mean. The food, the people. I have to tell you about Maria Park sometime."

"And you never called Bernie? He never knew?"

"Bernie, well, that's a whole other story." Paula stood and walked to the window, opened the drapes and stared at the parking lot.

Anna said, "Paula, it's not for me to tell you what went on here. It's Bernie. I can fill in some of the blanks, but you need to see him. Tomorrow. Tomorrow, we'll drive up there."

"Oh, boy," Paula said. "I really want to see him, but oh, boy."

Anna drank the last of her coffee. "Yep. Me, too."

Thirteen

Anna picked her up the next morning and drove to White Plains. It was a quiet ride. Paula was nervous about seeing Bernie, and Anna was still angry at him, but didn't want to tell Paula why.

"I don't think we should just march in and surprise him," Anna said. "He'll be thrilled to see you, I'm sure, but it's probably not a good idea to startle him. I should have called the nurses' station this morning and let them know we were coming."

"It might be a shock when he sees me," Paula said. "The night I decided to go to Europe and find Lyle, it didn't go well. In fact, we had sort of a conversation with flying dishes."

At the Wellness Center, they signed in, got visitor badges and moved cautiously to Bernard's wing. Anna peeked around each corner and kept checking behind her.

"Anna?" Paula said. "What?"

"There's an old boyfriend here," Anna said. "You just never know when one of them is gonna pop up."

They stopped at the nurses' station and explained the situation, as well as they understood it themselves.

"We're a little concerned about today's visit," Anna told the nurse. "You see, Paula here is Bernard's wife, which he doesn't know for sure, and at their last meeting, months ago, she threw a plate at him."

"And it was a Nieman Marcus, too," Paula interrupted. "I was too angry to pay attention to what I was throwing. I thought it was the Melamine."

"And the last time I visited, Bernie neglected to mention he had seen an old boyfriend of mine that broke my heart thirty years ago, and for a moment, I wanted to kill him. Not the boyfriend, Bernie."

"Maybe we need security," the nurse said, "for Mister Holloway's protection."

Anna smiled and mumbled. "That's actually not a bad idea, all things considered."

The nurse brought one of the therapists with them to room one-fourteen. She pointed at Anna and said, "I'll keep an eye on her, you stay between the patient and his, um, her."

Anna went into the room first. Bernie was taking a nap in a chair, so she nudged him a little bit and stepped back. He sat up and said, "I didn't expect you back, Anna. Certainly not so soon. I hope you'll give me a chance to explain."

"Yes, of course, Bernie, but not today. Not now. There are other bridges to burn first. You have another visitor."

Bernie was smiling, relaxed and expecting to banter for a little while with Anna. "Okay, I'm hoping it's Chloe, but the look on your face tells me it's not. Or if it is, she's only here to smuggle in your sword."

"No, it's not Chloe. Think in terms of flying plates."

The smile dropped off his face quickly and he stood up. "No."

"Yes. Sit, Bernie, and keep calm. She loves you and is worried about you, and this whole thing has been a muddle from the start."

"Oh god, Paula."

"Yes, of course, Paula. But you need to take a deep breath and stay calm." He nodded, and she opened the door. Paula was standing on the other side with tears rolling slowly down her cheeks and a pained look on her face.

"Bernie," she sobbed.

"Paula, I'm sorry. I'm so, so sorry."

She ran in, threw her arms around him and they both started crying.

The nurse looked at Anna and smiled. "We get a lot of that," she said. On her way out the door, she said, "He seems safe enough from you two, but I'll keep an eye on this room. If you need something, more tissues maybe, just wave."

Anna discreetly backed out of the room and wondered where she ought to go. As the door was closing behind her, she heard Bernie say, "I was so stupid, so rash, so—"

~ * ~

Paula kissed him and said, "I had to go, Bern. I had to get those papers. I know how hard it was on you, but I had to go."

"Oh, the divorce papers. Did you get them? Did he sign? Are we, you, know..."?

"Yes. It took all this time, but I got them. And we are, legally. Lyle was not, you know, Lyle was not easy to deal with."

"Lyle was being Lyle. Oh, sorry, please forget I said that. I'm just so glad you're here."

She told the story again, as with Anna last night. The bogus call from the State Department, flying to Greece, Hercule, Skopje, Lyle's treachery, and unexpected change of heart.

Bernie's last comment was, "The little Greek man really punched him in the nose? Good for him. I wish I had been there to see that."

"I wish you had been there for any of it. I missed you so much, Bernie, but I couldn't get in touch with you. The phone number, did you...?"

He stood and walked to the door. "We should walk, honey. I have some stuff to tell you, and, um, walking might be easier."

They walked down one long corridor and back, Bernie moving slowly, before he started talking. "Okay, here it is. I...oh, how do I tell you this?"

"Can it be that bad?"

"The night I walked out, I slept in my chair in the office. And I drank. I drank a lot. The next day, I walked around Manhattan and thought about you. And drank a lot more. When I got home, you were gone. So much for *Ozzie and Harriet.*"

"What?

"Nothing, just a dopey fantasy of mine. My point is you were gone, and I thought, I really thought, my life was in the dumper. "

"Ah, Bernie. What did you do?"

"I did what unattached, very stupid men often do. I went to Vegas and hooked up."

"'Hooked up? You 'hooked up?'" She wasn't sure she knew what that meant.

It took a long time before he could tell her. "I met this woman. All I remember is she was very kind to me. Supportive. She said she wanted to be my good luck charm, and when I sobered up the next morning, we seemed to be..."

"You seemed to be..."

"We seemed to be, um, married." They were standing outside his room on each side of the door, facing each other. Paula looked straight ahead with no expression. Bernie, red faced, didn't know where to look.

They stood like that until the nurse who had accompanied Anna into the room walked toward them with a concerned look.

"Everything all right here? This isn't about more tissues, is it?" she asked.

"We're fine," Bernie said, without looking away from Paula. "We just stubbed a toe on a bit of my stupidity."

Still staring at him, Paula said, "The hell we did stub a toe. We, no *I,* just got crushed by an avalanche."

"Mister Holloway," the nurse said, "your face is red and your hands are trembling. Let's go in so I can check your vitals." She took his arm and led him inside. Paula didn't move. She stood at the door, trying to align herself with a new nightmare. After a few minutes, the nurse left. Paula didn't move until she saw Anna making her way slowly down the hall.

"Anna, I can't stay. I just can't," she said. Anna just nodded to her, and they walked out of the building.

Outside, a misty rain was beginning, just to complete the miserable morning. Anna said, "I'm so sorry, Paula. I didn't know how to tell you."

Paula still focused straight ahead, said, "I guess not everything that happens in Vegas stays in Vegas."

~ * ~

When Bernie said, "I'm so, so sorry," Anna had quietly backed into the hallway and wondered where she could wait for Paula without running into Aloysius. The cafeteria was out, and it didn't seem right to just walk the hallways. She went back to the parking lot and sat in her car listening to a CD for a while, but got bored. There was a garden path around the circumference of the building so she walked slowly down the path looking at the trees and plants and trying to label some of them. Her mother was always good at identifying foliage and always pointed out something new to Anna. As usual, when she thought of her mother, flowers or no flowers, she thought automatically, *Thanks for everything, Mom.* It was still April, so not everything had bloomed, but green buds were beginning to show on the trees, the grass was filling in the muddy spots and becoming more green than yellow.

Around the back of the building, the path widened into a patio overlooking a small meadow. There was one man sitting with his back to her and Anna thought, *"Of course, it would be him. He's gone for decades, and now I can't avoid him."*

She considered turning around and going back to her car but thought that would be churlish and weak.

Deep breath, here we go. She walked around and stood in front of him. He was staring down at the flagstones as if they held an important message, and it took a minute before he looked up.

"Anna," he said with a smile, "I've been hoping..."

She said nothing, just stood and looked at him. In the afternoon daylight, and without a cafeteria table in front of him, he was a very different man. He was much thinner, his broad torso seemed to slip down into his stomach, and the eyes that had always been so lively were pale, watery, and unfocused. His voice, though, was the same. Even without putting on the brogue, he still had a commanding, deep, rumbling bass that gave him gravitas. His illness had not diminished that.

"If I explain, dear Anna, will you listen? I couldn't blame you if you said no. I couldn't blame you if you..." He took a slow, deep breath and stopped talking.

"No, Aloysius, not now. In time, yes, I think, but not now. I'm just glad to see you, believe it or not, and I want to hold on to that. Selfish, maybe, but I just want to hold on to the feeling that I am glad to see you."

"I understand, Anna. I do, indeed. But it's time you're asking for, and I'm afraid time is the one thing I can't promise." He smiled again and those tired eyes showed a brief flash of life.

A nurse's aide came through the double doors onto the patio and called, "Mr. McMahon, I'm glad I found you. It's time for your vitals check, and don't you think it's a little chilly out here for you?"

He slipped into his brogue. "Ah, well, sure enough, I lost track of the time in conversation with this lovely lassie. We were discussing my misspent youth. I'll come right back in, Nurse Deborah, and submit to your gentle ministrations."

Deborah asked, "Did you bring your...where is your walker?"

"Oh, it's double parked somewhere. Bloody thing only slows me down, anyway. I only needed a few minutes of fresh air."

"Mister McMahon," she pronounced it with three syllables, 'Mac-ma-hon,' "you stay here. I'll bring out your walker. Please wait until I bring it back." She trotted back into the building and came out quickly carrying a walker. She helped him up and they started walking back to the building.

He looked sadly, weakly, at Anna, and she said, "Soon. I promise we'll talk soon." He just nodded and moved slowly away. She walked back into the building and was surprised to see Paula standing alone outside Bernie's room. Her blank expression told Anna almost everything she needed to know, and the comment about Las Vegas completed the Bernie and Sherilyn saga for her.

~ * ~

Anna pulled into the first strip mall she saw. Paula sat, mute, still staring ahead. Anna got the biggest, sweetest coffee drink she could find and when she returned, Paula was outside the car in the light rain, leaning against the door, still stone faced.

Anna put the coffee on the roof and took both of Paula's hands. "On the plus side," she said gently, "you're safe at home with friends. He still loves you. He's an idiot, they all are, but he still loves you."

The drive back was somber for both women. Paula was angry, but uncertain as to whom she should be angry at. Sherilyn was a good candidate, but so was Bernard, and she had to admit, some of the fault was her own. She shook her head a few times, breathed noisily a few times, but said nothing.

Anna thought about Aloysius and heard herself saying "At sixes and sevens" out loud and remembering what it meant: complete, almost numbing, confusion. She was still angry at Bernie, but happy Paula was back. Her feelings about Aloysius, now revealed as Mister McMahon, were a Mulligan stew of anger, nostalgia, pity, and curiosity. She understood why he had run all those years ago, but where had he been, and why had he come back? A little guilt was thrown into the mix when she recalled she hadn't talked to Bernie about Chloe's problem.

When Anna pulled into the parking lot of the Best Western, Paula broke the silence. "A drink? On me?"

In the hotel bar, a glass of red for Anna and a Chablis for Paula, they struggled to talk. Paula had no idea what Anna was upset about, and Anna had only a sketchy idea what had been happening to Paula for the past months.

Paula sighed. "It just keeps getting more complicated," she said. "This is like a Marx Brothers movie where nothing makes sense, and I don't know what to do. And that woman! Sherry? Gaaaah! I never met her but I hate her!"

Anna just nodded, her eyes turning red, her eyes downcast. Paula reached across the table and took her hand."

"Jeez, Anna, I'm sorry. I haven't paid any attention to you at all. Obviously, something is wrong. Something is bothering you."

Anna sniffled. "You won't believe it when you look at my wrinkles and grey hair, but it's boyfriend trouble. I ran into an old beau up there the other day, and it's, well, it's...I don't know what the hell it is."

"That romance stuff doesn't go away, does it? I'm fifty-two, and look at the situation I'm in."

"Paula, I don't know the situation you're in. I know it involves Bernie because you were married to him—"

"For about two minutes, a hundred years ago. And now this woman, this Sherry—"

"Sherilyn, I think."

"Oh, Sherilyn. That's actually a nice name. Very pretty. Anyway, she has moved into my life. I don't even have a place to live anymore."

"Oh, yeah, I didn't think of that. Sherilyn is in Bernie's apartment. Your apartment."

Paula shook her head sadly and sipped wine. "Hotels are too expensive for a long term. New York is too expensive for a long term. I called a cousin who lives over near the Delaware Water Gap. I'm hoping I can stay with her until I figure something out."

"It's good to have relatives."

"Well, sometimes. She's a mailwoman." Paula laughed.

Anna hesitated a moment. "Sorry, she's a what?"

"That's how she describes herself. She works for the post office, and she tells people she's a mailwoman. Not a mailman, or a mailperson, a mailwoman. She's eccentric, but she has an extra bedroom, so..."

They both stared at their wine glasses for a minute or two. "She's quick to point out the jokes about 'going postal' are not true and insulting to postal workers. That incident at Disney World between her and Tinkerbell was not her fault, she says. She swears Tinkerbell threw the first punch. And the time she kicked the ostrich was just a case of mistaken identity."

"Oh," Anna said, trying to keep a straight face.

"To be honest, Anna, she scares the hell out of me, but I don't have a choice. The rest of my family is even further away, and if I'm gonna see Bernie and get out of this mess, Lydia is my best option."

Another long minute of staring at their wine glasses. "If you're interested, and not allergic to cats," Anna said, "you can stay with me and Mrs. Roosevelt until you figure something out."

"Mrs. Roosevelt? You mentioned her on your answering machine. But you have a roommate? I really don't want to intrude."

Anna laughed. "Oh, no. No. Mrs. Roosevelt is my cat. I call her that because she gets a little snooty when I get familiar and call her Eleanor."

~ * ~

Paula checked out, groaned and turned pink when she saw the bill, and put her luggage in the trunk of Anna's car.

"This is well above and beyond the call of duty, Anna. And very much appreciated. For what it's worth, Bernie always liked you, always trusted you."

"It's curious with Bernie and me," Anna said. "Sherilyn thinks there is something, you know, romantic between us, but no. Never. We throw jokes at each other, rain or shine, good days or bad, and we laugh. I appreciate that about him, I think he does about me, too."

"He is funny. When he gets on a roll, he breaks me up. That's not why I married him, but probably part of it."

Anna said, "If he hadn't made a career out of editing a humor magazine, he would have grown into a cantankerous old codfish yelling at kids to get off his lawn."

For the last few miles, they drove up Lefferts Boulevard, a wide, busy local street, rather than taking the highway, just because Anna wanted to be in the midst of stores and people and normal life. "I have one stop to make first, Paula. I want to show you *The Schoolhouse*, my pride and joy."

"You're teaching?"

"Ha, no. I think it's more like I'm being taught. Let me show you and I'll explain it all."

They went in the side door, it still being a little chilly to open the front screened-in porch entrance, and Paula looked confused. Anna said, "It used to be a pre-school, but everything else is adult. Bright colored walls and Felix the Cat, little person's toilet, but adult furniture, computers, fax machine. A little of this and a little of that."

"I still don't get it."

"This is my magazine, Paula. We call it *The Schoolhouse*. After Bernie got sick and I was forced into retirement, thank you Sebastian, I started my own magazine. This is where the magic happens. I hired writers, illustrators, and a web designer, and we're putting out a small magazine, more of a humor journal, monthly. I'm in debt, I'm working my senior-citizen butt off, and I love every minute of it."

"This is your magazine? You built a business?"

"Still building it. It's a work in progress, but it's showing signs. It's definitely showing signs."

Paula walked around for a few minutes while Anna sat at a computer and checked *The Schoolhouse* website and submission emails which had been growing week by week. She would have some reading to do, and the team would have some decisions to make.

Before she left, she checked her personal email. As usual, lots of ads for rival magazines, insurance, software programs to make your life easier, garden appliances to make your life easier, nutritional supplements to make your life easier, and one for hand-crafted rugs. One message, flagged in red, stood out. It was from Chloe. She opened it, and the words jumped out at her, upper case, and in large font, "ANNA, HELP!! I'VE BEEN FIRED!! CALL ME!"

She called to Paula. "Paula, we have to go. An emergency at *Aplomb*. It's time to go, anyway. I imagine Mrs. Roosevelt is getting lonesome, too."

When they got back to Anna's, she called Chloe immediately while Paula unpacked her suitcase in the second bedroom. Mrs. Roosevelt, bored, curious and hungry, hopped up on the bed and watched her intently. Paula sat down and rubbed behind her ear by way of introduction.

Chloe was a bit more subdued, having had most of the afternoon to calm down. "I knew something was coming," Chloe said. "Donna wouldn't even look at me, and there was this quiet, funereal feeling all day long. Sebastian waited until the afternoon to do the dirty deed."

"How about Mike? Did they fire him, too?"

"No. I don't think so, but I haven't talked to him. I just ran out. He probably went to class tonight, but nothing happened to him that I could see. He's probably steamed about me getting canned, but what can he do?"

"Ah, Chloe, I'm so sorry. I don't know what to say. This whole situation is swirling around like crazy and getting more and more confused. I spent the afternoon with Paula, and—"

"Paula?"

"Bernie's wife, Mrs. Holloway. She's going to be staying with me for a while."

"With you? Oh, right. The other Mrs. Holloway is in her house. Or somebody's house. Oh, here's another call…it's Mike. Let me get back to you later. Thank you, Anna. Thank you for, you know…"

~ * ~

Robert and Carla were the first to arrive at *The Schoolhouse* for the next Tuesday meeting. It was raining, and the door was locked.

"We can sit in the car until she comes," Carla said. "I'm sure she won't be long."

"Oh, wait, I remember she told me about a key." He reached under the mailbox to where Anna had taped a key. "Gotcha," he said to Carla.

"My hero," Carla said. L.T. came in just as Robert was hanging up Carla's raincoat.

"No Anna yet?" L.T said.

"She's been a little off lately," Carla said. She turned to Robert. "We should have her over to dinner. We'll stuff her with pumpkin cheesecake and Cherry Kijafa. It'll turn her right around."

"The last time we did that your cousin ended up spending the weekend on our couch," Robert said.

"How did I know she couldn't handle her Kijafa?"

Anna came in carrying Mrs. Roosevelt. She stood in the doorway looking at them blankly and then said, "Is everyone here?"

"No, Anna. Not quite. Miriam and Jasmine haven't made it yet."

"Oh, okay," Anna said. "I need a few minutes to print out some stuff anyway." She hung up her coat and turned on one of the computers. Mrs. Roosevelt strolled regally into the kitchen.

Carla made coffee, Robert put out cups, cream, spoons, and napkins. Jasmine and Miriam walked in together, shaking off the rain.

"Traffic is really gnarly out there today. Glad y'all made it," L.T. said with a smile.

Miriam called over to Anna, "Sorry to be a little late, boss. There was a flood on Ascan Avenue and traffic backed up for a block."

"It looked like almost three feet of water," Jasmine said. "One intrepid pioneer with a BMW tried to drive through it. I guess he thought Beamers could float. Turns out they can't."

"Maybe that's something you can draw, Jasmine," LaToya said. "You can title it, 'Just when you thought it was safe to go back to Ascan Avenue.'"

Anna was busy feeding pages into the copy machine. "Sixes and sevens again," she mumbled. She went to the table and passed out the copies of what she wanted them to read that morning. "Two submissions off the website," she said. "And one each from Carla and Robert. I really like Robert's piece because it shows how the quality of life has deteriorated in the last few years and is dragging us all in a downward spiral toward complete chaos."

The room went silent until Mrs. Roosevelt jumped onto Anna's lap.

"Oh! What are you doing, Mrs. ...?" Anna yelled.

"Anna," Jasmine said.

"Anna," Miriam said softly. "Anna, something is wrong. You haven't been yourself for a week now."

Anna sat quietly, avoiding eye contact. "Yes. I know, and I'm sorry. I apologize, and I apologize to you, Mrs. R."

"We're all friends here, Anna," Robert said. "You can tell us, or don't tell us, whatever works for you, but know we are on your side."

She was quiet for another minute, just petting Mrs. Roosevelt.

"Thank you, Robert. Thank you all. I'm okay, really. Nothing dire or life threatening. And I really don't want to talk about it."

The room went silent again, not even a meow, just Felix's tick-tock. Carla and Miriam were both about to speak when Anna said, "Yes. Yes, I do want to talk about it. You are the people I am most comfortable with, so yes, let me dump on you for a minute."

"Dump away," Jasmine said. "Unload, unburden, jettison,"

"Spaceman!" Miriam said. Everyone turned to her.

"Oh, sorry," she giggled. "I was thinking of The Jetsons."

"We have coffee," Carla said. "And L.T. brought some donut holes, and we have time. Go to town, girl."

"Okay," Anna said. "I'm 'Jetsoning' now. It's been a hellacious week. A friend, more than a friend, from my old job, Chloe, got fired by the same third-rate office troll that forced me into retirement. I just saw an old flame I thought I had forgotten about, and he still sets my hair on fire. I can't believe it, but he still does. And he's not well, not well at all.

"I have a house guest as well. And although she is a lovely woman, and we are fast becoming friends, it isn't easy to rearrange your whole routine when there's another person in the mix. She is the least of my problems, though.

"What's really grinding my gears are all these submissions. I'm up until two o'clock every morning combing through these submissions for gold. I'm sending you the good ones, and you guys are helping a lot, but I'm the gate keeper. They all go through me before I parcel them out to you, and I'm seriously overwhelmed. When I started this magazine, people told me I was biting off too much. I blew it off, but I'm finding out they were right. I think I need help."

"Oh, oh, I forgot, Anna. I'm sorry," Robert said. "I found someone I think might work out. He retired a few months before I did, and the way L.T. knows movies? This guy, Gerard, knows books. Reads 'em, quotes 'em, talks about 'em, loves 'em."

"So, Robert, you think he can help? Can he sift through a pile of submissions, and there are some real stinkers, and pick out what's good?"

"I think he's worth a shot. He's a little quirky, but..."

"Well, quirky is pretty much standard here at the wackadoodle *Schoolhouse*, so, when can I meet him?"

"I'll give him your number, and you can set it up."

"Okay, let's get back to it, let's talk about the next issue. Here are the pieces I spoke of, two off the internet, the doorbell piece and the spoof on awards shows, and one each from Carla and Miriam. And, oh, thank you all for your support and patience. I will do my best to pull it back together. As my mom used to tell me when I was sad, 'Just let a smile be your umbrella, and you'll get rain in your mouth.' So, here we go. This is what I have in mind for the next issue. Please read and comment:

THE SCHOOLHOUSE
Casual, Collegial and Classy

The Reason Things Don't Fit
by
Robert Bronner

Here is a list, far from complete, of things in my life that don't fit. Right foot shoes, my wedding ring, most of the screws and bolts I have ever bought and ended up at the bottom of my tool box, a bedroom door (there is a 'right-handed' door and a 'left-handed' door. Who knew?) another bedroom door (bought a 32 incher, needed a 30 incher), my Irish walking hat, the world's most orange sweatshirt. And now sadly, dolefully, I must add another to this cheerless list.

I bought a strike plate for the new bedroom door today. The strike plate, for those lucky enough to be unfamiliar, is a rectangular piece of metal that fits into the door opposite the funny shaped cylinder thingy that sticks out from the edge of the door and goes in and out when you turn the handle. And yes, 'funny shaped cylinder thingy' is a respected technical term coined by a home maintenance think tank in Podunk, Iowa, in their commercial park just west of East Podunk, Iowa.

The funny shaped cylinder thingy will, if the stars are in alignment and a soft breeze is wafting over your non-dominant shoulder, inserts snugly into the door frame in a hole cut into the, yes, the strike plate. Effectively, that keeps the door in place and stable, so the strike plate is a commodity all doors need. It is a universal and integral component of a door, and without a strike plate it is not truly a door, it's a flap.

You would think, wouldn't you, the strike plate into which the cylinder thingy inserts would not need to come in different sizes. Like hamburger buns, and bucket hats, and twist-off wine bottle caps, such a simple thing seems like a 'one-size fits all' kind of situation. But oh, how naive of you. And me. The one I bought was about a half inch longer than the space carved out for it.

That extra half-inch had no purpose whatever, other than to ensure it would not fit into the door jamb. So, it didn't fit and I needed to go back to the hardware store and find one that would. Which I did, and at the store I asked the hardware expert (he had to be an expert because he wore a brightly colored apron and an unmistakable air of superiority, even indifference) about the need for different size strike plates. I noted, with some firmness, how inconvenient it is to find something so simple could be so wrong.

"Well," he opined, "precision is a hallmark of modern building technology. We have a whole aisle of screws and bolts. Lumber comes in dozens of depths and widths, not to mention lengths. Even bricks are baked into a variety of shapes and sizes. We have fourteen different sizes of paint brush, eight sizes of paint rollers, and a paint tray for every taste. An educated consumer would think a screw-driver is just a screw-driver, but oh, not so. In humanity's long ascent, we have moved from caves to huts to ranch houses to palaces to space stations, but not without an enormous sacrifice to convenience. As John Barrow has elucidated... are you familiar with the work of Barrow?"

I had to admit I was not.

"Mr. Barrow has affirmed, in his somewhat circular and opaque style, that the universe is not constructed for the expediency of its inhabitants. We have no reason to anticipate convenience in its structure. On reflection, I think we have no choice but to ascribe to his world view."

I could only nod, nonplussed as I was. But I did notice his nameplate before he turned to go and polish the acoustic tiles, or whatever. The gold nameplate told me all I needed to know:

George
Ontological Hardware Associate

How to Read a Book in the Age of Information
by
Carla Bronner

There was a time when reading a book was a simple four step process: put on your glasses, turn on a light, open the book to where you left off, and begin. But reading in the twenty-first century, like taxes and television, has gotten complicated.

The first thing you have to do is get a computer. That way, whenever you see a French word, or a Latin phrase the author hasn't bothered to translate, you can look it up.

For example, I came across the word 'lagniappe' the other day. I was sure a lagniappe was a breed of South American monkey that's been taught to play canasta, but no. A lagniappe is "a small gift given to a customer by a merchant at the time of purchase." I tried for a day or two to fit 'lagniappe' into conversation. I failed, but I know it's there when I need it.

Most of us are familiar with *Veni, Vidi, Vici*, Caesar's way of saying "I came, I saw, I conquered." But try this one on for size: *Caesar si viveret, ad remum dareris*. It means, 'If Caesar were alive, you would be chained to an oar.' Certainly a handy phrase to memorize, in any language.

The second thing is to make sure you have Google at the ready, so if a person you're not familiar with is mentioned you can look him or her up, see a current picture, a birthday, and see who he or she married/ divorced/ lived with or sued. A reference to Harold Ross (turns out he was the original editor of *The New Yorker Magazine*), led me to a reference about Robert Benchley which led me to a quote by Dorothy Parker. Dorothy, a dog lover, once named her dog Woodrow Wilson, "Because he was so full of shit." Safe to say Dorothy was a Republican. Also safe to say, I now know more about both Woodrow and Dorothy than I knew before. And, as with much in this millennium, more than I want to know.

Third, when reading a book, always make sure to check the Internet Movie Database (IMDb) to see if it had been made into a movie, who starred, and if there was a remake. *A Star Is Born* has been made four times. But all you really need to know about *A Star Is Born* can be summed up in two words: Judy Garland.

The Great Gatsby has been made six times and was a success each time. (Don't give me Leonardo DiCaprio. Robert Redford is the quintessential Jay Gatsby). Apropos of nothing, the author of *The Great Gatsby*, F. Scott Fitzgerald, once observed, "The victor belongs to the spoils." To this day, no one really knows what F. Scott meant, and being dead, he is in no mood to tell us.

I am a reader, dyed in the wool. When I die I want to be buried with lots of books because, well, you never know. But here on this plane of existence, I occasionally flout conventional wisdom by putting the computer away and reverting to the still satisfying tried-and-true four-step process. I'm an old school gal, and it works just fine for me.

Annual SMACC Awards
by
Roger Karapace

Chip: Welcome, folks, welcome! I'm Chip Sunshine coming to you live from the Red Carpet, that's right, I said the Red Carpet, just outside the Crossroads Hotel/Motel and Brushless Car Wash. Alongside me is my charming co-host and runner up in the 2005 'Miss Ain't I a Peach' contest, Rosemary Gitaklu. How are you this morning, Rosie?

Rosie: I'm just rarin' to go, Chip! I've been looking forward to this moment since I got up this morning!

Chip: Well, me too, Rosie, sort of. This is the Third Annual Sign Makers and Content Contributors Award Show. It would have been the Fourth Annual Sign Makers and Content Contributors Award Show, except for last year's hairdresser strike that blocked traffic all across the downtown area and forced the cancellation of this much-ballyhooed event. However, the hairdressers are back, standing proudly next to their dryers, and we are ready to go!

Rosie: As you know, Chip, the Association of Sign Makers and Content Contributors, A-SMACC for short, awards a snazzy little statuette of an open hand to those sign makers and content contributors that it feels have best represented this vibrant field of commerce during the past year.

Chip: Yes, Rosie, like the Oscar represents the best in the movie industry, and the Grammy represents the best in the music industry, being acknowledged by A-SMACC means you are at the top of your craft.

Rosie: Look, Chip! Here comes our first nominee!

Chip: Yes, Rosie, and I would recognize him anywhere. He is Impala de Cervantes, who created the popular "Fines Doubled in Work Zones." His work is up for an award in the Hold onto Your Wallet category.

Rosie: And coming up behind him is a new face to the Sign and Contributor industry, Lincoln Tolstoy, vying for A-SMACC in the Best Supporting sign painter category. Many critics have found his work muddled and difficult to understand, but the general public seems to love it.

Chip: I thought his "No Cellular Phones Beyond This Point" was a work of genius, Rosie. And I think few can argue with that.

Rosie: Yes, notice the use of the complete adjectival referent "cellular" rather than the more pedestrian "cell." I wholeheartedly agree, Chip. A work of genius.

Chip: And here comes last year's winner in the Natural Disaster category, Toyota Hemingway, renown for both his "Bridge Out" and "Emergency Exit Only: Alarm Will Sound if Opened."

Rosie: I read he had a team working for months on that one, Chip.

Chip: And it obviously paid off, Rosie. It's become an instant classic. I think he is a shoo-in for an award this year, and in my opinion, if anyone should be A-SMACC'd, it's Toyota.

Rosie: While we have a few moments between the nominees, Chip, let's tell the folks about some of the categories up for consideration this morning.

Chip: Great idea, Rosie. In the Eye Strain Category, we have 'Alternate Side Parking Tuesday And Thursday 8-11, Fridays 10-6 Except October Through April.'

Rosie: In the Tell You Where to Get Off Category, we have 'Exit,' 'Exit Left,' 'Right Lane Ends,' and 'All Traffic Must Exit.' I think that last one is my personal favorite.

Chip: In the Mindless Obedience to Authority Category, we have 'Yield,' 'Stop,' 'No Littering,' 'No Turns,' 'Line Forms Here,' 'No Stopping,' 'No Standing.'

Rosie: And finally, in the Oh, Thank God, Just in Time Category, we have 'Men,' 'Women,' 'Ladies,' 'Family,' and 'Handicapped.'

Chip: What a great lineup Rosie. It just seems to get better every year.

Rosie: Well, except for last year during the hairdresser strike.

Chip: Yes, you were affected by that, weren't you, Rosie? Didn't I hear something about you having to do your own hair during the strike?

Rosie: I'd rather not talk about it, Chip. Do we have another nominee moving toward us on the Red Carpet?

Chip: Yes, Rosie, it's Ford Maddox Thurber, and he's coming over this way.

Rosie: Well, hello Ford, and thanks for joining us.

Ford: Hello Rosie, and hello, Chip. What a wonderful event!

Rosie: Congratulations to you on the nomination for your newest contemporary hit 'No Texting While Driving.' A brilliant piece of work.

Ford: Thanks, Rosie, but you know it really is a team effort. As the front man, I get a lot of the credit, but it takes a lot of work by a lot of people. The sheet metal guys, the riveters, the post-hole diggers, paint mixers...the list goes on. It really is a group effort.

Rosie: Well, that really is true, Ford. And it takes a big man to admit it.

Ford: Thanks, and by the way, your hair has almost completely grown back.

Rosie: But I really don't want to talk about it. Perhaps we'll see you inside at the award ceremony, Ford. Thanks for stopping and good-bye now.

Chip: Well, Rosie I think that may be all the celebrities we'll get to see this morning. It's almost time for the award ceremony to begin! We should be getting inside. It's time for someone to get A-SMACC!

Rosie: Why, you're right, Chip. Time sure flies. Well, so long everybody, from the Red Carpet outside the Crossroads Hotel/Motel and Brushless Car Wash. It's time to begin the Third Annual Sign Makers and Content Contributors Award Show. We'll see you all next year at the Fourth Annual Sign Makers and Content Contributors Award Show! I hope!

The Doorbell That Cried Wolf
by
Fiona Albright

At the suggestion, insistence really, of a patronizing neighbor who has one, I recently bought and installed a video doorbell. The term 'video doorbell,' clearly an oxymoron, makes as much sense to me as a four-door telephone pole, but in the current age, descriptions of common objects must be carefully parsed, as if I didn't have enough to do.

The suggestion was seconded by a grandchild before I could stop her. Grandchildren are, of course, a profound blessing. They are a reminder of how rich life can be once your own children are grown and gone.

The video doorbell, not unlike a non-video doorbell, is designed to notify me when there is someone at my front door. A halfhearted screech will sound on my cell phone each time something of reasonable size approaches my tranquil estate as a warning of either skullduggery or worse, mail.

This seems like a good idea, but the devil is in the details. It's the concept of 'reasonable size' where the scheme goes off the rails. Mail is delivered once a day; packages, maybe once a month. And yet, I get that halfhearted screech, breeeep, about twenty times a day. I get it when a car, seventy feet from the door, happens to go by. I get it when leaves happen to drift within range and when snowflakes have the temerity to descend into its jurisdiction. I can only be grateful that bees and butterflies are, for now, not an issue.

I have learned to ignore that *breeeep* of impending disruption, and so have missed visits from friends, trick or treaters (not a great loss), Christmas carolers, arrivals of family, notification that I won the lottery, and delivery of those gold ingots I ordered.

On the plus side, the neighbor who originally suggested I get this instrument of torture came to the door the other day and I was able to ignore him completely. That is technology put to good use.

I think I'll invite that grandchild for a visit.

Things That Go Beep In The Night
by
Edward Allan Golding

Inanimate objects have developed insidious methods of getting my attention. I know 'development' is not an attribute historically ascribed to inanimate objects, and that worries me. Lately, it seems, everything beeps at me: phones, computers, my car, smoke alarms, even my oven. They all have crucial, urgent messages that simply have to be attended to, *post haste, pronto, tout de suite.* If I don't listen, I'm in danger of ruining dinner, burning down the house, driving with a door open, losing my document, and missing a call from the attorney of my long-lost uncle who has left me his Olympic Luge bobblehead collection.

They all seem to 'know' what I should know, and that's where it gets creepy. Epistemology, the science of knowledge that goes back to ancient Greece, concerns itself with 'what do we know, and how to we know it?' The 'what' and the 'how' are challenging enough, but one of the things that unnerve modern life is a shift in the concept of 'we.' 'We' used to be limited to Homo sapiens but seems to now be expanded to include Hardware sapiens.

My GPS 'knows' when to make that tricky left turn to get to my cousin's barbecue. My clocks 'know' when to gain an hour in the spring and lose an hour in the fall. The motion sensor in the family room 'knows' when to turn the lights on. The problem is that the GPS doesn't 'know' I hate my cousin and don't want to go to his barbecue where his dog will hump my leg, the burgers will be burned, and his children will confirm the value of family planning.

The clocks don't 'know' that I have put in a lot of overtime lately, and the thought of one hour's less sleep is as welcome as Christmas carols in November.

The motion sensor doesn't 'know' there is a load of laundry to be done, a pile of bills to be paid, and the remnants of a pizza dinner to be cleaned up, all of which I can avoid if the room is still dark.

I suppose we can assume they 'know' some things, but not others. Nor do they seem to understand the meaning of the phrase "Shut! Up! Now!" regardless of how shrill and desperate the tone.

They also do not seem to have any sense of timing, even the clocks. Actually, especially the clocks, which tend to beep, buzz, and vibrate mostly in the wee small hours of the morning. Since I am my family's designated device whacker, it is my job to find whatever it is that needs to communicate and stop it. I have learned to wear moccasins to bed to protect my toes when stumbling around in the dark, and also to keep a ball peen hammer nearby for obvious reasons. The moccasins also come in handy when walking across shards of shattered electronics.

In unguarded moments, I pine for those days when new technology meant a more efficient plow, or moveable type.

Those things knew their place.

Fourteen

Paula was gradually returning to life and sanity after her adventure in Skopje and her misadventure with Lyle. She went to bed early, slept late, cooked for Anna, spoiled Mrs. Roosevelt, and worried about Bernie. At Anna's suggestion, she went to Herman's for coffee and a newspaper, but only one time. He was yelling at his nephew in German, but turned to her quickly with a big, friendly grin. She got her coffee, forgot about the newspaper, and left quickly.

She called Northeast Rehab every afternoon to check on her husband, now known beyond any doubt to be her husband, but she would only speak to the nurses. Only by the second week, when asked if there was a message for Mister Holloway, was she able to say, "Please tell him I love him."

She wanted to hire an attorney and confront Sherilyn but was concerned about how a legal battle would affect Bernie. Most evenings when Anna got home, Paula was busy in the kitchen with tears in her eyes. Over dessert one evening, Paula told Anna more about her time in Skopje, and told her about the discouraging phone calls home, and unanswered emails and letters.

"That doesn't sound like the Bernard Holloway I know. I can't defend him, Paula, but he had that coronary not long after you left."

"I know that now. But I just couldn't understand it. I thought he had abandoned me," she said. "I realize now, if she was living there, it was her."

Bernie spent most days in his recliner, guilt-ridden and morose and determined to get well so he could repair the mess he was in. Sherilyn visited once. He could barely talk to her and was trying to avoid a shouting match. Fortunately, she had been more than liberal with her perfume that morning, and his sneezing fit cut their visit short. He wrote letters to Paula, but couldn't send them. He asked about using a computer to email her, but couldn't find words to explain away his guilt. He spoke to his doctor about his unusual situation, but the doctor would only suggest that the stress of a divorce or a lawsuit would probably be dangerous. "Your wife," the doctor said, "the one with the perfume and the voice, seems like a difficult person."

"You have no idea," Bernard said.

~ * ~

Anna lived in one of the smaller apartments in the complex where she and her mother had settled twenty-five years earlier. The neighbors were quiet, the management was responsive, it was warm in winter and cool in summer. She had seen a generation of people come and go. Children grew up, new ones were born, older neighbors died, and throughout all the changes around her, it still felt like home. She had a new couch, a good reading lamp, and a ten-year-old television she never watched. Mrs. Roosevelt had two cat beds and a food dish that was always full.

Anna and Paula finished dinner and waited for Mike and Chloe to come for a drink. Paula was putting the dishes in the dishwasher and trying not to think of the one she had thrown at Bernie.

"This is the last time I will say this, Anna, I promise. You are a saint for letting me stay here."

"I've lived alone since my mother died, Paula. It's taken some getting used to, but I honestly and truly enjoy your company. And your cooking." Paula's family had owned a restaurant in New Jersey before they retired to Arizona. She had been a sous chef and *maitre'd hotel* at a beach resort not far from Atlantic City. That was where she had met Bernie.

When Mike and Chloe arrived, Anna made the introductions. "This strapping lad is Mike, and the lady, I think you know, is Chloe."

Chloe and Paula shook hands. "We didn't actually meet, but Chloe sort of pointed me in the right direction."

"Chloe, will you help me in the kitchen for just a minute?" Anna asked.

She handed Chloe a tray of cups and saucers and said, "I want you to think about something. Don't answer me tonight, just give it some thought and call or write me in a day or two, okay? I want you to come to work for me at *The Schoolhouse.* I can only pay you for part time, and I'm not sure how much I can pay you, but we can work that out. Anyway, I don't think what I pay will reduce your unemployment, so that's good. This isn't charity, or friendship. I really do need your help going through submissions. Please say yes, but don't answer now, just think about it."

"You really are Bernard's wife?" Mike asked when they were all settled in the living room, and Mrs. Roosevelt was walking between their legs.

Paula sighed. "There was some question about that for several months, Mike, but yes, I am."

"Does Sebastian know about you?" Chloe asked. "Or his aunt?"

"Not yet," Anna said. "Paula and I are going to 'rock, paper, scissors' to see who gets to tell them."

"Or maybe I can do Sherilyn," Paula said, "and you can do Sebastian."

"Okay," Anna said with a wide smile, "but I want them to be together when it happens. I want to see both jaws dropping at the same time."

Mike said, "Look, Anna, Mrs. Holloway, I'm sure there's some crazy backstory to all of this, but Chloe asked me here to see if you could help us. You know they already fired her and things are not looking so good for me, either. I caught up to the H.R. guy, Simon, and he's not the pal I thought he was."

"How do you mean, 'not a pal?'" Anna asked.

"When he first got complaints from distributors and suppliers, Jordan asked me if I would give him a heads up about Sebastian, and I did. Not like any of it was secret. All I did was repeat what was screamed at me and listen to what people were whispering about."

"Mike's desk is near the coffee station," Chloe said.

"I really thought someone would do something, or at least say something to Sebastian. I'm getting calls from all over that shipments are late, suppliers aren't getting paid on time, the magazine is getting thinner, and mostly, that it's just not funny. What's that saying about fish stinking from the head down? I'm starting to worry *Aplomb* is smelling a little fishy."

"So, you told Jordan Simon about all this, and what did he say?" Anna asked.

"He got very indirect, you know? Slippery. Like a congressman asked about a shady campaign contribution. He asked me if Sebastian was Bernard Holloway's nephew." He looked over at Paula, but she had no reaction.

"Ah," said Anna. "The boys' club."

"I said I think he is, because what do I know? So he tells me, with a smile, Mister Holloway fronted twenty-five percent of the start-up money for *Aplomb*. Therefore, Sebastian is the nephew of one of the primary investors in the magazine."

"I get it," Anna said. "That makes Sebaceous pretty much bulletproof."

Paula said softly. "So now, Bernie's reputation is protecting this phony nephew. 'Hoist by his own petard.'"

They all looked at her. "I heard that somewhere," she said. "I think it means Bernie screwed himself."

Anna said, "The part I don't understand is, why you, Mike? Why were you even asked if that would be the response? Is the Simon guy a friend? Why were you sent over with us, anyway? I remember you were at Corporate for a few weeks when you were hired, but there was some kerfuffle about where you would be working. I know you're a one-man department, but I was never sure why you were moved to us from Corporate?"

"They had their reasons," Mike said.

Anna blinked. "'Reasons.' That's a little vague, no?"

"Anna, he has a condition," Chloe said, a little too loudly.

"Oh," Anna said after a moment. "That."

"And I'm working on it," Mike said.

"He is," Chloe said.

Paula looked from one to the other, confused.

"Oh," Anna said again. "I was afraid maybe you were, you know…"

"Afraid he was what?" Chloe said. "He's fine, he just has a condition."

"You were afraid I was what, Anna? What?"

"Okay," she said, reluctantly. "Spying. I thought you might be spying for Corporate, and I didn't trust you."

"Oh, wow, Anna. You didn't trust me? From day one?"

"Not 'didn't trust,' Mike, just, you know, I needed to watch you."

"Damn. Damn, damn, damn."

Chloe looked at Anna. "Anna, that's just not fair, Mike has—"

Mike said, "Let me get it out all in one shot. I was friendly with Jordan Simon, but no one asked me to spy. They moved me over to your office because of my condition."

"It's called hyperhidrosis," Chloe said. "And it's a natural thing that just means he sweats too much."

"Sweats?" Paula said.

"Yeah," Mike said, "sweat. And then, you know, I smell like I've been sweating. Like I haven't washed. And I do wash. I wash so much I should have wrinkles. So, they moved me over, but I have not spied for anyone. Well, okay, for Simon, but that was really doing my job because I've been getting complaints Sebastian isn't doing his."

"Mike, I'm sorry," Anna said. "I didn't—"

"And Chloe didn't know anything about it. Nothing. She did not deserve to get fired." Mike was raising his voice and pointing at Chloe. "She does not deserve this," he yelled.

They all sat quietly for a minute, just looking around at each other, startled. Paula started to go back to the kitchen but decided not to. Anna coughed. Mrs. Roosevelt disappeared into the bedroom.

Chloe smiled. "Mike, I know you're being supportive of me, but we're among friends here. Please."

Mike frowned and drew a deep breath. "I'm sorry, everyone. I'm sorry I lost it. I just, well, I'm just totally fed up with all this stuff. Donna being suspicious, Jordan being a suck up, Sebastian being a pissant. Just fed up."

There was another long, uncomfortable silence that even the stately return of Mrs. Roosevelt couldn't distract. Finally, Anna said, "Mike, I'm sorry. I didn't understand. I should have, damn, I should have trusted you more."

Paula said, "I never heard of this hyper whatever thing. Is there something you can take for it?"

Mike smiled at Chloe, and she smiled back. "Yes," she said. "There is a treatment. Some kind of shots."

"I started already. An endocrinologist over in Floral Park. A Doctor Burns and his wife have a joint practice."

"I was thinking of writing something up in your magazine, Anna," Chloe said. "There's a little funny thing about the bathrooms in the office."

"Bathrooms aren't usually my kind of humor, Chloe," Anna said.

"Maybe not funny as much as cute, but probably not many people will get it. The practice is Doctor and Mrs. George Burns, and the bathrooms are labeled, 'George' and 'Gracie.'"

Paula looked confused, but Anna got it.

"Oh, that's great, Burns and Allen. The old radio show. Classic, just classic, but I have to agree with Chloe. Not many people will get it."

~ * ~

After a quiet weekend, Anna was at *The Schoolhouse* going through some submissions when someone knocked softly on the side door and stepped in. He was tall, well-dressed, and smiling.

He said quickly, "I'm a friend of Robert Bronner. I hope I'm not disturbing you, Miss Pennington. I don't have an appointment, but I was out doing errands, and I took a chance you would be here."

It took a minute, but Anna said, "Oh, you must be Gerard."

"Yes, I am. Robert called and told me you are looking for someone to help with a flood of articles and stories coming in for your magazine."

"Yes, but in fact, I may already have found someone, Gerard."

"Oh, well that works out, actually. Robert wasn't aware, but I'll be moving soon. I am heeding the words of Horace Greenleaf Whittier who famously said, 'Go rest, young man. Go rest.' I plan to put my feet up, sip sugary drinks, and let the rest of the world go cry.'"

"Oh, 'let the rest of the world go cry,' I see. Where are you moving to?"

"I have family in Nevada."

"Nevada. I've heard it's very hot in Nevada. Like Arizona."

"Yes, but you know the old cliché, 'It's a dry heat.' And like Franklin Deficit Roosevelt once said, 'If you can't stand the heat, quit bitching.' Pardon my language, that was Mister Roosevelt, not me."

"Ah, I see." Right on cue, Mrs. Roosevelt sauntered in from the kitchen.

"I won't take up your time, Miss Pennington, but Robert told me you started a magazine here, and I wanted to see for myself. An ambitious project, I think."

"A man's reach should exceed his, grasp..." Anna said.

"...or what the hell is it for?" Gerard finished.

"Yes," Anna said. "Exactly. 'What the hell is it for?'"

"Well, I'll leave you to it then. I'll get back to my errands."

"Gerard, when you were working with Robert, what was your job?"

"I was in payroll. I'm really very good with numbers."

~ * ~

"I just do not understand what is going on with that man," Sherilyn said.

"What happened now, Aunt Sher?"

"I went to see him, right? Dutiful wife visits her husband when he's sick. It's a two-hour drive to 'Hell and Gone Rehab' but, fine. I do it out of concern and affection. Really, how could I not?"

They were in Bernard's apartment, formerly Bernard and Paula's apartment. Sebastian was sitting on the floor thumbing slowly through the collection of CDs under the stereo cabinet. Sherilyn was focused on her computer game, unscrambling words, and focused on earning digital smiley faces.

"You're very good to him, Aunt Sher," Sebastian said without looking up.

"Well, he barely paid any attention to me. And within two minutes, he was sneezing so much it brought a whole platoon of nurses in. And they asked me to leave, like *I* was the problem. Not only do I have to worry about his heart, but what in the world is going on with his nose? He's sneezing all the time. Is his heart connected to his nose? That can't be, can it? I don't get it."

"Sneezing, huh?" Sebastian said. "I wonder what that's all about."

"Well, give me some good news, hon. Is everything okay at work? Did you talk to that Human Resource fellow?"

"Yes, we had a long talk. A couple of them actually. Uncle Bernard's name still carries some weight, and we got it all straightened out. And I fired the girl that was making all the phone calls, all the accusations."

"You fired her? No, you didn't. Tell me you didn't fire anyone."

Sebastian stopped looking through the CDs. He took a few minutes to put them all back in the cabinet. "I'm gonna borrow this Bach concerto for cello. It's Yo-Yo Ma."

"It's what? What are you talking about, Yo-Yo? And, in case you forgot, I am your Aunt Sherilyn. Your mom is still in Seattle."

"It's the musician's name, Aunt Sher. Yo-Yo Ma. He's Chinese, I think. Or Japanese or something."

"Wait, wait, what were we...oh, yeah, you said you fired someone. You fired someone, Sebastian?"

She was only half-focused on the conversation. The letters in her computer game were L I C A M E, and she was struggling to make a word of them.

"She was the one stirring up everything, Aunt Sher. And you told me I should do it."

"I told you to fire her? I never did."

M I C A L E? Nope, no smiley face.

"Don't you remember when you signed in to that rehab place to visit Bernard? You saw the sign-in the list of who had been visiting him?"

She stared at her computer for a minute. "Oh yeah. That one who's friends with Anna. Chloe, right? And Mark?"

C A M E L, she thought. *No, not enough letters.*

"Mike, her boyfriend. I can't do anything with him because he's not technically in my department. He still works for Corporate, and they seem to like him. But you told me the girl was dangerous, and I quote, 'Something has to be done about her.' So, I did."

"Oh," she said, and then figured out the word: MALICE. "Got it." Smiley faces all around.

Fifteen

Paula finally was able to write a note to Bernie. She was not the type to send a get-well card. She preferred sending a handwritten note, but her monogrammed stationery was in a drawer in her apartment, if it hadn't been thrown away. She wrote instead on plain, white printer paper. After four crumpled attempts landed in the wastebasket, she found the words she was comfortable with:

"Bernard,

Please, please, don't give up on us. I have not given up on you."

Your wife,

Paula"

She thought for a moment of capitalizing 'wife,' or writing it in red, or at least underlining it, but resisted. He would figure it out. She addressed the envelope, sealed it, and propped it up on the dresser.

At the end of the week, Anna made plans to drive to Northeast Rehab to visit Bernie and probably look in on Aloysius. Having seen his condition, she didn't want to wait too long. At seventy-four, the deaths of friends were still wrenching, but no longer surprising. She was confident Bernie was on the mend, but this was Aloysius. She had forced him into the shadows for so long, pushing him out of her mind, ignoring his ghost, dodging memories that could only turn sour, that his loss now, she knew, would hit her very hard.

Paula thought about going with her but was afraid she would either crumble into tears or angry recriminations. She reminded herself that he was recovering from two heart attacks and marital acrimony would not be helpful. Instead, she asked Anna to deliver the note and told her, "I don't know what else to say."

The other times Anna had visited, she was nervous about seeing either Sherilyn or Sebastian, but not this time. As long as she could keep the confrontation away from Bernie, she would be happy to go toe-to-toe with either of them. Or both.

Bernie was at a physical therapy session when she arrived, so she sat in his recliner and tried to plan what she would say to Aloysius. She gave up quickly. It had been thirty years since he left. What words could make a difference?

Bernie came in looking like Bernie of the old days. He was dressed in jeans and sneakers, had color in his face, a little bounce in his step, and gave her a big smile.

"Anna," he said. "Still friends?"

She smiled and was silent.

"I'm sorry I haven't been able to help with your friend's situation. Chloe?"

"He fired her. Your nephew. Your nephew, who isn't really your nephew, fired her."

"Seabass fired her? On what grounds?"

"That's a multiple-choice question, Bernard. Because he thought she was the one complaining to HR about him? Or, because she wouldn't go out with him? Or, because she had the gall to come here and visit you? Or, because she was seen actually speaking to your lawful wife when Paula came to *Aplomb* looking for you? Why he would fire her is a real poser, but I would say all of the above."

A nurse came in to check his pulse and blood pressure. She said hello to Bernie, and nodded at Anna, but got the hint when neither responded, and left quickly.

They sat quietly for a minute or two, Anna looking in one direction and Bernie in another. She was about to leave when he broke the silence. "I haven't heard from Paula. I hope you have," he said.

"She's staying with me."

That surprised him. "Oh, of course. That's me being stupid again. I didn't even think of where she would be living. She couldn't go back to the apartment, could she?"

"It might have been a little awkward with another wife on the premises." Another long silence. "I like her a lot. She's a really good cook and a really good listener, Bernard. I guess you remember that much."

"Yes."

"We talk at dinner. I tell her about Aloysius, she tells me about you. She tries not to, but she tells me a little about the time she spent in Skopje, and how abandoned she felt."

"Skopje?" he said. "That name sounds like someone is hacking up a hairball."

"Yeah, not funny Bernard. The important word there was not 'Skopje,' it was 'abandoned.'"

He sat on the edge of the bed and looked down at the floor for another awkward few minutes. "Are you going to see Aloysius?"

She waited until he looked at her again. "Changing the subject? That won't help either." She handed him the envelope and walked to the door. "Read the note, Bernard."

~ * ~

She went back to the main desk and got directions to Aloysius' room. She asked for Mister McMahon, being sure to pronounce all the syllables. His door was open. He sat in a recliner looking out the window. He saw her and smiled.

"So, Mister McMahon, is there a new first name that goes along with it, or is it still Aloysius?"

"Yes. Aloysius then, Aloysius now, and a name I'm proud to bear. Thank you for coming back, Anna. I wasn't sure you would."

She sat on the bed and took his hand, surprised at how cold it was. "I said we would talk, and I meant it. Please, tell me about you. I want to know what's going on with you now."

"Oh, it's the same old thing, you know. 'A tale told by an idiot, full of sound and fury, signifying nothing.'" The pale, shrunken body belied the man she remembered, but the voice certified him as her long-lost Aloysius. It was resonant, theatrical, and memorable.

"Hamlet, right? No wait, Macbeth."

"Macbeth, and who better?"

"Who better for what, Aloysius? To think of himself as an idiot? To feel sorry for himself? Boo-hoo. His castle is surrounded and the hag sisters disappeared. Might as well just sit and look out the window until the hearse comes."

"Anna, you don't know."

"You're right, I don't. And you haven't told me anything. I ask you one question in thirty years, and I get Shakespeare."

"Anna—"

"It's a simple question from an old friend. What's going on with you? And please, no blarney."

He stared out the window for a while. An airplane went by, they heard people passing in the hall, the overhead lights hummed softly. He sighed, she waited.

"Well, it's my heart, dear Anna. Unlike the Grinch, it has not grown three sizes, but parts of it have narrowed to a point where the only solution is to go under the knife. And what these smiling blatherskites are recommending scares the bloody, flaming hell out of me."

"Open heart."

"I've been fluent in the English language my whole life, and I know for a certainty those two words do not belong together. Hearts remain closed, dear Anna, in the space created for them by the Almighty himself. Hearts are only open in bad poetry."

She remembered another of his words. "That's codswallop, and you know it. You haven't been living in a cave, Aloysius. You know they do this surgery all the time, and people recover. You can have this surgery and live for years. You can go back to your life, wherever it is, and live."

He grunted. "I'll be the Tin Man, with a heart from the Wizard."

"No. You'll still be Aloysius, a smiling blatherskite in your own right, but you'll have a functioning heart. You'll have to take medicine and eat right and take care of yourself, but you'll live. It's not Oz, it's real life."

"Truth be told, Anna, I'm just scared. I've seen films, I've read up on this. Do you know what they do?"

"I do, Aloysius. And I know it's terrifying."

"They crack a man open like a walnut, is what they do. And they keep his blood flowing by some fiendish machine from hell while they do what plumbers usually do to pipes, but to a heart. *My* heart." He shook his head and sighed, and Anna thought for a moment he might cry. "This is not the world I was born into. It's no longer my world, Anna, where a thing like that can be done. For good or ill, this is no longer my world."

He wouldn't say more about the surgery, but asked her to visit again soon, and smiled when she said yes. For a moment, his tired eyes brightened.

She held his hand without speaking for a few more minutes, and then left. "I'll be back, and we'll talk again," she said at the door.

She walked back to Bernie's room, lost in thought, on automatic pilot. As soon as she was inside the door, he said, "I know what you must think of me, Anna, and..." He stopped when he saw the tears on her face.

She sat on the bed, not looking at him, not speaking.

"Anna," he said. Silence. Not even crying.

"Anna, what can I do? How can I make this right?" Still not a word.

"Anna, please."

Finally, she stirred. She breathed deeply and looked at him.

"You have to get better, Bernie. You have to do your exercises and take your medicine and eat right and you have to get out of here. You have to fix this mess you got into."

"I—"

"And don't you bail on me! You can't give up. People are giving up, but you can't give up, Bernie. You may not think so right now, but you are important to a lot of people."

"Anna, I..."

She stood up and went to the door. "You. Can't. Give. Up." She stopped, opened the door a few inches and then looked over her shoulder at him. "You have someone who loves you, and not everyone has that. Get healthy and fix it, Bernie." She turned and left.

~ * ~

She was back the next morning to visit Aloysius, careful not to bring up his surgery. They sat on the patio, he in a wheelchair, she on a bench, enjoying bright sunshine and a cooling breeze. There were other patients and visitors and a few children, presumably grandchildren, the older ones staring at their phones and the younger ones running across the meadow.

She tried to start a conversation with him; the weather, a few people left they both knew, her new magazine, but he did not respond. He looked at her when she spoke but looked away when she stopped.

He reached and took her hand. "I'm usually a bit spunkier in the morning, so this is the right time for that conversation I owe you."

"At this stage of the game, boyo, do you think either of us owes anything to anybody?"

"Yes, I do. Like the drunk says, 'beyond a dadow of a shout.' And truth be told, dear Anna, I need to tell it more than you need to hear it. So, once again, I am begging your indulgence."

She sighed and nodded, and he began. He looked out at the meadow, at the children playing, and occasionally over at her. She watched him carefully for signs of fatigue or over-excitement, but he maintained a casual, even tone. He slipped into the Irish brogue once or twice, but mostly it sounded like a confession.

"Born and raised in Donegal," he began. "I always thought it a musical name, and maybe it inspired me to become a musician. In my salad days, I played the pubs and clubs around Belfast. Heady days, dear Anna. I was a fair hand with a fiddle, and didn't embarrass myself with a flute, either. Never lacked for a bob or two to buy a pint. Heady days."

He stared across the meadow and spoke quietly of the day he and his brother were arrested. Their crime, in those dangerous and distrustful days, was to be young and near the scene of an attack on a local shop. "We had that 'lean and hungry look' and that's all it took back then. Sorry to pull The Bard back into the fray, but Shakespeare always said a thing about as clearly as it can be said. We had the look and it was enough.

"I spent a week in a cramped cell, and my brother spent, I don't know, I think three weeks. Seamus had a way with words, if you know what I mean, and let them know what he thought of the English and of law enforcement in general. Accordingly, he was not treated gently. He was never a temperate soul, but the time in chokey changed him. Turned a proud man into an angry one. I saw him only once after that, may he rest in peace."

"You were both innocent?" Anna asked.

With an effort, he pulled himself back from the past. "You, more than anyone, have no reason to believe what I say, Anna, but I swear to you, I was never a violent man, nor was Seamus until that time in jail. After they let him out, spittin' and swearing, he joined up and marched off, the damned fool. He decided to fight and I didn't. I'd had more than enough of bombs and fires and sirens in the dead of night. Seamus knew someone who knew someone, and I emptied my savings to buy some identity papers, and to emigrate."

"Aloysius McCaffrey," Anna said. "Of the Carrickfergus McCaffreys."

"Yes. My alter ego. I think, though I'll never know for sure, Squire McCaffrey spent a few years over here looking for work as an artist. I can draw a little, no worse than some, and Bernie Holloway laughed at my captions. He hired me, I met this spitfire that ran the office, and the rest, as they say, is mystery."

"Am I tiring you, Aloysius? I don't need to hear anymore. It's all over and done for me."

"I'm holding up so far, dear Anna. And as I said, I need to tell it more than you need to hear it. And there isn't much more. Just give me a minute or two."

Anna stood and watched children on the lawn chase each other. In her mind, bombs exploded, fires raged and people screamed until

Aloysius began again. "After I slipped that note under your door, cursing myself for a coward, I boarded a train to Florida. You would think a twenty-four-hour train ride down the East Coast of these United States would prove memorable, but I don't think I even looked out the window. It seems I had something else, more likely *someone* else, on my mind."

He found a job as a maintenance man in a Sarasota resort hotel, and settled in. His boss, Mr. Epstein, had some early misgivings about him, but Aloysius was conscientious and quiet, so he left him alone.

He smiled. "So, there I was, an Irish man, working for a Jewish man, in a resort owned by WASPs. Quintessentially American."

The immigration people found him eventually but didn't know what to do with him. They blustered and threatened him with jail, but other than occasional visits and bureaucratic jargon, left him alone. The immigration issues in Florida in the nineteen-nineties were not concerned with Ireland.

He had his first attack as he was stepping on the bottom rung of a ladder to change a light bulb. He sat on the floor until the pain subsided, went home early, and didn't tell anyone. Anna thought, but didn't say, *quintessentially American. Quintessentially male.* After the second attack, a more serious one, he decided to come back to New York. "Better hospitals up here. Something told me not to be just another Florida geezer."

They both gazed at the meadow for a few minutes, silent, lost. Aloysius began to hum an old favorite, "The Parting Glass."

"Ha," she said. "I remember The Chorus doing that one to close the show. And at the last line, Katherine would step forward and speak it, 'Good luck, and joy be with you all.' It was a great finale."

"Those women could sing selections from a tax return and make it sound beautiful. They were that good," he said. Anna was quiet, wondering if she should say what she was thinking.

"I had nightmares about the crash for months after," Aloysius said. "That stupid man. That stupid, blithering man." He was thinking about the captain of the Staten Island Ferry. "That thick-headed gobshite that fell asleep at the wheel."

"Do you remember that Katherine had a daughter?" Anna said. "Only a baby at the time."

"I do remember. Haven't thought about it in quite some time, but I remember a little girl. I recall her wrapped in a pink blanket.

"You saw her. Recently."

He looked at her, startled. "I saw her? When can I have...?" She waited, his mouth dropped and he said, "Ah, Bernard's visitor. Oh, Anna. Things do come back around at a man, don't they?"

"Her name is Chloe. You should meet her, Aloysius. You will like her, and she wants to meet you."

"I don't...I don't know. That may not be a good idea."

"She is Katherine's daughter, Aloysius. I know you will like her, given a little time."

"Katherine's daughter? How could I not like her? That's not the..." He was silent, smiling, looking out again over the grass. "I see. You think maybe she can change my mind about the surgery."

She shook her head. "I wasn't thinking that at all. I think you're making a mistake, but your mistakes are your own, Aloysius. I'm thinking of Katherine, and of Chloe. If for no other reason, you should meet Chloe for their sake."

"Oh, Anna. Oh, dear Anna. There is a craftiness in you. Caring, but crafty. I remember now what attracted me to you in the first place."

She smiled and remembered, too.

"I thought her father had moved away with her. She found her way back here, I'm supposin'."

"Her father moved to Springfield, partially to get some help from his sister with infant Chloe, and partially, probably mostly, to get the hell away from Staten Island."

"Springfield. That's Missouri, right?"

"No. Springfield, Massachusetts. She grew up with a loving family, her father, aunts, uncles, cousins. And they did right by her. She's a lovely girl, Aloysius."

"And you kept in touch, of course. A very Anna thing to do."

She smiled. "Yes. I knew her family wanted as much distance as possible from the accident, and New York, and all of it. They talked to her about it, of course, but *sotto voce*. You know what I mean by that, right?"

"Sure. Soft voice. Keeping things quiet."

"But I felt Chloe should have some connection to her mom's life. That was arrogance on my part, I guess. I sent birthday cards, holiday cards, little gifts, and when she got a little older, I visited a few times. I got some hard looks, but the family tolerated me as long as I didn't upset Chloe. I didn't know Katherine that well, anyway. Not as well as you."

"And eventually Chloe came and found you here in New York."

"She has a degree in English. Her aunt is a technical writer, so maybe it's in her DNA, and she knew I worked for a magazine."

"You got her a job."

"Sure. It wasn't hard. She had a good resume and, as soon as I told Bernie who she was, well, what else could he do?"

He shook his head and laughed a little. "That pretty colleen is Katherine's daughter. Things really do have a way of coming around at a man, dear Anna. It may take some time, but they do come around."

"I won't hound you, Aloysius, but, yes. Katherine's little girl. And she knows almost nothing about her mother's life in New York. About the Chorus. About all the good times you had with her. You should meet her. And yes I *do* think it's a good idea. Good for both of you.

Sixteen

The following Tuesday, Anna and Chloe arrived together for the staff meeting. Anna had emailed everyone that Chloe would be joining them. Anna went around the table making introductions, and Chloe, smiling and nodding, tried to keep the names straight.

"I've known Chloe since she was a girl," Anna said. "She worked at *Aplomb* for a few years as a copy editor, and my hope is she will function here as my right-hand woman; and in time, everyone's right-hand woman. I am delighted to have her with us.

"Robert, I did meet and talk with your friend Gerard, but he is planning to move to the Southwest. I'm not sure he would have worked out anyway."

"Yes, he called me and said he's moving to Arizona, The Sunshine State."

LaToya said, "Robert, I think Florida is the Sunshine State."

"Oh, of course it is, but try telling Gerard that."

Anna laughed. "Okay, we have some things to talk about, and a few submissions to evaluate, but in between, please take the time to say hello and welcome Chloe. Coffee will be ready soon, as usual, and I stopped for some muffins. I'd like to get the next issue planned out as much as possible. I won't be working tomorrow, Chloe either, and maybe for another day or two. I have a sick friend that needs some cheering up."

She talked for a few minutes about the progress of the magazine; increased advertisement, including an ad from Herman's Deli, an increase in the number of articles included, and an increase in both the number and quality of the online submissions. "Online subscriptions are up as well," she noted, "and to a lesser degree, the local subscriptions. We're small, but we are growing. We are being noticed. I'm elated with all of this, and I recognize the success is due to your hard work and talent."

"Wow," Carla said. "The last time I got a compliment at work was, well, I never got a compliment like that at work."

Anna continued, "Robert has two things going on for this issue. A humor piece called *What Were We Talking About Again?* and a heads up on the decisions made recently about the next year's fiscal budget.

"And a big thank you to Robert staying on top of civic issues. I think that's where our increase in local advertising and in local subscriptions is coming from."

"I have a short piece I'd like everyone's comments on," Jasmine said. "I'll print it out after the meeting, and please, be honest. There's a reason I'm an illustrator and not a writer."

Anna looked down at her note pad. "Let's see, introduce Chloe, check. Gerard, check. The next issue, check. Increase in advertisement, submissions and subscriptions, check. Thank you to all, check. I think that covers...oh, wait. Coffee, calories and conversation is next on the agenda. Let's take care of that one. And then we'll pull back together and plan out the next issue."

Chloe had always felt comfortable at cocktail parties and social situations where she didn't know people, and was soon chatting comfortably with Robert, Carla and Miriam.

Robert said, "Miriam, I don't know if you had a chance to look at the piece we wrote for the next edition, but we were thinking of you."

"Yes," she said. "Anna forwarded it to me. I think she wanted to be sure that I wasn't, you know..."

They both knew enough to wait.

"...upset. And I wasn't at all. In fact, for a few sentences, I thought it was about fishing. Actually, I was kind of hoping it was about fishing. I caught a trout one time and it was, you know..."

They both expected her to say, 'exciting' or 'fun.'

"...slimy."

Carla said, "Miriam, when he was writing it, I was thinking about you too, but honestly, and please don't laugh, I couldn't remember your name!"

Miriam tried, but she couldn't help laughing out loud.

The Schoolhouse
Casual, Collegial and Classy

What Were We Talking About Again?
by
Robert Bronner

The trout, a full-grown ten pounder, moves effortlessly through the rushing water toward food, the single object of all his being, on the surface. With a last final thrust he snatches at the fly, gobbles it down quickly, and moves on.

It used to be that easy. Names, places, numbers, events came to me naturally. I could grab what I needed from my brain like that trout gobbling a fly and move on. Now, not so much. My trout floats slowly in a more or less upward direction, and the fly dodges and leaps and stays just out of reach. The name of someone I've known for years, the phone number I just looked up, the first thing on my to-do list, all seem to be flies just out of reach.

Some things do still rise to the intellectual surface, but almost nothing I can use immediately. Like lines from old songs. Really, how many people can sing every word of the Mills Brothers' "Paper Doll?" For me, no problem. I can remember the moment I first saw the girl who would grow into the woman who is now my wife. The memory is in black and white, and the smells have faded a little, but the other details remain sharp. Her hair, the shiny metal handrail, the cream-colored tables, the clocks that told me how late I was for class. Her hair.

I can remember the moment Bill Mazeroski hit that homerun. In a more graceless age, like this one, he would have earned the same middle name as Bucky Dent.

Wait, where was I? Uh, trout...Mills Brothers...Late for class again....um, oh yeah, I remember. Or rather, I don't remember.

There are strategies, of course, to deal with a fading memory. Like the coverup when a name just won't come to you "Hey, how you doin' buddy, old timer, young fella, lady, good lookin'?" That'll get you by until you can apply the alphabet approach. This involves going through each letter of the alphabet to see if that will help catch the fly. Alice, Adrian, Amy....Barbara, Betty, Carl, Charley, Connor... This is a wonderful technique I have employed for years, and it has never worked. At least not that I can recall. I usually end up calling him "buddy" or her "lady" for the rest of the day. I pretend they don't realize that I don't know their names, but in time I always get that sideways glance that tells me I'm busted.

There is a variety of vitamins to help you regain mental sharpness, and I have purchased several. I don't know if they work, because I never remember to take them.

Meditation is another remedy for memory loss, based on the notion that the problem is not really memory, but focus. So, I have sat in a darkened room in a comfortable position and counted slowly while focusing on my breath, and it really does work. Afterwards, I find myself refreshed, re-vitalized and centered. And when an occasion arises when I need to recall something quickly, it is easy for me to be completely focused on the fact that I can't.

There are more routine treatments as well, like making lists. My uncle used to leave lists on the kitchen table to remind him to buy cereal, on the stairs to remind him to get the oil changed, etcetera. But he could never find his glasses to read the lists. And once he found his glasses he didn't remember the reason he wanted them in the first place was so that he could read the list. "Well, at least I have my glasses," he would mumble, while his engine seized, and he had nothing for breakfast. I haven't reached that stage yet.

Like outrageous life insurance rates and annual prostate screenings, memory loss is the price of remaining on this bank of the River Styx. At least I still have my sense of humor. Speaking of which...a priest, a minister, and a rabbi order a drink from a blond bartender, and she says, she says, uh. The blond bartender says to the priest, minister and rabbi, um...

Oh, never mind. It wasn't that funny, and you probably heard it anyway.

Painting The Kitchen
by
Miriam Seger Glasner

There are some jobs in life that don't end with retirement. A few years ago, we did the living room, the hallways, and bedrooms. I remember thinking, actually promising myself, I would not be painting in this house again. Not ever, never. Even then, this body was announcing clearly that it was no longer the appropriate tool for all of the squatting, bending, stretching, and lifting required for the task.

So, of course, here I am on this cloudy Friday afternoon, the last day of winter, painting the kitchen.

The word 'painting' is inadequate and misleading. When you paint a room, the spreading of paint on walls is the easiest and most satisfying of the required activities. There is also, in no particular order, moving furniture (including the refrigerator), sweeping all cobwebs and woogies out of the way, emptying cabinets, repairing dings and dents in the walls, taping corners, and, of course, hosting the internal debate on whether the human race should have moved out of caves in the first place.

It is, I'm happy to report, a smallish kitchen, and the color chosen is similar to the old color, so it should be a relatively quick job (I love that word 'relatively;' it modifies reality, it obfuscates, it sometimes flat-out lies, but it does so with elan and panache).

I heard once the quickest way to get a divorce was to wallpaper the bathroom with the one you love. So, I was smart enough to wait until my husband was out of town for a few days. When he returns, he'll inspect my handiwork for globs where I bobbled, and speckles where I spackled. But he loves me, and I'm sure my hard work will pass muster. I just hope he remembers to pick up some Advil.

Van Hokkh
by
Jasmine Hargrove

I went to an exhibit of Van Gogh's paintings last Sunday at a museum, about an hour and a half east of Albany, about three hours from New York. A long trip, but it was Van Gogh. I still have 'The Starry Night' poster I bought when I was in high school.

Everybody knows Van Gogh: red hair, intense stare, cut off his ear to impress a girl. He was different, and his paintings were different: thick daubs of paint, everything kind of swirly. And bright, very bright. A few of his paintings can almost make you sweat.

What people don't know is how to pronounce his name. It isn't Van Gogh, rhymes with 'You're too slow.' But 'Van Hokkh,' the sound you make after swallowing a moth, and nothing rhymes with that. But then Van Gogh was Dutch, and there must be a lot of moths in Holland, so Van Gogh or Van Hokkh is a very common name. You can't throw a severed ear in Holland without hitting a Van Hokkh.

What surprised me, and probably shouldn't have, was the crowd at this museum. I could not get into the parking lot, and I clocked a full half mile of parked cars before I found an open space on the street.

Inside the museum, of course, the exhibit was packed. There were a few dozen paintings and a few sketches, but it was 'scuze me, 'scuze me, 'scuze me, oops, sorry' to get anywhere near most of them. In that kind of environment, the delight that attaches to being a member of the human race fades rapidly. I admired many of the paintings from a distance of fifteen or twenty feet.

Vincent died, poor and depressed, from a self-inflicted gunshot wound. Poor and depressed largely because he only sold one painting during his lifetime. One. Ironic, then, that people cluster at museums around the world to say 'scuze me and squint from a distance at his work. Even more incongruous, his paintings have sold for as much as fourteen million dollars. That kind of money will buy a lot of paint, or a whole box of prosthetic ears.

The moral of this story, if there is one, is genius, or talent, or skill, or even something as pedestrian as hard work, is rarely recognized during its day. Often, not at all.

~ * ~

"I'll take my time getting there," Bernie told the nurse. "He's an old friend, he'll wait."

The phone was on top of the nurses' desk. "Bernie? It's Meyer. You're a hard man to get hold of."

"Meyer? I don't have a phone in my room. I had to walk down to the nurses' station. I'm really surprised to hear from you."

"I came up to Pennsy for a few weeks to do some trout fishing. Made the mistake of calling the office and they told me about your coronary. What the hell did you do that for?"

"Oh, you know. It seemed like a good idea at the time."

"I want to get over there to see you, but you know trout. Time and trout wait for no man."

"That should be embroidered on a pillow, Meyer."

"Is there anything I can do for you, Bern?"

"No, Meyer. I'm pretty well...wait, yes. That trouble you had with Carol—"

"Carolyn."

"Yes, her. Didn't you tell me you went to a detective agency?"

"Yes, and thanks so much for reminding me. I can usually forget all about it until I write the alimony check."

"Who are you kidding, Meyer? You haven't written your own checks in years. But can you remember the name of the detective agency?"

"Yeah, sure. Powell Associates. It's easy to remember because Dick Powell is the actor that played the detective, Phillip Marlow, in those classic noirs. Powell was really good, too."

"Powell the actor was good, or Powell the agency was good?"

"Both. When you call them, ask for Arthur Maalwyck. He worked my case, and he was very professional. Expensive, but worth it. He caught her fooling around with the guy we hired to do the landscaping."

"You're trying to tell me some guy was trimming your wife's rhododendron?"

Meyer laughed. "Same old Bernie, same old sense of humor. Get well, Bern, and stay that way. We'll talk again soon."

~ * ~

On the way to Northeast Rehab with Chloe, Anna had a *déjà vu* moment. At a traffic jam due to the same road construction, she saw the same hardhat leaning on the same truck. She was sure it was the same guy because only a few men can carry a beer belly that size.

"I shouldn't be nervous about meeting him, but I am," Chloe said.

"I understand. It isn't so much him as all the past stuff he brings along with him. Your mom, The Chorus, the accident."

"I guess."

"You'll like him, though. I'm sure."

"You'll stay with me?"

"Of course. I want to pop in on Bernie, but I can do that after."

As Chloe was signing in at the reception desk, Anna got an idea. She went to the nurses' desk in Aloysius' wing and asked about his condition and his progress. He asked if she was a relative.

"Well, not quite," she said. "I'm his fiancée." Chloe looked over at her but said nothing.

"You're engaged to Al?" he asked, eyebrows raised.

"Well, he asked me, and I said yes," she answered. "So…"

"I'll talk with Al," he said. "And he'll have to talk to his cardiologist."

Walking to Aloysius' room, Chloe said, "That was genius. You inspire me, Anna."

Aloysius was sitting up in bed with a magazine when they knocked and poked their heads in. He waved at Anna but focused on Chloe. "Hello," he said. "Thank you for coming."

"Hello, Mister McMahon," Chloe said. "I'm Chloe. It's very nice to meet you."

He looked at her closely. "Yes," he said. "You're the young lady I saw the other day with Bernard Holloway."

"Yes. I used to work for him at *Aplomb*, before he got sick."

"Of course. Anna told me that." He nodded, she nodded, and Anna nodded for a few awkward and silent moments.

Anna rolled her eyes and said, "Aloysius, we don't need to tiptoe. Chloe is Katherine's daughter. Chloe, Aloysius used to manage your mother's singing group."

More nodding from Aloysius and Chloe. Finally, he said, "Do you sing, Chloe?"

"No. I thought about taking lessons, but never got around to it."

"Your mother had a beautiful voice. And she really knew how to use it."

"I heard a tape of her once," Chloe said.

"You favor her," Aloysius said. "Especially the eyes, and the way you hold yourself. She would..." he stopped when he saw she was crying.

"I'm sorry. I don't want to make you sad." He looked over at Anna. "This is what I was afraid of. This is not a good idea."

"Oh, no sir. You misunderstand," Chloe said quickly. "It isn't sadness. It's...I don't know what it is. But please. I want to hear it. I want to hear anything you can tell me about her. I do. Anything."

Anna said, "Why don't you tell her about the time Katherine walked off stage, and no one knew why."

"Oh, yes," Aloysius said, smiling. "That's a good place to start. Very much at the beginning." He leaned forward, and Chloe did, too. "It's a Lion's Club event, as I recall, and the ladies are in fine voice until your mother steps back, turns, and walks quickly toward the exit. And I mean quickly. The ladies look at me, I look at them and we have no idea what the problem is. I follow her, because I'm worried, you know, but she goes into the ladies' room. She's back a few minutes later, pale but smiling. No, more than smiling. Blooming like a medieval Madonna. She finds her spot and goes on with the show. They finish a song, and she steps up to the microphone, proud as you please, and says, 'Ladies and gentlemen, I apologize for my quick exit a little while ago. I haven't even told my friends yet, but I'm two months pregnant, and my child just needed to have a word with me in the ladies' room.'

That was you, Chloe. That was your first appearance on stage."

Chloe laughed, Aloysius laughed, and after that, it was all okay. The awkwardness had been left in the ladies' room of that Lion's Club so many years ago. Chloe pulled a chair up close to the bed, Anna sat on the other side, both of them captivated, and Aloysius told Katherine stories for the next half hour. After another awkward silence, and at Chloe's hesitant request, Aloysius told her about the day the ferry crashed into the dock and the chaos and anger in its aftermath. Anna held back her tears. Chloe sat, hands in her lap, wide-eyed and rigid. There was no brogue now, no dramatic pauses or vocal theatrics, just a man telling a terrible story.

When Anna saw Aloysius was tiring, she nodded to Chloe and they made a reluctant exit. Anna touched his arm and Chloe kissed him on the cheek. "I'm very glad to have met you, Mister McMahon. I'm not just being polite, either. I am very, very glad we met, and talked about Mom."

Anna made a quick stop to say hello to Bernie. He was in a blue mood after a brief visit from Sherilyn, and didn't want to talk, but he asked her to deliver a note to Paula.

Chloe went to the ladies' room to breathe deeply, wipe off the tears and fix her make-up. When she came out, she said. "My god, Anna, no wonder you love him. That man can *really* tell a story."

Seventeen

They stopped on the way home for an early dinner, and when Anna pulled into the parking lot of her building, Chloe said, "That's Mike's car. I asked him to meet me here." He was in the car with the air conditioning on, despite the cool, early spring temperature. He got out quickly and kissed her.

"You had an okay afternoon?" Mike asked. "I know you were nervous about seeing him." Chloe didn't answer.

"Come in for coffee or a drink or something?" Anna asked. "If I know Paula, she's been busy all afternoon baking or roasting an ox or something."

Mike checked his watch. "If we go now, we can catch the early show, Chloe."

"Maybe that's a better idea. I need a little time to absorb everything I heard."

In the car, Mike was unsure about bringing it up, but he asked again about her visit with Anna's old, old boyfriend. He didn't know his name, nor did he know much about Chloe's mother. Stopped at a light, and feeling the pressure of an awkward silence, he asked how the visit went.

"It was good, Mike. And it was awful. Both."

"Okay, you don't need to say anything. I just want to know you're okay."

"I need time, that's all. Maybe later, after the movie. I want to tell you, but there's a lot to process."

They had opted for a gangster movie, not her favorite, so Chloe was able to tune out for ninety minutes and think. She was quiet as they filed out of the theater, and Mike knew enough not to try to draw her out.

In the car, she said, "It's still kind of early. I'm wrung out, but I don't want to go home yet. Can we stop somewhere for a beer or something?" They found a bar without too much noise and ordered beers. She sat next to him at first, but then shifted over and sat facing him across the table.

"It's a lot, Mike," she said. "Family stuff. My family stuff. Stuff people didn't talk to me about, and I've never asked about. I think everyone was afraid of it. I was afraid of it, too. I never even asked Anna."

She told him about Aloysius and his broken relationship with Anna, and, at first, Mike did not understand the connection. *The old, old boyfriend?* On her second beer, she talked about The Chorus, her mother, and the crash of the Staten Island Ferry.

"Aloysius was a friend of my mom and the manager of the group. There were three women. I've seen pictures, even heard a tape once. He was on the ferry when it crashed and, you know, and..."

"Oh, Chloe, I'm so sorry. I had no idea."

"No, you couldn't. How could anyone? Something so horrible..." They nursed their beers in silence for a while and then he drove her home. She slipped in quickly; he didn't even think of kissing her. She took her shoes off and fell asleep on the couch.

~ * ~

As Anna had predicted, Paula had just finished making a cinnamon pound cake. She cut two pieces and walked slowly into the living room, balancing the plates and reading the note from Bernie. "Things are getting serious," she said, and handed Anna the note.

"He's found a detective *and* a divorce attorney," Anna read. "Wow, the battle lines are drawn. I guess that's good, but it makes me worry a little about Bernie. She's not going to take this lightly."

"Sherilyn, right. Or the nephew either."

"The nephew," Anna said. "Right. How could I forget about the nephew?"

"Will you drive me up to White Plains tomorrow to see Bernie? I guess it's time I visited, mended some fences."

Anna said yes automatically, but quickly changed her mind. "Why don't you take my car? I don't want to see Aloysius again so soon. Today with Chloe was sweet, but gut-wrenching. He probably needs a break from me, too."

"Well, okay. If you want, I'll check in on your guy. Just poke my head in, say hello."

"Huh. 'My guy.'"

~ * ~

"How much can you tell me about her background, Mister Holloway?" Arthur Maalwyck said to Bernard. They were sitting on a bench in front of Northeast Rehab. "Anything at all might be helpful; otherwise, you know, it's that needle in a haystack situation." Bernie noticed that Maalwyck referred to 'situations' and 'scenarios' a lot.

Bernie was feeling much better. He was careful about doing his exercises and he was careful about his diet, but he was still worried about how a pitched battle with Sherilyn would affect him. "I'm embarrassed to say I know very little, Maalwyck. We met in Las Vegas at a time when I was, shall we say, not fully myself. She was charming and available, I think 'available' is the key word here, and we became close very quickly."

"'Close.' I take your meaning, Mister Holloway. It's a familiar scenario in my business, and often leads to a challenging situation. Especially with regard to a personage with a substantial reputation to consider." It had only been four days between Bernie's phone call with Meyer and the arrival of Maalwyck. Apparently, any friend of Meyer Lieberborg could be considered a 'substantial personage.'

Maalwyck himself was a study in grey and black. There was something about him, some visual trick which, when looking at him, seemed to make a person's eyes slide off center and not register anything. He wore black pants, a charcoal gray jacket and a black tie, no watch or rings Bernie could see. He was of average height and build, and had a clean-shaven face best described as bland. Short gray hair, and a scarcity of facial expression made Mr. Maalwyck an operative who was innately and perennially undercover. After their conversation, Bernie could barely remember what he looked like.

"I'm pretty sure she was not a resident of Vegas, just a visitor, a tourist like me."

"Oh, I would venture to say her vacation plan was very different than yours, Mister Holloway. But did she ever talk about her life before your encounter? Family, employment history, trouble with the law? These are the hooks I can hang my hat on, as it were."

"We never talked much, and when you meet her you'll understand why. Early on, there was communication of a much different sort, but not much talking. And then I got sick, so everything became about me. She did say she was from the Northwest and was sick and tired of the rain. She spent a lot of time out in the Nevada sun. I don't suppose that helps much."

"Oh, it does. It does." Maalwyck pulled a cigarette from its box, Marlboro, the kind Bernie used to smoke, and just held it between his fingers. "If I can get some dates and a good description, or better yet, a picture, I have a contact working arrivals at the airport. She's got a memory like a bookie. If the lady deplaned at McCarran Airport, Dotty will remember."

"I don't know if I have a picture. Oh, wait, yes I do." He reached into the lower drawer of the night table and took out a framed photograph with a written note on the bottom, "From me to you." It showed a woman posed in front of a fountain, fortyish, slightly overweight, with short dark hair and a smile that seemed to cause her pain.

Maalwyck held it for a moment and then sniffed it. "Her perfume is still on this. The scent could help with identification, if need be," he said.

"It sure doesn't help with anything else," Bernie said.

"Well," Maalwyck said. "I think I have what I need for starters. I have your check and your *bona fides* from Meyer Lieberborg. I'll be in touch as soon as there is something substantial, and a written report will follow about a week later. Do you have any questions for me?"

"No," Bernie said. "I think I understand the process, and the product. Do you have any more questions for me?"

Maalwyck had been on this job for eleven years. The one question he always wanted to ask, but never did, was, "How could you be so stupid?"

~ * ~

Sunday morning, Paula borrowed Anna's car and drove to White Plains. She was nervous at first, driving a little too slow, and being extra aware of the traffic around her. She hadn't driven since before she went to Skopje and was always an overly careful driver. She was glad it was Sunday morning and traffic was light. At the reception desk, she signed the register, as big as possible, as 'Mrs. Bernard Holloway,' and smiled brightly at the girl behind the desk. It occurred to her to check the other names on the register to see if Sherilyn or Sebastian were there, but then decided not to bother. *I'm visiting my husband. They don't count.*

She found Bernie awake and active, sitting on his bed dialing his cell phone. They had an awkward moment, but only a moment, where they just looked at each other wordlessly. Bernie just said, "Paula," and hurried over to hug her. She put her arms around his neck and just said, "Bernie." He took her hand and they walked out to the patio. It was early for visitors, and the patio was empty and quiet. They sat looking at the lawn and the flowers beds, just beginning to bloom.

"Your note was—," Bernie said.

"I had an idea driving up here," Paula said quickly. "I want to *not* talk about what happened, who was right, who was wrong. Should have, could have, would have. I think that can only cause new bruises. We're both so bruised already, Bernie. Let's not..."

"Yes, that makes a lot of...yes. No more bruises."

"Solutions," she said, "and repairs."

They sat looking out at the broad lawn, holding hands in her lap. Paula pointed out a robin pulling a worm out of the ground and hopping away. "Springtime," he said.

"Yes," Paula said.

"I have things to talk to you about," Bernie said, "not about what happened, but what's about to happen. When you came in, I was calling a rental agent about an apartment." He was still hesitant about saying 'we' rather than 'I,' unsure if, after all, she had made other arrangements. "I may need to stay at a motel for a while."

"Yes. *We* can do that," she said firmly.

He smiled and nodded at that. "I'll be leaving here soon, they all tell me, and I won't go back to our old place while she's there."

"You don't think she'll leave?"

"Not without a fight, but she will leave."

"I hate this, Bernie. I hate having to fight for something I know is mine. I hate having to hate someone, but I think I do hate her. It's not right, and it's not me, but I think I do."

They sat quietly together for another few minutes watching birds land, strut around and take off again. He said, "You and I seem to do best when we write, rather than talk. While I'm here, I'm going to be emailing you, if that's okay. I can get email here but haven't before, because, well because."

"I think that's probably a good idea. There's a lot I need to hear about. Private detectives, divorce lawyers, god knows what else. I want to be ready, too."

"It's all in flux now, all up in the air, and there's no telling how she'll react—"

"You haven't talked to her about any of this? Or the nephew?"

"No. I'm not sure if she knows you're back."

"Oh, she knows. I went to *Aplomb* looking for you. I met that person in your office. Anna calls him Seabass."

"Seabass. The once and future nephew. If he knows, she knows."

She pulled away and looked closely at him. "I need you to tell me honestly, Bernie, if you're strong enough for this, for a whole legal wrangle."

"Yes, I'm sure I am. It'll be a contest by proxy, Paula. I think my legal champion will *habeus corpus* her legal champion into a *nolo contendere* headlock and knock him right off his horse."

She kissed Bernie when she left, and he held her tightly. She found her way to Aloysius' room, knocked softly, and leaned in.

"I think you may be out of uniform," he said. "We have our greens and our blues around here, and both colors seem to require a stethoscope around the neck as an accessory. Don't worry, I won't report you this time."

She laughed. "I'm a friend of Anna, Mister McMahon. I promised her I would look in on you. I was just visiting Bernie Holloway."

"Ah, visiting the sick. A spiritual work of mercy. Bernie is a lucky man to have two friends like you and Anna."

"I'm a little more than a friend. I'm his wife."

He hesitated and looked at her quizzically for a moment. "That's a bit surprising. Scuttlebutt among the staff here paints Mrs. Holloway as somewhat vocal, and also, um, fragrant at a distance."

She frowned. "So I've heard. But that isn't me. It's a long story, but for a while there seemed to be two Mrs. Holloways. It's complicated, but you'll just have to take my word. I'm the genuine article."

"Well, if you're on a mission from dear Anna, I'm glad to make your acquaintance, Mrs. Holloway."

"It's Paula, please."

"Then that would make me Aloysius."

Two people came in behind her, one in green scrubs and one in blue. Both had a stethoscope hung neatly around their necks. "Oh, we didn't realize you had company, Mister McMahon," she pronounced all three syllables. She looked at Paula "I'm sorry, but we do need to take him away for a while."

"Oh, I wasn't staying. I just wanted to say hello and introduce myself. I'll tell Anna you're in good hands, Aloysius."

"If you would be kind enough, Paula, would you give her a message for me? Tell her I've decided to let them crack my walnut. She'll understand."

Eighteen

The Schoolhouse
Casual Collegial and Classy

At the staff meeting the following Tuesday, Chloe and Anna printed and distributed a short story and an essay that would be going into this month's magazine.

"I got these from Mister Dannell, the Superintendent of Forest Hills School District. I promised him two winners of a high school writing competition would be printed in *The Schoolhouse*. I have shared them with our resident teacher, and both have received the coveted Carla Bronner Official Okey-dokey.

Here they are:

This edition of The Schoolhouse *will feature the winners of the Forest Hills High School Creative Writing Contest. Two excellent pieces have been chosen by the school faculty; one short story and one essay, and we are pleased and proud to present them to you.*

Two, Build a Fire
by
Jared Kingston

Two-thirty a.m. The first day of the first month of the new decade. He had left the New Year's Eve party with an old song on his lips and directions home floating lightly on the surface of his alcohol-soaked brain. Within fifteen minutes he was lost, on the wrong road in the wrong county, driving in the wrong direction in an unfamiliar city. The snow fell heavily, and he watched it streak across his headlights. He glanced once in the rear-view mirror and saw a wonderland behind him, magically brightened by the streetlights, and disturbed only by his tire tracks. He guided the Caddy off the highway at an exit and moved silently through the dim, snow covered streets like a dog sled over a frozen trail. After a series of turns, a few lefts and a few rights in no particular order, he found himself on a wide, empty, and desolate street. It was as quiet as the moments just before an avalanche.

Suddenly, from his left side, a large white dog came trotting toward the front of the car. The man swerved quickly and jammed on the brakes, but the dog had already turned away and was loping toward one of the side streets. While the man focused on the dog, the car sputtered and died.

With clumsy fingers, he tried the ignition. Nothing. The starter hummed its little monotone melody, but the engine wouldn't sing along. Not knowing what else to do, he tried again, and a third time without result.

"Battery?" he asked himself out loud. "Starter? Tune-up maybe?"

He shook his head slowly as the answers swam slowly and languidly to the surface of his consciousness.

"Gas? Gasoline?" He turned the ignition switch and the fuel gauge needle stayed on 'E.'

He got out of the car, slipping a bit, and catching himself with his elbow on the inside car door, and angrily slammed it. Immediately a rush of snow and frigid air hit him, chilling and sobering him a little. He bundled his light raincoat around his chin and squinted through the snow for signs of life, or the miracle of a gas station. The only light was the haze from an occasional street lamp, and the only sound was the click of the traffic light as it changed from green to red. He spotted what looked like a phone booth and plodded toward it trying to remember his phone number. It *was* a phone booth, one of the old-fashioned glass coffin types, but the phone had been ripped out. He stared at the empty buildings all around him, full of dark holes where windows used to be.

Shivering again, he hurried to his car, but slipped and landed hard on his knee. He lay panting and grimacing for a few moments before trying to stand. His leg wouldn't take any weight, and he toppled back into the snow. Painfully, and feeling melodramatic, he dragged himself the remaining fifty feet to the car.

It was locked.

Frantically, he searched his pockets, rifling through them with thick, uncooperative fingers. Nothing. Fearfully, almost preferring not to know, he pulled himself up on his good knee and looked in the window. He stared, unbelieving, at the keys and gold key chain hanging from the ignition switch. He dragged himself around the car and checked each door, cursing when each was locked.

"Where the hell am I?" he shouted at the shadowy, forsaken landscape.

He saw the dog again, grimy and thin, trotting down the block, looking for shelter. It stopped for just a moment to sniff and stare at him, this alien creature lying in the snow, and continued on its way. Watching the animal move away from him, the man felt a strange conflict of emotions. Fear, of course. The reflexive, atavistic fear of wild animals. But he also felt a loss and yearning for something else alive in this barren wilderness. The dog meant that at least he was still on planet earth.

He dragged himself across the street to the open doorway of a building. He found a dry corner across from a shattered marble stairway, out of the snow and wind, and quickly fell asleep. Cold water trickling off the broken roof and down his neck woke him in the early daylight hours of New Year's Day.

He saw a wide stretch of what looked like a war zone framed in the open doorway. Graffiti, most of it unintelligible, added some color to the faded brick and stucco buildings. Mountains of rubble and charred lumber flowed from the apartment buildings into the wide, empty, snow-covered street.

There were three cars in the street, partially covered in snow. Two of them were nose-to-nose, wheels gone and hoods agape, like crippled animals that died in the act of mouth-to-mouth resuscitation. The third car he recognized as his Cadillac; gleaming, powerful, and worthless.

He shifted himself away from the dripping water, and a surge of pain burst through his left knee. He lay gulping for air, staring at the wall opposite him, recalling bits and pieces of last night and how he had come to this place.

He remembered singing, and watching the snow in the bright headlights, and a bridge—he clearly remembered driving across a long bridge.

He rolled onto his belly and began crawling in the same direction as he had been driving. It was not as cold as the night before, but the snow was just at the level of his shoulders, and it bunched and slid down into his shirt as he slid along. Within an hour, he was saturated with sweat and melted snow, and his arms ached from pulling the weight of his body. He had not seen a sign of life.

At an opening in the row of buildings to his right he saw, gray and stately and distance, a bridge.

"Bridge," he muttered. "Triboro Bridge." He looked around carefully and spotted a street sign, rusted and hanging at an odd angle: Charlotte Street.

Slowly, fighting fatigue and the alcohol from the night before, it all came together in his mind. New York City geography, the bridge, the burned-out neighborhood of the South Bronx, the blasted, war-zone atmosphere.

He fought back his terror. "A fire," he told the bridge. "Attract attention, get warm. I can do it, just need to take one thing at a time. One, gather up some stuff that will burn, and two, build a fire."

In the third building he searched, he found enough dry paper to get it started, and in the next building, dry wood and couch cushions. Giddy with hope, he pushed it all to the middle of the street and pulled the gold lighter from his pants pocket.

It took him twenty minutes to start the fire. His frozen hands would not do the things he needed them to do, and twice he lost the lighter in the snow. Finally, he held it between his trembling knees and rotated the striker with the heel of his unfeeling hand. On the fourth attempt, a small flame erupted.

Carefully, he lit one end of a rolled-up newspaper and cheered as the flame sprang up to consume it.

He heard or felt something next to him and saw a flash of green kick snow onto the pile and smother the fire. It was a boy, about fourteen or fifteen. He wore bright green pants and red sneakers, a fatigue jacket and a black beret. A wisp of a mustache was visible against his brown skin.

"Help me," the man pleaded. "For God's sake, help me, please! My car broke down a few blocks from here, and I think my leg is broken. Help me, please."

The boy stared at him, hands in his pockets.

"Just call the police, that's all. Just tell them where I am." The kid moved toward him slowly, circling until he was behind the man.

"There's something in it for you!" the man shouted. "Fifty bucks! No, a hundred! Just tell someone where I am!"

He felt hands grab him roughly from behind, penetrating and searching his pockets. He tried to strike at the boy, but he was so stiff, and his hands were so cold. He whimpered softly as the hands pulled the wallet from his pocket, the watch from his wrist, and finally, the gleaming gold lighter from his hand. Three vicious kicks in the back told him the boy was through with him. He didn't even turn to watch him walk away. He thought of screaming, but what was the point? He cleared a space in the snow for his head and lay staring at the distant bridge until exhaustion overtook him. He awoke in time to see the sun set behind the bridge. He knew it was very cold again, and wondered vaguely why he wasn't shivering anymore. There was no feeling in either of his legs now, and his hands and arms were too cramped and frozen to drag him along any further. Dimly, it occurred to him that he was going to die. He had been stupid, and this was the price he would pay.

The dog was back again, staring at him from a mound of snow thirty feet away. It sat quietly, licking the ice from between its paws as the man raged and cursed at him. He watched patiently through that night and part of the next day, alert for any signs of a fire.

In the morning, after the man had stopped moving, the dog crept closer until it caught the scent of death. It understood then, instinctively, that there would be no fire to be shared with this man. It turned away from the motionless figure, and quickly trotted off to find other men, men that could offer warmth, fire, and shelter.

A Tribute, Of Sorts, To March
by
Emily Brisbane

March is a swinging door month. From the winter side, I can see wispy, shadowy glimpses of the future: an empty beach, grass not quite green, a distant picnic in fading light. From the spring side, I see the jagged memories of the past: a frozen river, boots caked with snow near the front door, a leafless tree waving in the wind.

As March goes on, the door swings back and forth. Beach. Frozen river. Grass. Boots. Picnic. Leafless tree. March becomes the sum of these images streaked in sunlight, and washed in shadow.

March is:

A mudslide dragging shards of winter into the sun.

An old man limping down a narrow road, with half closed eyes, toward the warmth of his cottage.

Edvard Munch on the bridge, approaching spring and screaming at the memory of winter. Or, in dread of spring.

Driving through a long tunnel with small children, frightened of the dark, in the back seat. "We'll be there soon," you tell them, but they don't believe you, and with every minute the fear mounts that the tunnel has no end.

Falling asleep in a parking lot, with the engine off and the radio on.

March is a promise even cynics must believe.

March does have perquisites that define and nurture the promise:

Spring Training. Not exactly baseball, but a facsimile dressed up with the same sights, sounds, and equipment. Men who are old enough to know this is a game for boys, throw, catch, run, and hit for the pure joy of it. Baseball fans put on their rose-colored glasses and convince themselves it is still a game, and their team can compete with the Yankee deep pockets. In spring, scores mean nothing. Statistics mean nothing. The sun, the grass, the ball, the bat, the glove mean everything. It is over too soon.

St. Patrick's Day, when Americans, descended from a nation of unhappy, oppressed immigrants, romanticize their heritage. Yet somehow, no one recognizes the absurdity of this. Ireland isn't poor, it's rustic. Irish people don't live in apartments, but in cottages. It doesn't rain in Ireland, it 'mists.' Every smiling leprechaun slides down his rainbow into a pot of gold. I know all of this is true, because Hallmark Cards say so. Why would they lie?

March Madness. Perhaps the least distorted, least commercialized, purest athletic event in American life. Distorted, of course. Commercialized, certainly. But less so than the others. There are no seven-figure salaries. Well, okay, for the head coach, maybe, but that's it. There are no drug scandals, or gambling scandals, or point-shaving scandals. Okay, maybe among the starting five, but that's it. There are no performance enhanced drug scandals. Okay, maybe among the cheerleaders, but that's it. Despite the immoderate and distracting hype, the game is the crucial element, not the stars, not the halftime show, not the celebrities in the stands. It's the game. Can we dribble, pass, shoot, rebound, and defend better than you can dribble, pass, shoot, rebound, and defend? It's that simple and that complicated. Win seven games and you are the champion. In many respects, the NCAA basketball tournament is the high-water mark of civilization on earth.

Vernal Equinox. The first day of spring. Vernal refers to spring, and equinox means equal night. It comes from a Sanskrit word, "*vruxinoznal*," which means, loosely translated, 'a day when it is sure to snow.' People generally celebrate by wearing galoshes and dropping extra marshmallows into their hot chocolate.

Resetting The Clocks. People debate whether the correct phrase is 'spring ahead, fall back,' or 'spring back, fall ahead,' or 'please Mom, bash the alarm clock so I can go back to bed.'

March has never been anyone's favorite month, even though it is named after the Roman god of war. It takes too long, and has only one holiday. All the pieces of March seem small and fragmented. It's a beige and gray collage that lasts for thirty-one days, and when we look at it, we just hope it re-arranges itself into something reasonable in time for April.

Nineteen

Two days later, Bernie met with his cardiologist and his physical therapist and was discharged from Northeast Rehab. He was given an exercise program, suggestions for 'heart healthy' meals, a list of medications, and a fistful of prescriptions. He pulled away in a rented sports car, a little nervous about driving but still waving goodbye, and spent a few days at a Brooklyn motel until an apartment became available.

He called Sherilyn at his apartment, prepared, but hoping she would not be home, and left a message. "I was discharged from Northeast Rehab yesterday and am checking into a motel. You and I have a lot to discuss, but I need to pull some things together first. I'll be in touch." His cell phone was still somewhere in his apartment, and he had decided not to let her know where he was staying. Let her fume.

When Paula visited, they spent afternoons sipping iced tea, talking about the weather, about Anna and Aloysius, and about the changes at *Aplomb*. By agreement, they didn't talk about the past, and only a little about the future. The present, calm and careful, seemed to be sufficient.

Anna and Chloe spent the next few days at *The Schoolhouse*, adding some furniture, decorating, and laying out the next couple of issues.

Together they interviewed candidates for part-time sales consultant, and sent advertisements to a few more online writer magazines. The submissions continued to flow, and Anna felt the quality and relevance had improved noticeably. No more horror, no more aliens, and only an occasional teenage wizard.

Chloe spent an afternoon with Sam getting up to speed on managing the website, and proved to be more adept than Anna. She found some graphics to liven up the site, and some short cuts to tweak the process of sending a file. Anna could only say, "You can do that, really?"

They both noticed a few physical things around the building that needed attention: cutting the grass, trimming the hedges, replacing screens. "Yow, that's the one detail I forgot," Anna said. "I never arranged for maintenance. I don't even own a lawnmower."

Chloe had an idea. "I don't think we would need someone more than once a week, do you? How about Malcolm? I really miss Malcolm and his bad jokes."

Chloe called him. Malcolm agreed, and said he had all the equipment needed for light maintenance. The morning he came, he told a joke before he even said hello. "A termite walks into a tavern and says, 'Hey man, is this bar-tender?'"

"Oh, god, Malcolm, that is a new low in humor," Anna said. "The worst joke ever. I love it."

He flashed a big grin and said, "You know Anna, in this world you got to laugh."

Anna developed a daily practice of calling Northeast Rehab to ask about Aloysius, and always got the same evasive answer. "He had a restful night."

"Can you tell me any more than that? I'm his fiancée."

"I'm sorry, I can't. You should speak to his cardiologist."

"Friday?" Anna said to Chloe. "Let's take a run up there on Friday. I'll make an appointment."

~ * ~

Sherilyn, annoyed and concerned, called Sebastian at work.

"Do you know your uncle left that hospital?"

"Bernie left? When?"

"It's Uncle Bernie, and I was hoping you knew."

"No. How could I know?"

"You work in the same office, don't you? His employees are your employees. Hasn't anyone said anything?"

"No, Aunt Sher. This is the first I've heard of it."

She was quiet for a moment. "Well maybe you can ask that girl, Chloe. Oh, wait, you can't because you fired her. That was certainly a good idea."

"She wouldn't know anything, anyway. Even if she did, she wouldn't tell me. The boyfriend is still here, but he won't tell me anything either."

"Can you call the guy from human resources? You got kind of chummy with him."

"Oh, yeah, Simon. Yeah, he may have heard something."

"Well, if he does, you call me back immediately. Immediately, Sebastian. Don't take the time to listen to yo yo mama or whoever she is. Immediately." Sebastian happened to be listening to Yo-Yo Ma at that moment. He went over and turned it off. "I'll call Simon, but sometimes he's hard to reach. Maybe you could try calling Anna."

"Me? Call Anna? I really hate that woman, but I guess I have no choice, since the other one is gone, thank you very much, Sebastian. Just give me the number. I'll do it."

Paula was with Bernie, and Chloe was out with Mike when Sherilyn called. "Hello Anna, it's Sherilyn Holloway, Bernard's wife. How are you?"

After a moment's hesitation, she said, "Sherilyn? Oh. I'm fine, thanks." *Damn,* Anna thought. *This is why people screen their calls.*

"I have an odd question to ask. Actually, an uncomfortable question. I got a message that Bernard left the rehab center, but he didn't tell me where he was going. He hasn't come home, so I'm beginning to worry. Have you spoken to him?"

"I saw him last weekend. He seemed fine, but we haven't spoken since. Do you think you should call the police?"

"Oh, I think not yet. I'm just being a concerned spouse. He left a message that said he would be in touch, so I'll just give him some more time."

"Well, if you do hear from him, give him all my best. I'm thinking good thoughts."

"Yes, of course, dear. Thank you so much." After she hung up, she mumbled, "It's no wonder I hate that woman. She's just like those snooty nurses. Always so superior. God, some people."

Anna called Paula immediately and said, "Tell your husband the eagle has landed, and the well-known substance has hit the fan."

When Paula repeated that to Bernie his comment was, "Talk about your mixed metaphors."

~ * ~

They left early Friday morning, Anna driving, and once they were north of The Bronx, traffic was light all the way to White Plains. The construction crews were gone, as well as the orange traffic cones that always made Chloe nostalgic for Thanksgiving candy corn. The sky to the north was leaden, but closer to them the sun was peeking in and out from behind the clouds.

They signed in and asked for Doctor Dasgupta's office, the same cardiologist who had been treating Bernie. The physicians' offices were in the far corner of the building, a quiet, gloomy walk in the opposite direction from the patients' rooms. Anna checked in and said she was here to discuss Mister McMahon's condition and upcoming surgery. Chloe said, "Anna, you talk to the doc, I'll go visit Aloysius."

The receptionist overheard and said, a little too quickly, "Oh, you should wait. The doctor will be right with you."

And he was. He came out of his office with a smile and a handshake. He was tall and slouched, and had thick, dark hair with a widow's peak. They sat quietly for a moment in his office while he found a file and then turned to face them.

"Mr. McMahon was scheduled for coronary bypass surgery. I think you know we had discussed it for a good while, but he was hesitant and delayed too long. I'm sorry to inform you that he passed away yesterday afternoon. Please accept my sincere condolences."

Neither heard the rest of what he said, but learned later that Aloysius had been transported to White Plains Hospital for the surgery, and died there.

They carried each other to the parking lot and hugged when they got to the car. Neither could find any words until Anna said she wanted to drive to help clear her head. When she got behind the wheel, she began trembling, and couldn't get the key into the ignition. Chloe drove home. As soon as Anna lay down, Chloe called Mike to let him know she would be staying at Anna's apartment for a day or two.

~ * ~

It was two anxious weeks before Bernie got a phone call from Maalwyck, but the wait proved to be worthwhile. He asked if he could visit and speak to Mister Holloway in person, as the details of his report presented a 'somewhat complicated scenario.'

Paula had been staying with Bernie a couple of days a week and met Maalwyck at the door. Bernie introduced her as his wife. Maalwyck gave Bernie a surprised look, eyebrows up and head tilted. He was not used to discussing second wives in the company of first wives. "She's part of all this, Maalwyck," Bernie said. "She should hear it."

The three of them sat in the small anteroom, Paula and Bernie on the couch with her hand on his knee. "I'll leave you a copy of the full report," Maalwyck said, "but for now, I'll just hit the highlights. This case seems to have a lot of moving parts."

"You have no idea," Bernie said.

Maalwyck put his glasses on and read from his report: "The subject, Sherilyn Garafalo, nee Baldwin, a long-time resident of a suburb of Seattle, Washington, was employed as a sales representative in a jewelry store." Bernie cleared his throat and Maalwyck stopped. "Apologies. Much of this is not relevant. I'll skim down to the meat of the situation."

He mumbled to himself, scanning the page, and said, "Ah. Her sister, a ticket clerk at Seattle-Tacoma Airport, is currently under investigation for a minor role in a frequent-flyer mileage scam. Her brother-in-law, Sherilyn Baldwin Garafalo's husband—"

Bernie and Paula yelped at the same time, "Husband?"

"Yes. Her legal spouse at that time."

"He, Mister Garafalo, is thought to be, and is currently sought, as the primary organizer of that airline swindle. Mrs. Garafalo may have benefited from this activity by receiving free tickets to Las Vegas on more than one occasion. I say tickets, plural, advisedly, because there is some evidence that on one trip she was accompanied by a young man. My informant, a baggage handler at the terminal, made reference to a particularly loud speaking voice, and an unusually conspicuous perfume. She was close enough to the subjects to hear her refer to him as Sebastian."

"Wow," Paula said. "That's some informant."

"As I mentioned to Mister Holloway, this informant has a memory like a bookie. And both the lady and her perfume were memorable."

Bernie stood and walked around the room, rubbing his chin. "This is all good, Maalwyck, but I have to admit I was hoping for something more. I don't think peripheral involvement in a swindle is enough to nullify a marriage." He looked sadly at Paula, "We're probably in for an entrenched legal battle."

Maalwyck said, "There is more, sir. It seems a warrant was issued for Mrs. Garafalo's spouse, but never served."

"How does that help us?" Paula asked.

"It's a clear indication that Mister Garafalo made a quick, unscheduled exit, and so in all likelihood, Mrs. Garafalo is *still* Mrs. Garafalo."

They both gawked, open-mouthed. "They didn't have time to get divorced before he bolted. You think she's still technically married to him?"

"With that in mind," Maalwyck continued reading, "I've done a search of Washington State divorce decrees without finding the name of either Garafalo or Baldwin. I have my office doing a more comprehensive search, going back a full year, but it seems most likely she is still married to her first husband."

Bernie's eyes popped out. "And therefore, not *ever* married to me! What hypocrisy! That lying, projecting hypocrite. She played me like... like I was one of Meyer's trout."

Paula smiled at Maalwyck, who smiled back, thinking again of the question he most frequently wanted to ask his clients.

~ * ~

As soon as he closed the door behind Maalwyck, Bernie grabbed Paula and kissed her. And then kissed her again. "I think it's time to crank up the legal machinery and let loose the dogs of war," he said to her.

"Talk about your mixed metaphors," she said with a laugh.

The same afternoon, Bernie spoke with his attorney, a junior partner in a prestigious firm in Chicago where Meyer had incorporated his business, The attorney sent a registered letter to Sherilyn Garafalo with a copy to Sebastian Jenkins, referencing and quoting liberally from Maalwyck's report. The letter demanded she no longer 'consider herself or refer to herself as married to Bernard Holloway.' Further, the letter demanded, she is to vacate the apartment she shared with Bernard Holloway as of noon on Monday, May 12th, or be subject to the penalties for trespassing.

The letter came from the firm of Williams, Stuyvesant and Williams and was signed by Jewel Ingraham, with her address, phone number, email address, fax number and State Bar Association number under her signature.

"Wow," Paula said. "This is slamming the door, locking it, and posting a guard. And that's a good metaphor."

About ten days later, Ms. Ingraham received a letter from Jeremy Jackman, Attorney-at-Law, outlining 'Mrs. Sherilyn Holloway's position on her matrimonial status.' It explained, in language somewhat warm for an attorney, that Maalwyck's report was a bogus, inflammatory bundle of creative fiction; libelous, actionable, and devoid of anything worthy of litigation. Mr. Jackman expressed hope that his letter would put an end to these absurd claims, and Mister Holloway would regain his clarity of mind and return to his lawful spouse.

Jewel, well named, responded quickly that her firm was in possession of a folder of corroborating evidence, including a marriage certificate and, in particular, an appropriately dated divorce decree for the current Mrs. Holloway, Paula Holloway, from her previous husband.

She suggested further that to avoid exhaustive court time and significant legal costs, the principals meet somewhere on neutral ground and 'show their cards.'

They met in a hotel conference room, coincidentally the Best Western at Kennedy Airport. Sherilyn, Sebastian, and their attorney on one side of the table; Bernie, Paula and Jewel on the other. Sebastian took his earphones off. Bernie and Sherilyn only glanced at each other, but Sherilyn and Paula each did a full visual inspection of the other. Hairstyle, clothes, jewelry, makeup, shoes, speaking voice, all were examined and found wanting.

Attorney Jackman presented a marriage certificate from the State of Nevada, a receipt from the Bliss Forever Wedding Chapel and a copy of the bill for a weekend's residence at, another coincidence, the Best Western Plus in Las Vegas. "Marriage, celebration, and co-habitation," were all, in his opinion, evidence of a legitimate relationship. Sherilyn smirked, Paula turned pink and Bernie stared down at his hands.

Paula, from Bernie's description, expected Jewel to be a statuesque, atomic Amazon with eyes that could shoot laser beams. She was actually middle-aged, grey haired and had poor posture. When she spoke though, it was clear who owned the room. Cogent, articulate and focused, she compared the dates of marriage of each of the women, and then presented Paula's divorce decree from Lyle. Acting perplexed and confused for a moment, she wondered where the divorce papers were for Ms. Garafalo. She looked expectantly at attorney Jackman, and then at Ms. Sherilyn Garafalo. Jackman looked away, and Sherilyn turned the same color as Paula had earlier.

She then said that attorney Jackman was doing a creditable job representing his client but mentioned that her firm had an in-house investigation department, employed twenty-three lawyers and their hourly rates ranged from one-hundred fifty to three-hundred fifty dollars per hour. If necessary, she would not hesitate to call one of them in to consult. "I don't believe there is any criminal intent here," she smiled, "but the legal discovery process can clarify that, given time."

Sherilyn, angry now, said "You're just trying to frighten me."

"No, Ms. Garafalo," Jewel said. "I'm pointing out why it's in your interests to *be* frightened." Sherilyn, Sebastian and their lawyer had a brief and animated conversation in the corner of the room but said nothing when they came back.

Jewel waited a full two minutes and announced, "I'll wait to hear from you, and if not, I'll consider the matter concluded. And please understand that the May twelfth date in my original letter is not flexible, nor has it been amended by this meeting."

~ * ~

On Monday, May 12th, late in the afternoon, Bernie and Paula went back to their apartment. It was just as they had left it: Paula when she went to Skopje, and later, Bernie when he had his heart attack. He checked the refrigerator and poured himself some seltzer. Paula sat and cried.

A week later, Bernie visited *Aplomb*. A few people at their desks waved or said hello as he made his way between the desks and into Sebastian's—soon to revert to his—office. The desktop was empty, the stereo was on. "Mister Holloway," Sebastian said.

"Hello, Sebastian." He looked around the room silently. Sebastian said nothing. Bernie said, "I'm not here to be a problem, I just want to say hello and get the feel for the place again."

"Ah," Sebastian said.

"I understand you've developed a fondness for this desk. You're welcome to take it with you when you go." He turned and left.

~ * ~

Dearest Hercule,

I write this just after returning to my home from an engagement party of two of my new and very good friends, Chloe and Michael. I have written of Chloe before, and her fiancée Mike seems, to my mind, perfectly suited to her.

Let me catch you up on all the latest news:

My friend, Anna Pennington, wears a black armband now, and is still managing her humor magazine, The Schoolhouse.

Chloe has been formally appointed as associate editor. The magazine is growing, slowly but steadily, and they are both thrilled at its progress.

My husband (I do love using that word now), Bernie, is finishing his tenure at Aplomb Magazine, clearing up some distribution problems, and training his replacement. He will leave officially in a few weeks, and we will begin to plan our itinerary. Skopje remains central to our travel plans. Bernie wants to meet you, and thank you for all your kindness to me, and we want to sip ouzo, dine on moussaka and take selfies at Maria Park.

I think of you often, with respect and gratitude. I hope you are well, and still happy at the Embassy, and I thank you again for all your kindness and patience with me.

I will write again when our plans are more settled.

All the best,
Mrs. Paula Holloway

Meet Gene Murray

Gene is a retired speech/language pathologist living and writing in upstate New York. This is his third novel published by Wings ePress.

Over a long and happy life, he's been a smiling toddler, a reluctant student, a crossing guard, body surfer, and Mickey Mantle wannabe. He has a family, nuclear in more ways than one, that he cares for deeply and worries about in the 'wee small hours of the morning.' They are the star around which his wobbly planet orbits.

Writing has become the activity that keeps Gene balanced in these unbalanced times.

Other Works from the Pen of Gene Murray

Mcguffin - Two fans at the Woodstock Festival witness an inexplicable event, and their lives are affected by it until they meet and investigate thirty years later.

Rare Bird - A reluctant detective is persuaded to investigate the murder of an octogenarian, possibly for a rare book that has been in his family for generations.

Letter to Our Readers

Enjoy this book?

You can make a difference

As an independent publisher, Wings ePress, Inc. does not have the financial clout of the large New York Publishers. We can't afford large magazine spreads or subway posters to tell people about our quality books.

But, we do have something much more effective and powerful than ads. We have a large base of loyal readers.

Honest Reviews help bring the attention of new readers to our books.

If you enjoyed this book, we would appreciate it if you would spend a few minutes posting a review on the site where you purchased this book or on the Wings ePress, Inc. webpages at:
https://wingsepress.com/

Thank You

Visit Our Website

For The Full Inventory
Of Quality Books:

Wings ePress.Inc
https://wingsepress.com/

Quality trade paperbacks and downloads
in multiple formats,
in genres ranging from light romantic comedy
to general fiction and horror.
Wings has something for every reader's taste.
Visit the website, then bookmark it.
We add new titles each month!

Wings ePress Inc.
3000 N. Rock Road
Newton, KS 67114